SUPERNATURAL DETECTIVES

5

THE COLOUR–CRIMINOLOGIST

William Le Queux

FROM WHOSE BOURNE

Robert Barr

COACHWHIP PUBLICATIONS

Landisville, Pennsylvania

Supernatural Detectives 5: The Colour-Criminologist / From Whose Bourne
Copyright © 2012 Coachwhip Publications
No claims made on public domain material.

(Cover) Planetary Nebula NGC 6302: NASA, ESA, Hubble SM4 ERO Team

The Colour-Criminologist stories were published in 1917 as *The Rainbow Mystery: Chronicles of a Colour-Criminologist*, by William Le Queux (1864-1927).
From Whose Bourne by Robert Barr (1849-1912) was published in 1896.

ISBN 1-61646-131-4
ISBN-13 978-1-61646-131-7

CoachwhipBooks.com

SUPERNATURAL DETECTIVES

5

CONTENTS

THE COLOUR-CRIMINOLOGIST

FROM WHOSE BOURNE

THE COLOUR-CRIMINOLOGIST

William Le Queux

The First Colour: Green
THE MAN WITH THE CAT'S EYES

"What sort of employment are you looking for?"

I gave a start as I heard the voice, so completely did the question fall in with my thoughts. I had been sitting alone at the little table in the tea-shop, and now, as I looked up, I was astonished to see a tall, pleasant-looking stranger standing over me and returning my stare of astonishment with a friendly smile.

"I'm afraid I must have been talking to myself," I stammered apologetically. "I hope I haven't worried you. I didn't know you were there."

"Don't be alarmed," the stranger replied pleasantly; "I assure you that you have not spoken a word, so far as I know. Your secrets, whatever they may be, are safe."

"Then how did you know?" I began.

"Oh, I just guessed," he laughed. "Am I right?"

"Quite," I answered. "I certainly am looking for work of some sort."

"Tell me all about it," he suggested, taking the seat opposite me. "I may possibly be able to help you."

So it came about that, clutching at the first straw of companionship that came my way on the dreary surface of London's seething sea of humanity, I told him everything. Of my father's death I could scarcely speak, but of my life in the rambling old rectory, my duties as village organist, as secretary and housekeeper to my father, to say nothing of amateur parish nurse and peacemaker, I gave him so many unnecessary details that I suddenly realised I must be boring him dreadfully.

"Not at all, not at all," he replied in answer to my faint apology. "I am really very interested."

"Well, you see," I concluded, "I have to make my own living, and I am not at all sure how it is to be done. I taught myself type-writing and shorthand, with the assistance of our local schoolmaster, in order to be able to help my father with his literary work. Now you see I am quite alone, and my knowledge is very limited indeed. I am staying with some friends at Turnham Green at present, and I am attending classes in commercial subjects in order to qualify me for some post. My trouble at present is that I am anxious to get some sort of work which will, to be perfectly candid, reduce the financial strain."

"I see," said the stranger thoughtfully, and he looked at me with a curiously penetrating look, which, rather to my surprise, was not in the least disconcerting. "I quite understand. You would probably prefer a post as secretary to some literary man, rather than a job in a city office?"

"Oh, infinitely," I cried; "only I don't suppose I shall be able to get one."

"Oh! one never knows," the stranger replied, as he took a small pocket-book from his waistcoat pocket. "Here is my card. My name may possibly be known in a slight degree to your friends. If not, they can easily find out anything they want to know about me, and if you care to call on me to-morrow afternoon about this time I may very likely have something to offer you. Take the tube to Highgate and then take a Barnet tram. Good-bye."

He shook my hand and slipped away so quickly that I had hardly begun to thank him before he was gone. Truly London was a very wonderful city, I told myself, but I was not sure that I had done a wise thing in talking so intimately with a total stranger in a tea-shop. I turned over the card which I was still holding, mechanically.

JOHN DURSTON, LL.D., D.Sc., Ph.D.
LORRAN HOUSE,
EAST FINCHLEY. TOLLINGTON CHAIR OF PSYCHOLOGY.

So I had been talking with Professor Durston! The man who, so his supporters declared, would revolutionise the world with his scheme of education by suggestion; the man whom the halfpenny papers worshipped one day and laughed at the next, and who was said to be the greatest authority on the psychology of crime in the

cosy little house at Turnham Green in a ... —I was just nineteen at the time—to ... an even greater personage than I

atically, "there is always a strain ... mit there must be a lot of brains ... t on very reliable authority that ... ast year, of which the public have ... oned from Ireland, where he was ... meeting of the Cabinet."

...e?" I asked.

y is that one mind which is prop- ... l any number of minds which are ... a lot of bunkum, you know, but he ... should certainly go and see him, ... to you."

ing afternoon I presented myself at ... eal more nervous than I should have cared to ad... mediately I was shown into the professor's study.

My new friend came towards me with my card in his hand.

"Good afternoon, Miss Dalrayne," he said, "I am glad you have decided to come. Sit down, won't you. I have ordered a cup of tea for you."

"Thank you, Professor Durston," I answered.

"Mr. Durston, please," he corrected me kindly; "Professor is such a big mouthful and means so little in reality."

I confess that I was rather disappointed as I glanced hurriedly round the room. I had expected to see an *édition-de-luxe* of orderly chaos, if I may use the term, which had always existed in the study

---

Shearing was another of the male pen-names used by Marjorie Bowen, under which she published fifteen novels of historical suspense. They include *Aunt Beardie* (1940), set in post-Revolution France, and the better known *Airing in a Closed Carriage* (1943), a successful fictionalization of a classic real life case, the poisoning of James Maybrick, with the setting switched from Liverpool to Manchester.

For Her to See (1947) was another mystery inspired by a famous true crime – the Bravo case of 1876, which has fascinated criminologists ever since Charles Bravo met his end in mysterious circumstances. The book was filmed in 1948 as *So Evil My Love*, with Ray Milland and Ann Todd in leading roles. "The Chinese Apple", written shortly afterwards, is typical of Shearing at her rather dark and

at home. But instead of the rows of ill-assorted books, in their faded and tattered bindings, instead of the little piles of papers lying here and there, I saw only a neat and tidy collection of "elastic" book-cases, every book in which was calf-bound in a uniform library binding, and apparently every scrap of paper in the room was hidden away in a filing cabinet of which there were many. I had scarcely had time to complete my rapid survey of the study when the maid announced tea. My host led the way to the drawing-room— at least I called it the drawing-room for want of a better term. It was a large, long room, with a big bay window looking out on to the garden, and the scheme of decoration was entirely black, purple, and yellow. The ground-work of everything in the room, including the wallpaper, was black. Timid little country mouse that I was, I sank into a luxurious black-and-purple easy chair by the fire, and gazed round the room in astonishment. Mr. Durston smiled as he noted my surprise.

"You like it?" he asked.

"Immensely," I replied enthusiastically; "but it's rather, well, rather unconventional, isn't it?"

"Perhaps it is a little," he agreed; "though of course black-and-white is getting common enough nowadays."

So we talked of decorations and pictures and everything except the subject that was nearest my heart as we took our tea by the fire, but at last the professor came straight to the point.

"I want you to act as my secretary, and to undertake the responsibility of assisting me in my work in any other way. Before you decide whether you will come to me or not, I want you to be sure that you understand what your duties will be."

"I'm afraid I'm not at all clever," I apologized. "I should hardly be able to assist you in any way except by typewriting and that sort of thing."

"I am quite convinced that you can help me very much," he answered seriously. "I knew that before I spoke to you yesterday. I am doubly certain of it now. You are aware that I am engaged on what I hope is an original form of experimental psychology. I have a great deal of collegiate work to attend to, and I am also completing a book which occupies most of my spare time. I am very anxious to record some of my present experiences, the results of some of my current experiments, but I have not time. Now, I want you, Miss Dalrayne, to share these experiences, so far as is psychically possible, to witness my experiments and to record them for me from your point of view. That is, I wish you to write your own book about them."

"My book!" I exclaimed nervously. "Oh! I couldn't—but I should simply love to try."

"Then you will find it easy. If you really want to try there is nothing to stop you doing anything. But first you must realise what it is I want you to do. Look out of the window and tell me what you see."

I got up and walked over to the window. Rather to my astonishment there was nothing at all unusual to be seen.

"There is just the garden and the house at the foot of it," I remarked.

"That is what I want you to understand," Mr. Durston replied. "I want to give you a very elementary lesson. You can't see that house. No one ever saw a house yet. When you recognise a building it is by your sense of touch, aided by your memory, never by your sense of sight. Look again."

"Why!" I exclaimed, "it's hidden by a mist, a coloured mist."

"Yes," said the professor quietly, "that was all you saw before."

"But there is a house there," I insisted, "I saw it."

"No, you saw a series of colour shapes. By a sub-conscious process of analysis you recognised shapes that you have been taught to call walls, and windows and doors, and by another and quite separate form of collective mentation you decided that you had seen a house. All you could see really was a series of colour forms which you associate with the exterior of something that your sense of touch has previously taught you is a solid object, in this case a house. Look!"

"Why, there is the house!" I cried. "Where did that mist come from, then?"

"There was no mist," said Durston. "You lost your sense of sight for a moment; that was all."

"But how?" I exclaimed. "It's never happened before."

"That," smiled my companion, "is where I come in."

"Hypnotism!" I cried.

"Oh! dear me, no," he laughed. "Not even suggestion. It is a more simple and much less theatrical solution altogether, and that was what I might call a kindergarten form of the experiments I shall want you to record. These experiments will deal entirely with colour mentation. All you have to understand is that we have no means of seeing anything in this world except colour. Nothing else has any existence as far as our sense of sight is concerned. We cannot see a solid object at all. I want you to understand that when the brain recognises a tree, or a waterfall, or anything else, the eye only sees a series of colour shapes or forms. It is of course a very obvious and elementary statement to make, but it is the basis of all psychic development. Metaphysical psychology began in the wrong way. In order to have something to start on it conceived the hypothesis of the ego. Given a sufficiently plastic hypothesis one can prove almost anything, except that one's hypothesis is correct. The one acknowledged force is vibration, the predominant vibration is colour, and the least developed and most neglected and at the same time most important part of the only thing in man which has any individual existence, his brain, is what I call the chromatic centre of ideation. Colour exists not in what we call a coloured object but in the brain, the chromatic centre of ideation, that is where physiology and psychology coincide. A blind man 'sees colour'; in a light-tight room one could still see colour, and it is chromatic vibration which promotes the cerebral circulation which keeps the brain alive. You see what I mean?"

"Yes," I said, "I think I understand. It must be a very interesting subject."

"It is," he replied, "though of course I am merely putting the elementary principles of the subject in a very simple way, so that there shall be no chance of confusing you with terms. You see I devoted a great deal of thought to this subject and I have come to this conclusion: Every action, every thought, every movement of man, either consciously or otherwise, has its origin in a latent moral colour

image, and I have proved that the *chromatic centre of ideation*
that is properly trained is capable of recording the thoughts and
actions—that is, the vibrations and their results—of any number
of other centres which are not trained to resist the superior force.
Not only is the trained centre capable of recording these things by
chromatic visualisation, but it can also influence the untrained
centre to act in any desired way and from any distance. Now, every
man, woman, and child has a predominant colour note in the composition of the chromatic centre, because no person in the world
is normal. In a purely psychological sense the word 'normal' means
'perfect,' and perfection is an unattainable ideal. I don't want you
to think that when I speak of the predominant colour note I mean
a colour, or shade of colour, which one may prefer to another. I
have found that where this is most pronounced the colour is one
which the subject positively dislikes, and is frequently the cause
of aggravated mental disorder and insanity. You see what I mean?"

"Well, no, not quite," I ventured. "Are not insanity and mental
disorder two different terms for the same thing?"

"No," the professor replied, "certainly not. Insanity is, of course,
mental disorder, but the converse does not apply. Mental disorder
infers a knowledge of the disorder on the part of the subject; insanity, on the other hand, makes it clear that the patient is un-
aware of his disorder and believes himself sane. In the one case,
two or more colour vibrations have come into conflict without de-
stroying the relative value of the others; in the second case two or
more vibrations have conflicted with such violence as to render
the remaining colour vibrations nugatory. By my system the treatment of brain disease is a matter of discovering the offending
colour vibrations by means of telepathic colour mentation and
treating them by the use of constructive colour suggestion. This is
a branch of the work which you will not be troubled with for some
time, except perhaps incidentally."

"What is it I am to do?" I asked excitedly. "It is extremely interesting."

"The experiments I am conducting now," he replied, "are all
connected with colour mentation in relation to crime. This is very

largely a matter of necessity. I have trained myself to visualise the actions of others by receiving their chromatic vibrations, and then allowing my memory and my other senses and my acquired knowledge to give them an automatic appearance of reality, in precisely the same way that you did when you said you saw that house. At present my own centre of chromatic ideation is only capable of receiving messages from the most powerful of many around me. I have not yet succeeded in tuning what I call the chord of reception to different levels, and I discovered that the most powerful emanations arise from centres in which there is colour conflict resulting in criminal acts. At first this rather surprised me, and I felt it must be due to my long study of the psychology of crime; but on thinking the matter over, it appeared to me that the explanation is fairly simple. Mankind having succumbed to gregarious instincts many thousands of years ago, and having lived in colonies and communities for a similar period, there must have been social laws of one sort or another in existence during practically the whole of that time. It follows therefore that the man of to-day comes into the world with a strong, innate sense of his duty to the community. His home life and his early education, though not to a sufficient extent, still to a certain degree, strengthen and develop this instinct. He finds that there are certain bounds set out by law which he is not permitted to cross, and if he does he is met by certain deterrent punishments in every direction. Therefore it is easy to believe that the conflicting vibrations, which make a man blind to his hereditary instincts, his early training, and the probability of his own ultimate discomfort, may readily be stronger and more penetrating than other vibrations, which, acting either in unison or in conflict, tend to lead him in a less evolutionary direction. So what I am going to do is to continue my experiments on these lines till I have completed my chromatic cycle. You shall describe them in your own words and when they are complete I shall have them bound and put aside for reference. Then we shall get on with something else. Now do you understand?"

"You mean you are going to get in touch with the—er—the cases, Mr. Durston, and then tell me about them and I am to write them down?"

"No," he replied, "you are to get in touch with them too."

"But how?" I cried. "I haven't been trained, and I might not prove a suitable subject for training."

"That's of no account at all," the professor laughed. "I am quite capable of transmitting my impressions to you and I am confident you are a suitable subject, or else how could I have known yesterday that you were wondering where you could get work and whether you would make enough money to share a small flat with your little friend with the brown eyes."

I gazed at him in astonishment. It was perfectly true. My cousin Doris was doing illustrations for a firm of advertisement contractors, and our ambition was to take a tiny flat together at Hampstead.

"I suppose I ought to be afraid of you, Mr. Durston," I said, when I had recovered from my surprise. "But you are quite right, that is just what I was thinking about."

"Oh, you have nothing to be afraid of," he assured me; "but I shall quite understand if you prefer to throw up the idea. You are young and entitled to be nervous of such a scheme, but don't hesitate to say so if you are at all frightened. In any case, unless you have made up your mind already, I should prefer you to experience once the actual experiments before tying you down to anything definite."

As he spoke the door opened and a young man, rather good-looking, with a pale, intellectual face, and dark, thoughtful eyes, entered the room. I was most struck by the straight, almost stiff way in which he carried himself, and by the excellent cut of his neat, blue serge suit.

"Oh, I beg your pardon, uncle," he said, as he caught sight of me.

"Not at all, my boy; not at all," exclaimed the professor, as he strode forward to greet him. "You've just come at the right time. Let me introduce you. Miss Dalrayne, this is a spurious nephew of mine—I am his godfather, really—Arthur Bindold, Miss Dalrayne. I fancy, Arthur, we have found the subject of our search and the secretary in one."

Mr. Bindold looked at me with an air of such obvious surprise that I felt rather hurt for a moment, and more than ever determined not to betray my youth and ignorance if I could possibly help it.

"I must explain," said Mr. Durston, "that Arthur helps me in my work to a very great extent. He is absolutely no good at all from any psychic point of view, but he is a successful journalist, which means, at any rate, that he has common sense and tenacity. He does his best to discover the whereabouts of my cases, as you call them, and to verify my visualisations. I fancy he is coming round to the opinion that there is something in it, after all."

"Oh, there's more than 'something' in it," the other agreed readily. "I've proved that. But that doesn't make it any the less extraordinary."

"Well, I daresay you'd like a cup of tea," the professor suggested. For a few moments they spoke of personal affairs, and I picked up a manuscript book of music which was lying on the piano, and glanced through the music. It was a curiously wild, eerie composition as far as I could gather, with many modulations and changes of rhythm, and very difficult to play even for an advanced amateur.

"Play it," suggested Mr. Bindold, as he saw what I was doing.

"Oh, I couldn't possibly!" I laughed. "I hardly play at all; I could never play this. What is it?"

"It is a piece of my uncle's. He calls it 'The Dance of the Spirit of Power.' I think it is very wonderful. You should get him to play it for you."

"Some day perhaps I will," Mr. Durston replied; "when I'm very cross with you. Now what about this experiment? If you care to come into the other room, Miss Dalrayne, we may as well see how this idea works out with you."

"I'll hang about and have a smoke till you're ready," Mr. Bindold laughed; "I only upset the vibrations, or whatever you call them."

The professor led me across the hall to a large door just opposite the study, and I confess that as I followed him I began to feel a trifle nervous. But after the look of surprise with which Mr. Bindold had greeted me I was determined to go through with it to the end. In a few moments, however, my fears were drowned in curiosity, for I found myself in a room—for I suppose I must call it a room— such as I had never dreamt of before. We entered it from a small platform, through a narrow sliding door. Everything was in pitch darkness, and Mr. Durston helped me into a big easy chair, and then suddenly the place was lighted up and we were sitting inside a great white globe. This was sufficiently startling, but I think I was even more astonished to notice that our chairs were not at the base of the globe, but half-way up the side so that we could only see the white walls of the globe above us, and beneath us, and all round us. A terrifically powerful light burst from an aperture above our heads.

"Tell me," said Mr. Durston, in a curious monotone, "what colour is this place?"

"White," I replied at once.

"There is no such thing as white. Look again and tell me when you have changed your mind."

I glanced round the walls of the dome. Were they white? Was there a slight tinge of colour about them? Then I almost started out of my chair. The whole place was green, a vivid, liquid, transparent green. There could be no doubt about it.

"Green," I said in a whisper of excitement.

"Green," came the strange monotone from beside me. "Green—green—green."

I sat back in my chair with an involuntary sigh of contentment. It was a very wonderful sensation. A mass of transparent colour with no beginning and no end. I felt a singing noise in my ears, and the lights grew dimmer. I sat up, determined to keep awake. The colour grew deeper and deeper. Only two small specks of vivid green remained, close together, right opposite me. I leaned forward, fascinated, and suddenly shivered with a strange, intangible fear. Brighter and brighter grew the spots, darker and ever darker the surrounding gloom. Suddenly a soft glow began to surround the two bright spots. I shut my eyes, but the spots remained, and the soft glow grew in distinctness.

"It is a face," I cried; "a human face. Oh, hideous, hideous!" For there, gazing at me, was a man with the eyes of a cat. I felt a draught of cold air sweep over me, and then my fear seemed to leave me. I looked again and saw the man with the cat's eyes move his head; and then I noticed he was wearing a brown tweed suit and leggings. Then slowly the scene unfolded itself before me, and I began to hear the murmurings of voices. I was standing in a long room. Before a great open fireplace at the far end of the room sat an old man, huddled up in rugs. Beside him was the man with the eyes of a cat. The lips of the old man moved. I strained forward to hear what he was saying. Presently I heard the words ". . . a dying man, but you can't force me." He lifted his hand from behind his back, and in it he held a sheet of paper. The man with the cat's eyes leaned over him and laid a blotting-pad on his knees. "You shall," he hissed. "You shall." The old man's jaw dropped, his eyes wavered, he took a pen which the other gave him, and was about to write when, to my utter astonishment, the figure of Professor Durston appeared beside him and snatched the pen from his hands. The man with the cat's eyes uttered a hoarse cry and staggered away. He stood for a moment leaning on a small writing-table which stood by the wall behind the old man's chair. Then suddenly he opened the drawer and pulled out a revolver. His left hand clutched his throat, slowly he lifted the pistol with his right until at last it reached his temple. And then—

"Thank you, Miss Dalrayne," said the professor; "shall we go back to the drawing-room?"

I was almost too astonished to speak as I found myself on the little platform leading into the dome, but fortunately Mr. Durston gave me no opportunity.

"Please tell Arthur I should like to speak to him in the study," he said; "I shall be with you in a moment."

Left alone in the drawing-room, I felt a strange sense of elation, a curiously delicious feeling of power and life. I sat at the piano and saw "The Dance of the Spirit of Power" in front of me. "What a strange coincidence," I thought, as I began to try to play it. Before I quite knew how, I reveled in the weird music. My fingers and wrists seemed to be charged with electricity.

"Splendid!" cried the professor as I finished. "Not a wrong note anywhere, and very beautifully expressed."

I looked up and found Arthur Bindold standing over me with an expression of extreme interest.

"Do you mean to say you played that from memory after just looking through it as you did before?" he asked.

"Of course not," I laughed. "Why, here's the music, in front of me."

"In front of you, yes," he replied; "but still open at the first page, and you haven't turned over once. I've been watching you."

"Come, Arthur," said Mr. Durston, as he looked at me a little anxiously, I thought. "Miss Dalrayne will want to be getting home now."

He led me into the hall before I had a chance to reply.

"Think it over to-night," he said. "I will give you four pounds a week, and if you decide to come to me, let me know to-morrow on the 'phone."

Four pounds a week! And my very highest ambition had been two! I reached home with the same strange feeling of elation that I had experienced ever since I left the dome, but now there was more reason for it. However, I decided to tell my friends nothing more than the fact that Mr. Durston had offered me a post. And as I lay in bed, I pondered on my strange experience. It was all fancy, I told myself. I had been dreaming, that was all. But when I came down to breakfast and opened the paper I nearly dropped in the sudden shock. There, staring me in the face, were two photographs, one of the man with the cat's eyes, and one of the old man whom I had seen sitting before the fire. Below was the following paragraph:

"SUDDEN DEATH OF THE EARL
"OF RANELLERTON
"STRANGE DOUBLE TRAGEDY

"As we go to press, we are informed of the sudden death of the aged Earl of Ranellerton, and of the suicide of his younger son, the Hon. Basil Virlayer. It seems that last evening a shot was heard by one of the housemaids, who rushed into the library and found the earl dead in his chair, and Virlayer lying, shot through the brain, on the floor. The amazing part of the affair is that the earl was holding in his hand the draft of a will, revoking his previous wills,

and bequeathing all his unentailed property to his
son Basil, whom he was popularly supposed to have
disinherited. Further particulars will appear in our
later editions."

I had scarcely finished reading the account before I found myself standing at the 'phone. This was too uncanny altogether, and I
felt I must decline the offer, cost what it may. But when I got
through to East Finchley Mr. Durston had already gone out, and I
spoke with Arthur Bindold.

"So you'd better ring up about four," he suggested. "You are
going to accept, I hope."

And then something made me change my mind.

"Oh, rather!" I replied; "if he will have me."

"Good!" said Mr. Bindold over the telephone.

No. 2: Yellow
THE HOUSE WITH THE GOLDEN DOOR

"Well," said Arthur Bindold, as he threw himself into an easy chair by the window of my little den, "and what do you think of the work now?"

"I have had three months of an entirely novel and absorbingly interesting life," I replied enthusiastically. "I wouldn't have missed it for anything."

"You believe in my respected uncle and his colour-vibrations, then?" he asked idly.

"Yes," I said, "I do, and so do you really, you know, only you will never admit it in so many words. Why do you pretend to be so sceptical?"

"I'm not sceptical exactly," he laughed. "I have had ample proof of the soundness of the theory, but you see I feel that an excess of enthusiasm in the house might lead us astray. If we were all as tremendously in earnest as the professor and you, we should probably end in a madhouse. Besides I don't really understand it at all. I am quite content to do my share of the work and abide by the results, but you must count me out of the uncanny part of it, because it is beyond me altogether."

"You don't seriously mean that you don't understand your uncle's theory of colour vibrations?" I asked.

"Oh, dear me, no!" he replied lightly. "I can put that in a nutshell for you. My uncle believes, and I must say he appears to have proved, that the mind is very much the same as a wireless-telegraphy instrument, and that it is only susceptible to colour vibrations.

We can only see colours and colour forms, and we can never see solid objects. We only know an object is solid because we can touch it, or because we believe what we have been told. Therefore, as everyone speaking of an object mentally pictures that object, every thought must have its origin in some latent colour image, and an object only receives its solidity by the automatic operation of the sense of touch through the medium of the memory. But how he comes to sit in a room and see things which are happening miles away, I don't pretend to understand."

"Don't you see," I explained, "that if you can train yourself to suspend the action of the memory, that is, make your mind a perfect blank, your brain, which so long as you are conscious must either give or receive impressions, is bound to be affected by the colour transmissions of other brains which are making an active effort. It is only a matter of training and application to put the vibrations received into their proper order and relative significance, and you have a complete picture of what is going on in the mind which is transmitting. In nine cases out of ten, Professor Durston actually sees everything that the other brain sees, as, for instance, in the case of the Paulson Emerald, and again in the case of the Man with the Cat's Eyes."

"Well, I quite admit it, but I don't in the least understand it," he repeated. "Though if a young and healthy and jolly girl like you can get hold of it, I don't see why I shouldn't."

"Because you won't try," I retorted somewhat crossly; "you won't make any effort at all. Even if you made a black ring on the centre of a large sheet of white paper and concentrated your attention on that for a few minutes every day, refusing to allow yourself to think of anything else, you would be astonished at the results in less than ten days."

"All right, if you're going to get cross about it, I'll go and try," he replied.

"Yes, do," I said, and he strolled leisurely out of the room. I slipped a piece of paper into the typewriter and prepared to get on with my work Was Arthur right, I wondered? Was Mr. Durston, with all his marvellous brain-power and strength of character, playing with fire? Could the theory of colour telepathy, worked out to its logical conclusion, end in madness? Certainly there was nothing at all about the man, charming and gentle and fatherly as he was, which suggested anything except remarkable ability. Mr. Bindold was no fool, and I wondered if I had better keep a check on my enthusiasm before it robbed me of my self-control. I was only a child, to all intents and purposes, and I began to feel frightened for the first time since my original visit to Lorran House. I sat and mused as I gazed absently at the sheet of white paper before me. The professor was away in the country for the week-end, and he had left me a carelessly scribbled article which I had promised to have typewritten for him when he came back.

It was Saturday morning, and my cousin Doris and I had arranged a walk in the country. Yet I did not seem as if I could get on with my work. I sat there, idly wondering why I was not working, gazing without any fixed purpose at the paper before me, thinking of nothing in particular. Presently I tried to sit forward and lay my hands on the keys of the typewriter, but I found I was unable to move. Instinctively I stared at the white sheet, expecting from sheer force of habit to see there an explanation of my inertia. But the paper was no longer white. In the centre it was a deep grey, growing gradually lighter towards the edges. I watched it, fascinated. The mass of deep grey seemed to melt away from the middle until the edges were dark and almost smoke-coloured and the centre was nearly white again. Presently the white gave way to a faint tinge of lemon, which, in its turn, grew gradually deeper until it was the colour of burnished gold. Hardly daring to breathe, I saw a series of faint lines draw themselves across the grey, and other lines and marks appear upon the gold. Then suddenly I saw before me a perfect little vignette of a golden door in a grey stone wall. Then I shivered from head to foot in a sudden convulsion and the image was gone. Instantly my senses returned to me. I had received a colour-message from some one, whom I knew not. Possibly it might be from Mr. Durston himself. I looked at my wrist-watch and made a note of the time. It was twenty minutes to twelve. I took a sheet of paper and wrote a brief description of the picture I had seen and laid it aside for further reference. Then remembering the professor's repeated advice, "Never force anything, the brain cannot work consciously and subconsciously at the same time," I struggled to get on with my typewriting.

When I returned to our little flat I found my cousin hard at work on some illustrations, and as it began to rain while we were at lunch we decided to postpone the walk and spend a quiet afternoon indoors. I curled myself up in a chair by the fire and began dipping into the "Pickwick Papers." But try as I would I failed to keep my attention on the book, I could not rid myself of the picture of the house with the golden door. I tried to work out in my mind what it could mean and where the message had come from. Possibly Mr. Durston had been experimenting to see whether he could influence my mind at a distance, because hitherto we had been together during the tests; but, if it had emanated from some other source, the golden door must have played a very remarkable part in the mind of some stranger to have produced such a powerful impression. All our previous experiences had brought us in touch with crime—could the golden door be the dominating thought in the mind of some criminal? "Pickwick" fell unheeded on the hearth-rug as I pondered it all until presently I got up, and taking a piece of plain white paper pinned it on the wall in front of me. I looked at the clock and noted that it was twenty past three. I stared at the paper until my eyes ached, but I could see nothing. I began to feel drowsy, but still I tried to keep my mind a blank and concentrate my attention on the white sheet, till at last I heard Doris's voice.

"Come along, dear, tea!" she called. "Wake up."

I sat down at the tea-table, determined to make no further effort, but to leave my brain free to receive any other message, and Doris entertained me brightly with a description of her difficulties in satisfying the firms whose advertisements she illustrated and her own conscience at the same time. Presently I strolled across to the fire to get some hot water. As I stooped down over the fireplace I glanced idly at the sheet of blank paper which was still pinned to the wall.

"Have you hurt yourself?" cried Doris anxiously, as the kettle fell with a clatter into the grate.

"No, no," I replied hurriedly. "It's all right," but I felt far from all right; for, as I had glanced at the paper, I had seen a perfect picture of an extraordinarily beautiful girl, dressed—or rather, wrapped—in a flowing garment of some material such as cloth of gold, her magnificent red-gold hair flowing in gorgeous profusion about her shoulders. The image was gone in an instant, but that face is burnt into my memory to this day. So strong was the impression I received that I could almost see the lovely features wherever I looked. But my cousin was evidently anxious about me, for she told me I looked dazed, so I hurried out into the scullery, refilled the kettle and put it on the gas-ring. During the rest of tea-time I carried on a light conversation with Doris, but all the time I was trying to think of some way in which I could get to the root of the mystery. One thing was obvious; I was now able to receive a colour message without the presence of my teacher. Could I by any means transmit my impressions as Mr. Durston had transmitted his to me? If I had a sympathetic subject I felt sure I could. Why should not Doris help me? I had never really confided in her the nature of my work with Professor Durston, because I was afraid that, not fully understanding, she might have made fun of the whole things and that would have led to a quarrel.

Accordingly I thought out my plan carefully and decided to set about it in a roundabout manner. Later in the evening, when my cousin had finished her work and was resting before the fire, I handed her a magazine through which I was glancing and, pointing to an illustration, I asked her what she thought of it.

"In what way?" she asked.

"Well," I answered, "do you consider that a pretty girl?"

"Oh, heavens, no!" she replied emphatically.

"What do you call a pretty girl?" I asked.

"If you are trying to get at my work, you needn't imagine that the young brides I do for the 'How we furnished our home' advertisements is my idea of a pretty girl, because it isn't. It's the popular idea, but it's not mine. Now you're a pretty girl yourself, Leslie, a very pretty girl, though you look too horribly intelligent for the public fancy."

"Thank you," I laughed. "But what I mean is this. Have you been so long catering for the taste of the public fancy, as you call it, that you have forgotten your own idea of a beautiful woman?"

"Oh, I hope not," she protested. "Get me a sketch-pad and let us see."

"Oh! do," I cried, "make a colour sketch and just sit down and think of nothing except that you want to paint a beautiful woman— not anyone you have ever seen, but just some abstract idea."

"Is this some of your psychology stuff?" she asked suspiciously. "Besides, what's the good of colour at this time of night?"

"It's not any of my psychology," I laughed, "though it may have something to do with yours. And a face looks so uninteresting in black and white; beside, it's not the first time you've done colour work by electric light."

So my cousin sat down with a drawing-board and a box of colours in front of her, while I nestled on the arm of her chair and laid my hand lightly on her neck.

"Now, what is it you want me to do?" she asked.

"Just let your mind rest on the fact that you are going to draw some beautiful woman, whom you have never seen or thought of, but who is what you consider a really beautiful woman."

"What do I think of?" she asked.

"Don't try to think of anything," I suggested. "I just want to see what your brain will do by itself. If you start to think of something definite, you will probably draw some pretty girl you once met."

"That," said Doris, "probably sounds a lot easier than it really is."

I leaned over and switched off the lights, leaving only the reading-lamp on the table beside us alight. Doris sat quite still after a few somewhat flippant remarks. I sat beside her and concentrated all my attention on the face which I had seen, and, in view of the remarkable features and striking beauty, I found this comparatively simple. Presently my cousin sighed deeply and passed her hand across her eyes.

"Your hand is burning my neck," she said at last, in a drowsy voice, "it's . . . burning. . . burning . . . ."

Then suddenly, to my utter astonishment, she shook my arm away and, pushing me aside, seized a brush and began to work with the feverish frenzy of a maniac. I stood stock still, determined to see nothing, feel nothing, think of nothing but the image I had seen on the paper above the fire. And then Doris threw herself back in her chair with a little cry and I ran to her side. She got up and, dropping on to the sofa, began to cry softly. She was a little hysterical, and I thought it best to leave her to herself for a little and, hardly knowing what I dared to expect, I went over to the table and picked up the drawing-board. It may seem strange that, having brought every force of which I was capable to bear upon the achievement of the result I desired, I should have been at all surprised to see that result accomplished; yet I was absolutely amazed when I saw that I held in my hand the exact replica of my brain-picture. This was no fleeting image painted on the tissues of the mind, but a straightforward painting executed in real pigment.

"I'm sorry to be such a little fool," said Doris, with an apologetic laugh. "What is it like, anyway? Show me."

"It's very good," I replied lightly, "and I won't have you calling yourself names."

"Yes," said my cousin after she had examined it, "it *is* a beautiful face. I wonder why I chose a golden robe! I suppose it was to match her hair as nearly as possible."

I took the painting from her and laid it away carefully to dry after she had told me I could keep it for myself, and after that, thinking it would be safer to change the subject, I manœuvred the conversation into less turbulent channels until we went to bed.

The following morning we walked across the fields to East Finchley, and I called at Lorran House to, see Mr. Bindold.

"Of course," I began, "I know you will tell me that you simply don't understand it, but what do you make of this?"

Mr. Bindold took the painting I held out to him and listened attentively while I told him the whole story.

"At least you must agree," I concluded, "that it is very remarkable, even if you don't understand it."

"Yes," he admitted, "very remarkable; the more so as I am quite sure I have seen the face before somewhere."

"Are you sure?" I cried.

"Certain," he answered emphatically. "It is hardly a face that one would be likely to forget, and yet I have managed to forget where I have seen it and when."

"Does anything suggest the circumstances to you," I asked, "a dance or a dinner party?"

"No, I have never met her," Arthur declared, "but I have seen a photograph of her somewhere, in one of the 'illustrateds' or something."

But though I tried my best to help him and to suggest a number of places in which he might have been looking at one of the weekly illustrated papers, no suggestion of clubs, or railway journeys, or anything else I could think of conveyed anything to him at all.

"No, it's no good," he admitted regretfully at last; "but this is where my part of the work comes in. I shall find out."

And without more ado he strolled into the hall, took up his hat and stick and went out. Even though he sometimes threw cold water on the fire of our enthusiasm, Arthur was exceedingly helpful, and one could not but admire the quiet, business-like way in which he tackled anything tangible we had for him to work on.

After spending the afternoon at home, I returned to Lorran House to greet the professor on his return from the country. I was sitting at the piano when he came in, and as I noted the air of almost boyish freshness on his face I could not help thinking that Mr. Bindold's idle chatter of madhouses was about as unjustified and ridiculous as anything could be.

"Why, hullo, Leslie!" he exclaimed in surprise as he caught sight of me—for after my first month with him he had dropped the more formal "Miss Dalrayne"—"I hope you haven't been working over the week-end. You must have *some* recreation, you know. Arthur is everlastingly dinning it into me that you are working too hard."

"Oh no, I haven't been working, Mr. Durston," I laughed; "and it is very good of Mr. Bindold, but I am quite capable of looking after myself. I just dropped in for a chat."

"Ah!" he said, "that sounds interesting. Come and sit by the fire and tell me all about it."

"To begin with," I said, "I wanted to know whether you have been conducting any experiments over the week-end? I mean, have you been sending me any messages?"

"No," he replied; "none whatever. My whole being has been concentrated on golf. What have you seen?"

So I related the entire circumstances to him, adding a great many technical details with which I have not troubled the reader.

"Excellent!" he said as I finished. "And where is the picture your cousin painted now?"

"Mr. Bindold has it," I replied. "He went out this morning to see if he could identify the subject."

"I don't suppose he'll be able to do much with it on Sunday. I wish he'd come back; I should like to see it."

"It is a very remarkable face," I continued; "and the sketch is almost an exact replica of my mental image. I do hope we shall be able to find out who it is."

We had not long to wait before Arthur himself returned. He nodded to Mr. Durston as he entered, and tossed the sketch over to me with an air of triumph.

"Well?" I asked.

"On the back," he replied abruptly, and lighted a cigarette.

I turned the drawing over. On the back of it was pencilled: "Muriel Garringham, only child of William J. Garringham, American millionaire, chairman of the Garringham Traction and Transport Co., Ltd., of 134, Cadogan Square, W."

I read the inscription aloud.

"Good!" exclaimed the professor. "How did you get the information?"

"I went round the pictorial news-agencies until I found a man who recognised the face. He showed me a photograph—undoubtedly of the same lady—which they had on their file. Those were the only details he could give me. I then called on the Society Editor of the *Daily Argus*, a personal friend of mine, and told him I wanted to know all I could about Miss Garringham for journalistic purposes. He supplied a few of the missing links. It seems that Garringham has brought his daughter over to this country in the hope that she would make a sensation in London society, as she undoubtedly would. The ultimate idea is obviously to marry her into the peerage. Then the usual thing happens; Miss Muriel appears to be in love with a young American lawyer, a fellow with political ambitions, any amount of brains, and something like ten or twenty dollars to call his own. Then we come to an interesting rumour—mind you, I can only call it a rumour—to the effect that Miss Garringham has disappeared from home and eloped with the lawyer fellow. He is known to have arrived from America this week, and to have made several unsuccessful attempts to gain an interview with the old man. That is as far as I have gone, but I hope we shall be able to get to the bottom of the matter in a few days."

"There is more behind it than an elopement," the professor declared.

"The golden door and the penniless lawyer don't seem to fit in very well," I suggested.

"No," Arthur agreed. "Quite apart from your aspect of the affair, a commonsense—forgive me, I should say, a practical—view of the matter suggests that a man who is eloping with a millionaire's daughter would hardly be anxious to interview the father until the first fury of his anger had subsided a bit."

"What shall we do?" I asked, for I had a great opinion of Arthur's ability and judgement when it came to a question of action.

"Obviously get to know Garringham for one thing, and find the lawyer chap for another," said Mr. Durston. "I have no doubt I can manage the first, and I am sure Arthur will arrange the second part of the programme."

Mr. Bindold and I discussed the best means of finding the American, the hotels he would probably put up at, and so forth, while the professor sat and gazed absently at Miss Garringham's portrait. Presently he got up slowly and heavily, and laid his hand on my arm. I rose to follow him. He led the way across the hall and into the great white globe in which we had conducted most of our experiments, and taking our seats on the daïs, we fixed our attention on the dazzling walls which encircled us. Mr. Durston never took his hand from my arm, and I began to grow restless under what seemed to be a persistent pressure, but was in reality, as I learned afterwards, the merest touch, until, just as the weight was beginning to be unbearable, the white walls of the dome suddenly faded away into a dull grey mist. I sat breathless and watched again the unfolding on a much larger scale of the house with the golden door. It was identical with my miniature image of the previous day, but there was this difference in the setting. Before the door, crouching against it and looking towards us, was a hideous little hunchback, his face twisted up in a ghastly leer of lunacy, his eyes burning with the awful fire of madness. I must have cried aloud involuntarily, for I came to myself to find the professor shaking me.

"Come away, Leslie," he said anxiously; "come away. You'll be all right in a moment."

I staggered back into the drawing-room and drank a glass of cognac which Arthur handed me.

"How do you feel?" he asked.

"Better, thank you," I murmured. "I'm all right now."

"You had better rest a little while, my dear," said Mr. Durston kindly, "and Williams will drive you home in the car. Arthur and I are going to call on Mr. Garringham."

But, having elicited the admission that I might possibly be able to help, I insisted on accompanying them. As soon as the chauffeur could bring the car round we jumped in and drove off to Cadogan Square. As we alighted from the car we noticed a tall man talking excitedly to a policeman.

"I expect that is our American friend," said Mr. Bindold. "I will wait for you here."

Mr. Durston handed his card, with the simple message, "an urgent matter," written across it, to the butler, and we were admitted almost at once.

"Of course, your name is quite familiar to me, professor," said Mr. Garringham, a pompous little man who looked exceedingly worried, "but I don't think I have the pleasure of your acquaintance."

"No," said my companion abruptly. "Won't you sit down?"

The millionaire gave an almost comical start of surprise at this unusual request in his own house, but he promptly did as he was told.

"We have come to see you about your daughter," continued the professor.

"Oh, indeed," said Mr. Garringham, with a sarcastic sneer; "come to plead for her and that young scamp Prenton? I suppose. Well, let me tell you, sir, that she is no longer my daughter, and if I ever—"

"That will do," said Mr. Durston quietly, and the little railroad magnate, apparently recognising the force of a superior personality, gave up the uneven struggle and subsided. "Do you know a little hunchback, with a prominent chin and very dark complexion?"

"Fordyce," replied the other, "William Fordyce, my friend, one of my greatest friends. He has done nothing to assist my daughter in her—"

"Where is he now?"

"Well, as a matter of fact, he is in the next room; but I repeat that he has nothing whatever to do with the matter. He is my friend and I am very grateful for his sympathy in my trouble. My daughter is the apple of my eye and—"

"Would you kindly ask that Mr. Fordyce be shown in here, and tell him that you will be detained on important business for the rest of the evening?"

Mr. Garringham looked uncertainly from one to the other of us, wavered for an instant and then rose and rang the bell. When the hunchback entered a few moments afterwards I was surprised to notice that there was no trace of the strange madness which had been our chief impression of him in the dome. Mr. Garringham explained to him very plausibly, I thought, that he would be engaged indefinitely.

"All right, my dear fellow, certainly," said Mr. Fordyce. "Watson can have my car sent round and I will run along home," and with a cheery good-night he left the room.

"Now," said Mr. Durston, "We will follow, Mr. Garringham, and you shall accompany us in our car."

The millionaire rubbed his hand across his forehead with a dazed expression and nodded absently. As soon as the hunchback's motor had started off round the square, the three of us jumped into the car and set off in pursuit. We followed up Sloane Street to Knightsbridge, along Piccadilly and Shaftesbury Avenue to Oxford Street, until eventually we pulled up in a dreary little side street off Holborn. Williams informed us that Mr. Fordyce had stopped just round the corner and we followed, cautiously, on foot. We clung to the wall as we watched him take a key from his pocket and open the door of a dingy house, which looked like the outside of a warehouse. He shut the door behind him and we held a council of war outside. Presently the door opened again and a tall figure crept out. Mr. Durston flung his weight against the man and sent him rolling in the gutter and before he could recover his wits we had slipped inside and bolted the door. We found ourselves in a very ordinary square hall or lobby, with a cheap hat-stand and a dirty old mat, and I felt we had discovered a mare's nest. The professor opened the door at the end of the hall and started back with a cry of surprise. I stood on tip-toe and looked over his shoulder. There in front of us was the golden door, a great massive thing, set apparently in the wall of an old Norman Church.

We looked at each other in silence, and my friend stepped forward and tried the door, but it would not move. We followed the wall round, along some dark, dimly lighted cloisters and suddenly stopped dead as the sound of a fiendish, grating chuckle caught our ears. Then we quickened our pace almost to a run until we reached the end of the cloisters. Here we stopped by a narrow stair. Stealthily we climbed the steps, the hideous chuckle growing louder and louder, until at last we found ourselves on a narrow platform in front of a door with glass panels. Mr. Durston and I pressed our faces against the glass in breathless excitement, while I heard the "transport king" panting behind us. Then, as I took in the scene, I bit my lip to suppress an exclamation which might have betrayed our presence. We were looking into a large, glazed-in case, very much like a box at a theatre. Sitting in a luxurious easy chair, his hideous face distorted in a maniacal grin, was Fordyce, the hunchback. Below us was the most extraordinary sight that I have ever seen. A great hall, which had evidently once been a church, was one blazing mass of gold. The old pillars were hung with rich yellow silks, the floor was strewn with bright yellow Oriental rugs, on which were reclining a number of young girls clad in yellow robes. At the end of the hall was a large black divan and reclining on it, her face buried in her hands, her shoulders heaving with violent sobs, was Miss Garringham. Beside her, dressed in a red gown with a bright yellow sash, stood a swarthy negro with a fan.

Mr. Durston was the first of the three to recover himself, and, bursting open the door of the box, he pinioned the lunatic from behind. It was the negro who, in the midst of the uproar which our sudden intervention caused, showed us the way into the hall, down a narrow spiral staircase. In less than ten minutes the beautiful girl was safe in her father's care, driving back to Cadogan Square with Mr. Garringham and me, while the professor went for the police. When we arrived at Mr. Garringham's house we found Arthur and Mr. Prenton, the young American lawyer, waiting in the library, and by mutual consent we left the lovers together, the old man offering no opposition at all.

From the story she told us afterwards, it appears that Miss Garringham had been walking in the park one day, when a stranger came forward and, introducing himself, informed her that her father had met with a serious accident. She stepped with him into a taxi-cab and remembered no more until she found herself in the house with the golden door. She had been treated with the greatest consideration by her captors as, we discovered afterwards, had the other girls, and not one of them had seen the mad hunchback in that strange environment. After I had helped Miss Garringham's maid to see her to bed, Mr. Durston joined us with the information that Fordyce had been taken to an observation ward, where he was afterwards declared insane.

"Well, Leslie," said the professor, as the three of us were driving back to our little flat, "you've done very well indeed."

"Yes," said Arthur, "I think she deserves a reward. I'll get a box for Miss Doris and the three of us at His Majesty's for Tuesday night. What do you say?"

"Thank you very much, Arthur," I said.

No. 3: Red
THE MANCROFT STUDIO MURDER

I was sitting beside Professor Durston's desk one day, taking some shorthand notes from dictation, when the maid entered with a visiting card on a tray. Mr. Durston took the card, whistled softly, and passed it across to me.

"Recognise the name?" he asked.

"Edith Walton," I read. "No, I don't think I know."

"My dear Leslie," he exclaimed, "you evidently haven't read the paper lately."

He delved among a pile of newspapers at his feet and handed me a copy of *The Daily Telegraph*.

"Read that."

I looked at the headlines and remembered that I had certainly seen the name only the day before.

"The Mancroft Studio Murder," I said. "Of course, a Miss Walton is under arrest—Valerie Walton."

"This," said Mr. Durston, "is probably her sister. I had better see what she wants."

"Shall I leave you?" I asked.

"No, you had better stay where you are," my employer replied. "I have grown accustomed to rely upon your assistance already, you see."

I have recorded this trivial conversation for a particular reason. As the reader may remember, it was freely stated in the press and elsewhere at the time of the Mancroft Studio Murder, that the services of Mr. Durston were sought for by the police, and that, acting upon the advice which he was able to give them, the authorities themselves solved one of the most baffling mysteries in the annals of Scotland Yard. I hope I have made it clear that our first connection with the mystery arose from the fact that Miss Edith Walton called at Lorran House.

I make no apology for including this story in the series of colour impressions which I was collecting for our "Unbound Book," because, although it was something quite apart from our usual experiments and investigations, it helped to bear out the professor's theories of colour vibrations and to complete his chromatic cycle. I do not in any way attempt to explain the remarkable phenomena which we witnessed at this time; I simply give the facts as I know them. Spiritualists and students of the occult—as distinct from the purely psychic—may place what construction they like upon the incidents, for I have no suggestion to offer, and I never had any real opportunity of learning the views of my famous teacher on the subject. But to resume.

Miss Walton was shown into the study. She was a tall, slight, rather delicate-looking girl, with dark hair and eyes, and, as might have been expected, she was pale and agitated. As the professor had supposed, she proved to be the sister of the Valerie Walton who was under arrest on a capital charge.

"I have come to see you about my sister," she began. "You have heard—you must have seen it in the paper—that she has been arrested on a charge of murdering the man Anderson, at No. 5, Mancroft Studios, South Kensington."

"Sit down and calm yourself, my dear young lady, and tell us all about it," Mr. Durston urged gently.

"On Tuesday evening," the poor girl continued, "I was sitting at home waiting for my sister to come in for her evening meal, when I heard a knock at the door. It proved to be two detectives and a policeman. They asked for Valerie, and I told them she was out. They asked at what time she usually came home, and I said she was a little later than usual that night as she was going up to Oxford Street to buy a pair of shoes on her way home—we live at Clapham. Just then Valerie came running up the stairs and looked from the men to me in astonishment. The spokesman of the three stepped aside and asked her to come in. As she did so, they followed and closed the door behind them. Then the same man said, 'Is your name Valerie Walton?' Of course, Valerie said 'Yes,' and the man replied, 'We are police officers and you are wanted on a charge of murdering Philip Anderson, of 5, Mancroft Studios.' He also said something about anything she said being used in evidence against her. Valerie looked bewildered for a moment, and then burst out laughing. 'But I've just left him,' she cried; 'I left him in the studio about an hour and a half ago.'

"I saw the men look at each other significantly, and I realised that my sister, innocent as she must be, had made a dangerous admission. I told the officers that it must be a mistake and that they would find themselves in trouble if they were not careful. Then they informed us that Philip Anderson's housekeeper had heard a revolver shot, and had burst into the studio to find him lying shot through the temple. She ran downstairs screaming and opened the front door in time to see Valerie running round the corner. Of course, we were both dreadfully shocked, for though we did not like Mr. Anderson, it was a very terrible affair, but we neither of us realised that they really suspected Valerie of murder until they took her away. There was nothing I could do; I went straight round to some friends, and they promised to help me, and in the morning they took me to the police. I am to be allowed to see Valerie to-morrow. We have got a solicitor to look after her interests, but they all seem to think she is guilty. So I came to you to see if you could help me. It is impossible that Valerie could murder anyone. If only you could understand—if only—"

At this point the poor girl broke down altogether, and it was many minutes before I could comfort her, and make her understand that she was with friends. I assured her that the wisest thing she could have done was to come to Mr. Durston.

"Now, my dear young lady," said the professor, "you must try to calm yourself for your poor sister's sake. We must act quickly and decisively, for though I am confident that your sister is innocent, and that we shall be able to clear her, every minute is to her a year of agony. Now tell me, why do you speak of 'the man Anderson'? It is a term which suggests contempt."

"I couldn't bear him and neither could my sister," Miss Walton replied. "Valerie used to sit to him for her eyes, and she had known him for many years. None of the other artists at Mancroft Studios liked him, and Valerie only sat for him because he offered nearly three times the money anyone else did. He was in love with her, or at any rate he pretended to be. He asked her to marry him on one occasion, and when he noticed the involuntary look of disgust with which she greeted the question, he threatened to kill her. He repeatedly threw out sinister hints that he would not ask her again, and that some day she would be sorry she had refused him. Of course, Valerie used to laugh it off and take it as a joke, but, only the day before the murder, she told me that, when his present picture was finished, she would not sit for him again."

"I see," said Mr. Durston. "But what was the real reason for your sister's arrest?"

"The real reason?" queried our visitor. "That she was the last to be in the room with him, I suppose."

"That appears to me to be rather a reason for observation than for immediate arrest. The police are really very considerate. You say Anderson was shot through the head with a revolver? Where was the revolver found?"

Miss Walton gave the slightest possible start.

"In the street, just outside the front door," she answered.

The professor looked at her shrewdly and lay back in his chair.

"Now, Miss Walton," he said, "please remember that we are anxious to help your sister, and tell me, who did the revolver belong to, and where did it come from?"

Our visitor leaned forward suddenly and buried her face in her hands.

"The revolver was Valerie's," she sobbed.

"Now keep calm and tell us how she came to have a revolver, and how she came to take it to the studio with her. Had she any idea of protecting herself from Anderson, or what?"

"The pistol was given to Valerie by an uncle of ours, who was home from Canada. He used to take Valerie to a shooting gallery and taught her how to use a revolver, and before he went away he presented her with the automatic pistol which was found on the doorstep at Mancroft Studios. Valerie says she does not know how it came to be there, although she herself took it to the studios to show to a young artist with whom she is very friendly."

"And she left it with him, I suppose?"

"Yes, he used to tease her about it, and said she ought not to have a pistol about the house, and she told him to take care of it until she wanted it."

"Who is this man, and where is he?" asked the professor.

"His name is Donald Flockhart," Miss Walton answered. "He went over to Paris the day before the murder, and came back yesterday. He had seen the report in the Paris edition of *The Argus*, and returned at once."

"And the pistol was locked in his studio, or flat, or whatever it is, all the time—or at least your sister believed it to be."

"Yes, she quite thought it was."

"What about ammunition?" I put in. "Had your sister any cartridges? Did she leave them with Mr. Flockhart at the same time?"

"Valerie had no cartridges, I know, before the murder. She had used the last at the revolver-range, and only got there just what she wanted. We neither of us cared to have a loaded pistol lying about the rooms. But the extraordinary thing was that in Valerie's suitcase at the studio the police found some spare cartridges. The bullet that was taken from Mr. Anderson's wall—it passed clean through his head—fits the empty cartridge in the magazine of Valerie's pistol. They seem to have a complete story to bring against her."

"Well, we must do what we can at once," said Mr. Durston. "Leslie, will you ring up Arthur at his office, and tell him we should like to see him as soon as he is free?"

"Do you think the police will let you interview my sister, Mr. Durston?" our visitor was asking as I returned from the 'phone.

"I anticipate no difficulty in that," said the professor; "but I don't think the interview would do any more than perhaps help her to feel that she has friends who are doing their best for her.

No, the person whom I wish to interview is the housekeeper, and also the other artist, Flockhart. You see we are working against the police, and we must reverse their methods. They assume that, in view of their incriminating evidence, your sister's story is false; we must assume that, in view of our belief in Miss Valerie, her story is true. The police, I am sorry to say, are now looking for more evidence that she is guilty, and that is all that is really concerning them; we must look for evidence that someone else committed the murder, and I must say I think we shall find it."

"Oh, thank you, thank you!" cried Miss Walton pathetically. "I cannot tell you how grateful I am to you for your offer of help. You will let me know what is happening, I hope?"

"Certainly, my dear young lady, certainly," replied the professor; "you shall hear from us as soon as we have anything to report. I shall communicate with the police at once, and I assure you we shall not allow any grass to grow under our feet. Good-bye, and try to be as hopeful as you can."

When I had shown Miss Walton out, I returned to find Mr. Durston poring over the London directory.

"Well," I asked, "who murdered Philip Anderson! The girl, her artist friend, or the housekeeper?"

"None of them," he replied.

"Good gracious!" I exclaimed. "You seem very sure. I must say the police seem to have a black case against the girl. It is terribly sad."

"Yes, they have a strong case, but I think it stands on a rotten foundation, and I am quite certain that Miss Valerie What's-her-name is innocent."

"Is that just a conviction?" I asked interestedly, "or have you some reason for saying so?"

"My reason for saying that she is innocent is that her pistol was found on the doorstep. The police case is this: The girl was seen to be running away just as she naturally would do if she was going up to Oxford Street to buy a pair of shoes, and at the same time didn't want to keep her sister waiting for her. She left the studio at her usual time, as we can gather from the fact that she was so late for tea, and ran for a 'bus. The man was found murdered, and the girl's revolver was found lying on the doorstep. I think as soon as I see the door I shall be able to convince you that the revolver could not have been dropped on the doorstep by a fugitive murderess. It would be very difficult indeed to open a door and rush out and drop a pistol in such a way that it would stay placidly on the step. If she was running, the pistol would have bounced on to the pavement, or been kicked into the gutter as she fled. If she had been walking with an assumed air of innocence, shall we say, she would have picked the pistol up again, for she most certainly would have heard it drop. I think we must look for someone else. The other artist is a friend of the girl Valerie, and the housekeeper probably has no reason for committing murders."

"But what about the revolver?" I urged. "If Miss Walton didn't drop it there, the same argument applies to any other person who may have committed the murder. You see, if there is a reason to suppose that Miss Walton could not have dropped it, why, then no one else could have dropped it in similar circumstances. As the pistol was found there, it seems likely to have been dropped there by the fugitive. I'm afraid, Mr. Durston, that seems to be of very little help to us at all."

"Well, we shall see, Leslie," he replied. "I think you will find that I am right about the revolver anyhow."

"Oh, I expect you are, Mr. Durston," I admitted readily. "I know it is a very great impertinence on my part to suggest that you are not, but I couldn't quite see your point."

"All right, my dear," he laughed; "I don't mind how many opinions you express. And if you like I will tell you why I think we must look in some new direction for the murderer. The housekeeper I see no reason to suspect. The other artist, Flockhart, was, as pointed out before, a friend of Valerie's, and in my opinion this murder was committed by someone who owed the girl a grudge, and who, utterly fiendish and impossible as it may seem, carried out the whole plan in order to pay the grudge. Possibly, of course, it was a double grudge, but in either case I am sure that the murderer worked his plans out carefully and cunningly in order to cast suspicion on Valerie Walton."

"You mean that someone killed Anderson in order to gain a revenge over the girl and get her hanged for murder by arranging the evidence beforehand? It seems hardly credible."

"Unfortunately such things do happen, though," the professor replied, "and one has to be ready to take them into account. In this case I feel sure that the revolver was not dropped on the doorstep, but was deliberately laid there so that the housekeeper, or whoever else was first on the scene, should find it. Now I will ring up Scotland Yard, and get them to arrange for us to have access to the scene of the murder."

"Am I to come, too?" I asked.

"Yes, if you will, Leslie," said Mr. Durston. "We shall want all our resources in this matter, I fancy."

I ran from the study to my little den for my hat and coat, wondering what my country friends would have said had they known that the timid little parson's daughter, whose life had, only a few months back, consisted of a daily round of nursing and housekeeping, was now putting on her things to visit the scene of a peculiarly horrible murder with scarcely a tremor. Truly I had "found myself" since my first strange meeting with the professor.

When we arrived at Mancroft Studios we found a police inspector awaiting us. He touched his cap respectfully as the professor stepped out of the car.

"I was rather surprised to hear that I was to expect you, sir," he remarked. "Everything here seems perfectly above board and quite simple and straightforward. Young man makes love to a young woman and she resents it, he persists until one day the young woman pulls out a gun and puts an end to it. I should have thought it would have paid her to confess, seeing that everybody round here says he was a most objectionable man."

"I just wanted to have a look round, Inspector," the professor answered. "There are one or two points about this business which I can hardly understand from the reports I have received, and I should like to clear them up on the spot."

"Very good, sir," the inspector replied. "I am at your service. The young lady, I suppose, will stay outside."

"On the contrary," said the professor, "she will accompany us. This is my secretary, Miss Leslie Dalrayne, Inspector Orless."

I bowed to the policeman in response to his salute, and he looked at me as if I were some sort of new animal he had just heard of. As we entered the gateway of the little courtyard leading to the studios, the inspector pointed out the room in which the murder had been committed, and went into a vast amount of detailed measurements which so far as I could see had no bearing on the question of who committed the crime. Mr. Durston seemed to seize on one point at once, however.

"You say it is only four paces from the door of Anderson's studio to the outside door?" he asked.

"That is so, sir," the inspector answered. "And it goes to show that the young woman must have rushed out of the room with the pistol still smoking in her hand, opened the front, or as you say, the outside door, accidentally dropping the pistol as she did so, and fled."

"Candidly, Orless," said the professor, "I don't like your story a bit. I can't see it happening just as you suggest at all. You say the girl suddenly pulled out a pistol, fired at the man, and ran straight out of the room while it was still smoking. You say this because you feel that otherwise the housekeeper would have met her in the hall, although she had only four paces to go. You are trying to fit the case to the evidence; that will never do, we must fit the evidence to the case, and if it won't fit, throw it away. Now if the girl had only four paces between the studio and the street, and less than half a minute's walk from the front door to the back, how do you make out that the housekeeper heard the shot, ran up from the basement, opened the studio door, discovered the body, ran to the outside door, opened it, and arrived on the step to see the murderer *running away?* Now that won't do, you know, Orless, will it? That housekeeper is wrong."

"She most certainly said she saw the girl running away," the inspector declared; "but now you come to put it like that, it seems hardly feasible."

"So that little bit of evidence is knocked on the head," said Mr. Durston. "Now, you only have the revolver clue left."

"That and the fact that accused was the last person with the deceased, either of which would be very incriminating separately, but together they leave no room for doubt."

Mr. Durston paused on the doorstep and laid his hand on the inspector's sleeve.

"How do you know she was the last person with him?" he asked.

"Well," said Mr. Orless, "she admits it; that's good enough for anybody, surely."

"My dear fellow," laughed the professor, "how can you possibly take anyone's word for a thing like that? How can she know whether she was the last person there or not? All she can admit is that she left him at about a certain time; she can't say what may have happened after that. Still, let us have a look at the place anyway."

The inspector took a key out of his pocket and opened the door leading into the hall.

"This is the door through which you say she came, and then this must be the doorstep on which you found the pistol?" I asked.

"Exactly, miss," the inspector answered.

I put my shoulder against the door. It was operated by the appliance necessary to hold it open to prevent it pushing you into the street as you went out. I held it back with my hand and turned to the inspector.

"Which side of the step was the revolver, inspector?" I asked.

"On the left-hand side, miss," Mr. Orless replied, with a look of mingled surprise and disapproval. I glanced at Mr. Durston.

"The fact that the revolver was on the left-hand side of the step goes a long way towards corroborating your theory," I said. "The door would have to be held open with the right hand."

"Not unless it was someone in the house," said Mr. Durston; "because otherwise there would be no need to hold the door open."

"I'm afraid there can only be one answer to it all, sir," said the inspector, with an impatient shrug. "Everything seems to point to the young woman Walton."

I was not by any means so sure that it did point in that direction at all, and while I waited for the policeman to open the door of the studio I could not help feeling how ready the authorities were to take the first probability and do everything they could to clothe it with circumstantial evidence. Suddenly Mr. Durston gripped my shoulder heavily. I turned round startled, almost afraid he was ill, but his face was lighted with a smile of intense eagerness and interest. He leaned down and whispered in my ear.

"I think I have it," he said, "I am sure I have it, but it will take us all our time to prove it."

Before I could reply the inspector's voice interrupted us and we turned to follow him into the studio. There was nothing very remarkable about the place in itself, except that it was very artistically and tastefully furnished. Several of the artist's things were still lying about the floor, just as he had dropped them. Over a screen hung a white satin dress. Standing on an easel at the end of the room was a picture of a tall dark girl, with curiously lustrous and beautiful eyes. She was dressed in what appeared to be a red gown of some striped material, but when I went closer and examined it, I found that it was a painting of a white satin dress viciously daubed over with red paint. I pointed it out to the others.

"Yes," said Mr. Orless. "Of course, I saw that. These artist chaps get very irritable at times, you know, miss, and sometimes entirely destroy their own work. That means nothing, I assure you."

But the professor was staring at it as if it had given the clue to the whole thing. The inspector and I stood and watched him as his face worked and his eyes appeared as if they would drop out of his head. The perspiration was standing out in beads upon his forehead and his breath was coming in short gasps. I shuddered suddenly and caught the inspector by the arm. Presently Mr. Durston spoke in a low, hoarse voice.

"This man was not murdered," he said; "he killed himself."

He stared wildly about the panelled room, muttering to himself, "suicide . . . I know it . . . I feel it." At last he called to us to stand back, and as we did so he picked up the artist's palette in one hand and hurriedly switched off the lights with the other. Mr.

Orless gave a short cry of protest; I felt instinctively that we were about to witness some strange phenomenon, though, somehow, I was sure it would not prove to be one of our chromatic images. The inspector was shaking beside me in the dark, convinced I am sure that Mr. Durston had gone out of his mind. Presently the darkness was lightened by a dull red glow which seemed to emanate from a corner of the room. Soon I could make out the figure of the professor, crouched beside the easel, clutching the palette in a grip of frenzy. Then suddenly a figure sprang forward, threw a chair against the wall, jumped upon it and down again, and pushed the chair across the room so quickly that it was all over in an instant. Then I heard a faint click and then a clatter on the panelled wall and a chill thud. By this time the figure had entirely disappeared. I felt a cold shaking hand on my face and I screamed aloud, but it was Mr. Orless trying to find the electric light switch. When at last the light was on we found Mr. Durston, still leaning against the table, his eyes fixed upon the centre of the floor. I went up to him and shook him. He turned to me with a haggard look.

"Well," he asked in a tired voice, "did you see it? It *was* suicide after all."

Both Mr. Orless and I admitted that we had seen something, but we could not be very sure what it was we had seen. The professor raised himself and motioned to me to fetch a chair. This he placed against the wall and, after fingering the panelling for some moments, at last laid his hand upon a small spring which released a sliding door in the panelling. Then he put in his hand and drew out a bit of paper and a revolver, which was attached to a long piece of elastic. Together we bent over the paper. Truly it was a strange document. "Whosoever shall find this"—it ran—"shall know for the first time of how I, Philip Geoffrey Anderson, did wreak my vengeance upon Valerie Walton, who hated me because I loved her. I took from the room of her friend the revolver which she left there, and I bought another which took the same size of bullets. I placed a discharged cartridge in the magazine of her own pistol, and as I saw her out I laid it on the doorstep. Then I rushed back to my studio. I took from the secret cupboard, where you have found this,

the revolver, which you have also found. I held it to my temple and
with my finger and thumb released the trigger. Then, as I fell, the
elastic which you see drew back the pistol to its hiding-place and
closed the door in the panelling. I pray that this has happened as I
had planned it and as I had rehearsed it so often, that Valerie may
suffer as she has made me suffer, and die as she has made me die.
P.G.A."

"Come, Leslie," said Mr. Durston, as he handed the paper to
the inspector. "Mr. Orless will see to everything now, the release
of Miss Walton, and everything of that sort. I want you to see me
home, Leslie. I'm tired, very . . . very tired."

No. 4: Blue
THE SONG THAT WAS NEVER SUNG

"Who is that singing?"

It was Professor Durston who spoke. Arthur Bindold looked up from, his paper in surprise.

"Singing?" he asked; "I don't hear anyone singing."

"I thought I did," I said. "In fact, I'm sure I did. It seemed to be coming from that corner over there; a low soft voice singing a few bars of a very melancholy refrain."

"Then it *was* someone," Mr. Durston repeated emphatically, "for that is exactly what I heard myself."

We were silent for a few moments, listening for the sound, but Arthur was positive we were both dreaming.

"If you could hear it, *I* ought to be able to," he declared stubbornly. "It may have been somebody outside; but there was certainly no singing in the room. Possibly one of the maids in—"

"Listen!" I cried. "There it is again!"

Professor Durston jumped to his feet, an expression of acute interest on his face. The music stopped again, just as it had done before.

"It sounded nearer this time!" he said thoughtfully.

"Somebody in the grounds," Arthur insisted. "As I said before, probably one of the maids."

"That wasn't one of the maids, Arthur," I assured him; "and who would be in the grounds on a night like this?"

"Well, anyway it was very strange," my employer declared. "It seems to have stopped now."

I was much impressed by this curious incident. True, there may have been someone singing a little way off, and, owing to some strange condition of the atmosphere, the sound had travelled more than usual; but there was such a poignant note of grief in the music that I confess it almost made me shudder. I could not imagine who could be singing such a refrain at such a time. Suddenly it struck me that, late as it was, it might be some beggar woman on the drive, and I ran to the front door and looked out. But, no, all was silence, save for the steady drip, drip of the rain. I returned to my work feeling a trifle uneasy, somehow, for what reason I could not tell. I was sitting by the fire in the drawing-room at Lorran House, correcting the typescript of the professor's treatise on "Cerebral Circulation," which I had finished that afternoon. It was an absorbingly interesting thesis and, though I had read it twice before and typed it out as well, I soon forgot the few bars of music in my interest in my work. If anyone ever doubts that Professor Durston was the greatest authority in the world on thought transference and colour vibration, let him read "Cerebral Circulation." My employer's discovery of thinking in colour set the world agape, and in this treatise he sets out more fully than in any other of his works the theories which have made his name a household word through the world. The reader who has followed my humble efforts to record some of Mr. Durston's cases is aware that he proved it possible actually to visualise the thought of his subjects, and to see *happening before him* thoughts which had not at that time been put into action. Moreover, he was able, as in my own case, to transfer his powers to others. He believed that no thought wave ever dies; that it is taken up by other minds and reinforced, and then sent on its journey again. He proved that, by visualising in colours, it was possible to materialise any thought wave that happened to be "current" at the time.

"You seem to be very interested in it, Leslie," he said to me as I pored over the manuscript in front of the fire.

"I am," I said; "intensely. I think it is wonderful. I have nearly finished correcting it, and I am going to read it again when I have time."

"Put it away now, my dear girl," he said with a kindly smile. "You have far too much of this work, I'm afraid. We shall be having you ill one of these days, and that would never do. What we should do without our little Leslie I simply don't know."

I laughed. The work was difficult, and sometimes there was a great deal of it to do; but I had learnt to identify myself so thoroughly with Mr. Durston's theories, that I am afraid I sometimes felt toward the articles, lectures, and books I typed for him as if they were the children of my own brain.

"There's no fear of my being ill," I declared. "I'm as strong as a horse, and I'm too keen to want to be ill and miss any of it."

"Well, dear," said my employer, "when we have collected the cases that are to make up our 'Unbound Book' you shall have a right royal time. The day the book comes back from the binding we shall set out on a long holiday. We'll go abroad, if you like. Leslie shall do as she likes with us. Is that fair?"

"It sounds gorgeous," I declared, laughing; "but I've no doubt that when that time comes you will have started something fresh, and I shall be far too interested to want to go abroad. It will probably end in our spending Saturday to Monday in the New Forest."

Arthur looked at me thoughtfully for a moment.

"What an enthusiastic little girl it is!" he exclaimed.

"Well now, run along home, dear," said Mr. Durston. "You've been at it too long already to-day. Arthur will see you to the tram. I'm sorry the car is out of action; of course, that would happen on a wet night like this."

I ran upstairs and put on my hat, and in a very few moments I was standing in the hall, while the professor was helping me into my mackintosh.

"You mustn't do any more to-night, either," I warned him, shaking my finger playfully in his face. "You know you've done enough, too."

"I'm going to sit in front of the fire with a little hot whisky and a cigar, and dream for a couple of hours, and then I'm going to bed. Will that do?"

I nodded assent.

"It sounds splendid," Arthur said, and I felt a little bit mean to drag him out into the wet, and I began to tell him I could quite easily go to the tram by myself.

"Of course not, Leslie," he replied, "as if I should be likely to let you go out at—"

Suddenly a cold shiver ran down my spine.

"Listen!" I cried. "Listen!"

For through the hall came the weird, insistent crooning which we had heard in the drawing-room. I cannot describe it, except that it was a minor refrain droned in a strangely beautiful contralto voice.

I stood and shivered from head to foot.

"Come, dear," said Mr. Durston, laying his hand on my wrist, and instantly the singing ceased. He led me into the dining-room and poured me out some brandy. I took it and was grateful for it, which was a most unusual thing for me. I think I may say without boasting that I do not often shiver with fear, and fear it undoubtedly was.

"Didn't you hear it?" I asked anxiously.

"Yes," he said slowly. "I heard it, Leslie. It must be in the road."

I looked at him closely.

"It was not in the road," I declared. "You know it was not."

"I told you you were working too hard," he said, patting my hand gently. "You had better have a day's rest to-morrow."

"Perhaps I am a little tired," I agreed; "but I shall be all right in the morning."

They both tried to persuade me to stop the night, but I insisted on going home. I knew that my cousin Doris, with whom I lived, would be waiting for me.

"Come along then," said Arthur. "I'll see if I can get a taxi at the corner."

So feeling very much better, I set out with Mr. Bindold. We did not succeed in finding a taxi—one never can on a wet night, the only occasion when some of us have any use for them. There was nothing for it but to go by tram.

"I'm coming with you," said Arthur.

"There's no need for you to do that," I declared. "I always go by tram to Golders Green and then take the tube."

"I'm coming with you," he said, with a note of finality.

"Thank you," I said simply.

I must admit that I would have been very sorry had he left me to go home by myself; but it seemed a shame to take him all that way in the rain. I was always glad of Arthur's company, although I had little of it, for, although he practically lived with his uncle Durston, I was always so busy there that I had not much opportunity of talking to him. Yet there had sprung up between us a curiously intimate friendship. True, there had been no protestations of friendship on either side, but it would have been impossible for us to have worked together, and to have run the risks we did together, without taking a good deal for granted. And Arthur was a splendid contrast from the psychological work, too, so that when he came in to tea it seemed a thorough rest and change for an hour or so. He was exceedingly clever, and was making his name felt in his profession, but he was not a practical psychic, and he did not even pretend to understand some of the cases in which he nevertheless gave us his invaluable assistance.

"I have something to say to you, Leslie," he said when we were safely seated on the top of the tram.

"Nothing very dreadful, I hope."

"I'll try and let you down lightly," he replied. "But, joking apart, Leslie; I'm very worried about you. I am quite sure that your employment is not the most healthy thing for you. I have the greatest admiration for your abilities—my uncle says you have more brains in your little finger than all the men in his class at the college have collectively, and I quite agree with him. But at the same time you are a young and beautiful girl—forgive me for saying so, but you are—and you are not having any of the pleasures and enjoyments which a young girl ought to have."

"I'm gloriously happy in my work," I protested.

"That's what I think is not good for you," he continued. "These psychic experiments are a great strain on your nerves, and so long as you have the excitement of novel investigations to keep the strain from telling on you, it will be all right. But when that excitement ceases, I'm afraid you'll have a breakdown."

"It is very good of you, Arthur, to take so much interest," I said; "but I am very well and very happy, and I wouldn't change places with anybody for anything."

"I'm glad," he answered quietly. "It makes a big difference to me to hear you say that. I don't want to tell you yet what a difference it would make to me if you did break down, Leslie, because I haven't any right to. But do, do take care of yourself."

I looked out of the window; the rain was beating on the glass. What did he mean? He could only mean one thing. Somehow I felt as if I were in a different world at once. I had not had any time in my short but busy life to think of anything of that sort, and it thrilled me through and through. From which you will gather that I was very fond of Arthur. I laid my hand on his knee for a second.

"Let's be good friends," I said; "always very good friends. It won't always be nothing but work."

At that moment we reached Tally Ho corner, where we had to change, being on an Archway Road tram, which we had taken in preference to standing in the rain. We got off and crossed the road. Just as I was stepping on to the kerb I experienced one of the most strange sensations I have ever known. I felt compelled to turn round, and yet, somehow, I dared not. I clutched hold of Arthur's arm.

"Good heavens, Leslie!" he cried. "What is it?"

I did not answer, but, summoning all the courage I could muster, I deliberately turned my head.

Some yards away I saw a faint blue mist, about twice the size of a human figure. It seemed to be following me across the road.

"Leslie! Leslie!" my companion cried, and his voice seemed very far away. I could only just feel him shaking me, and I have a dim recollection of Arthur hailing a passing taxi and thrusting me into it. I lay back in the cab shaking like a leaf. My head was burning like a lump of hot coal, my feet were as cold as ice. In a few minutes— though it seemed hours to me—I managed to pull myself together.

"I'm sorry if I scared you," I said apologetically. "I wasn't feeling very well."

"You must get right into bed as soon as you get home, and I will go and fetch a doctor."

"Oh! I shall be all right," I protested, with a pitiful attempt at a laugh; but I was feeling far from well. My whole being was possessed by a hideous, unknown fear. I did not know whether to tell Arthur what I had seen or not. I felt sure he would put it down to nerves and overwork, and be very sympathetic but not very helpful, so I decided to wait until the morning and tell Mr. Durston about it. The cab bumped along the Finchley Road while Arthur rubbed my hands, which were still stone cold. Suddenly I did a thing which I must say I think I have never done before. I shrieked at the top of my voice. Just behind me, so close that I knew if I leaned back my head would touch it, someone was crooning the haunting melody into my very ear.

I have no recollection how I got home. Arthur tells me I fainted in the cab as we were going up the North Road, and he told the man to pull up at the first red lamp. By this time, however, I had come round and, as the doctor was out, he drove me straight home and carried me upstairs. I cannot explain how it is although I had recovered from my fainting fit, I can remember nothing till I found myself lying on my bed, my cousin standing over me. Doris, for all her artistic temperament and charmingly dilettante ways, was the most practical little woman in the world when it came to an emergency, and after a few minutes of her skilful and sympathetic treatment I began to feel better.

"You silly old dear," she said chaffingly. "You shouldn't do things like this, you know; it isn't allowed."

I smiled. It was a treat to be in one's own room, out of the cold and driving rain. Mr. Durston had been quite right, too much psychology had affected my nerves. I looked round at the curtains which Doris had designed and then, passing on to more lofty thoughts, had left me to make. I looked at my pictures and the little odds and ends that make for home, and came to the conclusion that there could not be very much the matter with me after all. Then I sat up and glanced in the direction of the pier-glass to see if I looked any worse than I felt.

"Leslie!" cried my cousin, "what is it, darling, what is it?"

I could not reply. I stared into the mirror, fascinated, horrified. I moved my arm slowly, hardly daring to think what I might expect. The arm of the reflection moved also. I turned my head; the head turned simultaneously in the glass. I opened my mouth and closed it again. Yes, there could be no doubt, I was looking at my own reflection. Yes, it was I, Leslie Dalrayne! That hideous hag, with long, coarse grey hair, great black rings beneath her eyes, toothless and dishevelled, was I! I clenched my hands and bit my teeth. The ghastly apparition opened her mouth and began to sing— sing—

And again I lost consciousness.

It was a merciful providence that robbed me of my sense this second time, for I feel convinced to this day that I should otherwise have gone mad. When I came to myself Arthur was standing over me, his face pale and anxious, and the doctor was with him. I stretched out my arm and took Arthur's hand.

"I shall be all right," I assured him; "I only want a good night's sleep."

The doctor was one of those young men who ask a great many questions and then take no notice of the answer when you give it, and I did not feel like making myself appear ridiculous in the eyes of a man who would not understand my case if I told him, so I merely said that I had quite suddenly felt ill, but that I couldn't really remember anything about it. He nodded his head sagely, gave me something which, he said, would make me sleep, and said he would call again in the morning. Wherein he proved himself wise in his generation. His sleeping draught was certainly effective and, though it may have been largely that I was tired out, I fell asleep in a few minutes, still holding Arthur's hand.

It was nearly eleven o'clock the next morning before I awoke. Doris was sitting by my bed.

"Well, darling," she asked, "how do you feel now?"

"Feel?" I exclaimed. "I'm all right. Why, what time is it?"

"It's a quarter to eleven, but you mustn't get up, dear. Lie in bed and have a real lazy day."

And then I remembered the circumstances of the night before. I looked round instinctively for the mirror, but it had been taken out of the room. Doris was not risking any more experiences of that sort, evidently.

"You gave us all quite a fright last night," said my cousin.

"I'm awfully sorry, Doff," I apologised, "I was tired, I suppose. A bit overworked, that's all."

"Added to which you turned the flat into an hotel."

"Into a what?" I exclaimed.

"Well, we've had Mr. Durston and Mr. Bindold here, anyway," Doris replied. "Mr. Durston slept in the spare room, and the bed must have been inches too short for him—you know we furnished for lady visitors—and Mr. Bindold has been sitting in front of the studio fire all night, in case you might want something."

"Are they here still?" I asked.

"Yes, and both apparently dying to see you," she answered.

"It's most awfully good of them. Do you think they might come in here?"

"Considering you held a reception in here last night, I can't see that it matters much," said my cousin airily. "I'll tell them."

"Doris," I called after her, "before you go I want to tell you something. I've come to the conclusion that Mr. Bindold is rather nice."

"You dear old thing!" Doris laughed in reply; "as if I didn't know you'd come to that conclusion long ago."

"Oh! how could you?" I protested. "I didn't know myself!"

Arthur and Mr. Durston came in a few minutes afterwards. They were both exceedingly sympathetic and anxious. I assured them there was nothing at all the matter with me and we proceeded to talk of anything except the topic which was foremost in the minds of all of us. Presently the professor hinted to Arthur that he wished to speak to me alone.

"Now, Leslie," he said solemnly, as the door closed behind Mr. Bindold, "I want you to promise me something. If ever this happens

again, remember that I can help you. Make up your mind that I am
helping you. You understand, don't you? If ever you have an experience like that of last night, fix your mind on me."

"Indeed I will," I promised readily; "but last night I was too
frightened to think of anything."

"Never mind, dear," he said kindly, "it's all over now."

"I wonder if it is!" I mused. "I should like to tell you all about it."

"You needn't, Leslie," he said. "I know."

I had not realised till then that what was passing through my
mind so vividly was probably registering in his too.

"I wish I'd thought of that at the time," I said; "I should have
been so much happier."

"I don't want to talk of these things while you're not feeling
well, Leslie," he continued, "but would you prefer to take my advice or do as the doctor would tell you?"

"I'll do anything you wish," I declared emphatically.

"Then I should like you to follow this up. I shall be with you.
You need not be afraid; understand you shall not be afraid. Any
doctor would tell you to let the matter drop; but I am convinced
that, unless you go through with this, and let us see where it leads
us, you will not get rid of last night's unpleasant experience. It
will be repeated."

"What am I to do, Mr. Durston?" I asked.

"Lie in bed and read a novel until I come to fetch you," he said.
"I shall not ask you to do anything to-day, but to-morrow I shall
probably want you."

"I am ready whenever you like," I replied.

So I stayed in bed all day, and Doris read to me and toasted
tea-cakes in front of the bed-room fire, and I felt ever so much the
better for it.

It was not till late the following afternoon that I saw the professor again. My cousin came in and told me that he wished me to
get up and come with him at once. I dressed as quickly as possible
and found him pacing up and down the studio.

"Ah! Leslie!" he greeted me, "how are you?"

"Fit for anything, Mr. Durston," I replied.

"Good!" he exclaimed. "Get your things on and come out will you? I think I may have something to show you that will interest you. When you have seen it you must come back here and go on with your rest for a few days at least."

I slipped into my things and the professor and I got into a waiting taxi and drove off west. We pulled up in Leicester Square and walked up a side street for a few yards. Mr. Durston knocked at the door of a great, gloomy-looking house and we were admitted by a man in livery. We were requested to sign our names in a book which was printed with the name of the Da Capo club, which, as I was told afterwards was a sort of night club frequented by bohemian musicians. As we were fulfilling the formalities the manager came up to us.

"Good evening, professor," he said affably; "you have not been long away."

"No," said Mr. Durston, "I just ran out to Hampstead and back. Has my man been yet?"

"I fancy he's here now, sir," said the manager. My companion nodded approval and we went down a flight of stairs into a basement which had been turned into a sort of music-room. There were long benches round the walls and three or four low divans about the floor. At one end of the room was a grand piano, by far the best piece of furniture in the whole building as far as I could see. There were a few small tables dotted about the room, and seated at one of these were two men; one an elderly, stout man, with large, protruding eyes, dressed in a greasy frock coat and a floppy French cravat. Opposite him was a thin, dark Italian-looking man wearing a black Homburg hat. I looked at these two men closely, but I did not feel that either of them was of any particular interest to us.

"Sit down, Leslie," said Mr. Durston in an undertone, "I've ordered a coffee for you."

The waiter brought my coffee and a whisky and soda for my companion, while I sat and glanced idly round the room. Gradually my gaze turned to the far end, and as it did so I felt myself growing slowly colder. Mr. Durston laid a hand on my arm.

"Don't be afraid, Leslie," he said, "don't be afraid."

Then, as I had always found before, when I had the professor with me, I knew no fear. I simply became intensely interested. I deliberately stared up the room. In the far corner slowly moving towards us, I saw the same blue mist which had terrorised me at Tally Ho corner.

"Here it is!" I exclaimed, almost beneath my breath.

"The mist?" asked Mr. Durston.

"Yes," I replied. "It seems to be coming to us."

"Don't let it frighten you," he said again. "Remember it is only thought transference." But I was not in the least frightened. I watched the faint blue haze growing closer and closer until we seemed to be looking at each other through a thin cloud of blue smoke. Then suddenly I saw a figure following it. It was an old man, with long grey hair tumbling over his shoulders. He tottered towards us, and just as he passed us he raised his head for a second and I looked him straight in the face.

I gasped with astonishment. It was my reflection of the night before. The old man went past us and sat down at the piano. For a moment his hands wandered idly over the keys; his touch was like velvet and the beautiful liquid notes of the magnificent instrument created an amazing contrast with the dishevelled creature on the stool. Suddenly he stopped, and then slowly and softly he played the strange, eerie melody which we had heard at Finchley. Mr. Durston rose to his feet and strode over to the piano.

"That is a very beautiful thing you are playing, Mr. Lereton," he said, and I recognised the name of a man who had been the greatest pianist of his time. "Might I ask what it is?"

The old man peered at the professor.

"I don't know you, sir, I don't know you. Go away," he quavered.

"My name is Durston," said my friend.

"Well, well, perhaps it is," said the other querulously. "What is it you want?"

"I was asking the name of that beautiful little melody which you were just playing."

"Ah, that! Ah! that has no name, sir. No, sir. That is the song that was never sung. No, sir, never sung. I wrote it for my wife and before I finished it she died. They tell me that when my wife died I went mad . . . yes, mad. So some day I shall finish this song and everyone that sings it shall go mad, too. Yes, sir, mad. It can be done. Anything can be done in music. But it isn't finished yet; no, sir, it isn't finished. . . ."

The poor half-witted old man was babbling away, his eyes fixed on the ceiling, when Mr. Durston touched me on the arm.

"Come, Leslie," he said; "we don't want to stop here."

"I think you will have to put that in our 'Unbound Book,'" said the professor, when we were discussing the case later. "It shows you what thought transference can do. The mad obsession of twenty years in the brain of a lunatic musician came very near to costing you a complete collapse."

No. 5: Orange
THE BROKEN CUP

From among the several cases which would have sufficed to complete the chromatic cycle of our "Unbound Book," I think I must choose the strange adventure regarding the Broken Cup. It was the great strain which this affair placed upon my employer, and the mental effort of retaining control over superior forces, that brought the first sign of nerve collapse. Mr. Durston himself would have liked me to give the Broken Cup narrative to the world, if only for the reason that it proved he was not alone in his theories.

"Leslie," he said to me one day, as we were sitting in the study over an early cup of tea, "have you ever seen anything like this before?"

He handed me a small black thing, made of ebony or of some similar substance, shaped like a lozenge and of about the same thickness. One side was quite blank, but on the other was a curious device. In the middle of the black surface was engraved a tall Venetian goblet; curled round the foot of it was a long black snake, and the device was outlined in a bright orange colour, which looked exceedingly effective against the sinister background.

"No," I replied, "I have never seen anything like it. What is it?"

"I'm not sure what it is," my companion replied, "but I fancy it will bear some great significance in my life—perhaps in yours also, Leslie."

"How did you get it?" I asked, "and what do you think it means?"

He looked at me with a smile which seemed to have something of pathos in it.

"I have no idea at all what it means, my dear girl, or even how I came by it," he admitted. "I found it in my pocket this morning when I got up and, except that it is some decorative design or badge, I cannot fathom it."

"You have seen it before?" I asked.

"Not in reality. I have not actually seen this lozenge, but I have seen the design. The orange cup on the background, yes, I have seen that thousands and thousands of times—in my mind. As I lie awake it flashes on my brain at nights; sometimes I see it before me in the street, sometimes it stamps itself upon the pages of the book I am reading. Yesterday when I was lecturing at the college, I saw a great orange goblet gazing at me from the blackboard in front of me, and now I find this solid seal, or whatever it may be, in my pocket!"

"What can it mean?" I cried anxiously.

There was no hallucination about the lozenge. That was solid enough, and therefore it must have found its way into the professor's pocket by some quite ordinary means. I wondered who could have put it there and why.

"I really don't know what to make of it, Leslie," Mr. Durston admitted, "but I am most certainly going to find out. I shall want you to help me this time by keeping out of it altogether. It may be dangerous, and I will not have you running into danger to satisfy my psychical curiosity. I don't like the look of this at all, not at all."

Of course, after my experience of Professor Durston's psychic manifestations and his practical experiments in colour vibration and telepathy, I must confess that the thought of the orange goblet and the black snake left me rather cold. I felt that my friend was exaggerating a little when he said that there might be danger for me. During the year I had worked with him we had only had one experiment which had not involved danger of some sort. What, then, was the mysterious, hidden peril which he spoke of now?

"I fancy there is one thing you have forgotten, Mr. Durston," I ventured to suggest.

"How do you mean?" he asked with interest.

"Well, you see, you decline to take me into your confidence over this stupid lozenge thing, but you have not stopped to consider that you have trained me so well that if anything happens in connection with that device, my mind will register it and visualise it almost immediately. I shall know about it almost as soon as you do yourself."

"Yes, Leslie," he admitted, "I had forgotten. I have trained you too well. If, then, you are determined to go through with this, let me tell you why I speak of danger. You may think I have some definite form of danger in my mind, but I have not. I speak as I do because, among all our experiences, this is the first in which we have been brought in contact, at the beginning of the case, with a physical rather than a psychical manifestation."

"You mean it is a real object that we are dealing with and not a visualised picture?" I asked.

"Not so much the real object," he replied, "as its real presence. What I am most struck with at present is the undeniable fact that this seal was found in my pocket, and that, therefore, someone must have put it there. You and I, Leslie, probably know more about colour vibration and what is known as mental telepathy than any other two people in the world, and therefore we are entitled to regard it as a very remarkable thing that this adventure—for it looks as if it would develop into one—should have begun with a solid and obvious fact, and not with a mental image."

"All of which suggests," I replied hopefully, "that there will be no danger. Surely otherwise we should have 'sensed' it at once."

"That may be so," said the professor; "but the fact remains that I did receive a very forceful mental image of this seal before I came by the solid object, and I have a feeling that it may be dangerous. If you would prefer to have nothing more to do with it, say so, my dear, and I shall quite understand."

"Dear Mr. Durston," I cried, "I have been with you in everything since I first came to typewrite for you. You have been kindness itself to me and I am intensely interested in all your work, so I shall stay right in, whatever happens."

"Thank you, Leslie," my friend replied, obviously relieved. "Of course there may be nothing in it all, and I shall take all the care of you that is possible."

"So that's all right then," I laughed eagerly. "Now let us begin, shall we?"

Professor Durston was very ready to commence the experiment at once and without more ado we made our way into the great white globe in which most of our experiments were made. In this strange room, designed for the one purpose of enabling us to concentrate our minds on some mental picture to the exclusion of all other thoughts, I have seen some strange sights. In Professor Durston's now famous treatise on "Colour Vibration and Perception" the dome is scientifically described at great length, so I need only remind the reader of its general appearance. It was quite round, and there was not a crack or crevice to be seen in it. On one side of the great concavity, as it were, set half way up the wall was a sort of platform on which were two great chairs, where the professor and I sat. Above our heads there was an opening, through which a terrific flood of light was thrown into the room from four great arc lamps. As the reader is aware, the whole object of this room was to assist the experimenter to keep his mind a perfect blank, or, in other words, to suspend the conscious activity of the mind. For my own part, I frankly confess that, after my first experience in the dome, I found the blazing white sides of the bowl so dazzling and fascinating that they reduced me almost at once to a state bordering on trance. Yet as I stepped on to the platform that day I was prepared for disappointment; I felt that there was something much more of the material world than of the psychic world in the strange device of the orange goblet. As we took our seats the professor handed me the lozenge.

"Hold it in your hand," he said.

I clutched the symbol in my left hand and fixed my whole attention on the great white space before me. Presently the lights seemed to fade away and very soon there rose before me a huge black lozenge, bearing the same device which I held in my hand. I admit I was disappointed. I had hoped that my brain would have been capable of visualising something further, and not merely repeating to me a sight which I had just been studying. And then, just as I was letting the image slip from my grasp, it suddenly grew brighter and the snake that lay coiled at the foot began to twine slowly up the stem of the goblet. Up and up it went, slowly and deliberately, until it raised its hideous head above the cup. Then it seemed to draw its coils together sharply, the stem snapped, and the glass fell into a hundred pieces. Mr. Thurston brought me to myself as he jumped up, with an exclamation of anger, and strode from the platform. I tried for some moments to continue the experiment alone, but the trivial incident had destroyed my attention and I was compelled to give up in disgust. I returned to the study and found to my surprise that Mr. Durston was not there. I looked out in the garden for him, but he was not to be found and, when I questioned the servants, one of the maids said she had seen him put on his hat and walk off down the road. I went on with my work as well as I could, but, as it happened, I had very little that I could get on with by myself. When at last it was time for me to go home, and still the professor had not returned, I rang up Arthur Bindold and asked him to come round and see me.

"What's all the trouble, Miss Dalrayne?" he asked when he arrived.

"Well," I replied, "there is no trouble that I know of, but it is possible there may be. Your uncle went out without a word to any-one some hours ago, and he has not yet returned. It is very unlike him, especially as we were in the dome at the time."

"Oh?" Arthur asked; "anything of any special interest?"

I told him of the lozenge which his uncle had found in his pocket, and of my image of the broken goblet and the snake.

"Did you see nothing else that could possibly have given you a clue?" he asked.

"No," I admitted, "absolutely nothing. And I have no idea what Mr. Durston may have seen, as he simply got up and went out."

"Who has this curious sign?" Arthur asked, and I took it from the drawer in which I had laid it and handed it to him.

"It might be anything," he said when he had studied it carefully. "It is probably some inoffensive curio which my uncle has picked up in one of his absent-minded fits and forgotten all about."

"But," I protested, "he is far too sensible to worry about a thing like that, unless he felt sure there was something behind it."

"Oh, that might be nerves or anything," laughed my companion. "I don't see anything very alarming about it, but I will take it to the police and see if they can suggest anything. You had better come with me, for if my uncle is face to face with any danger of a material sort, we can't do better than get a little solid help from the authorities. And you know two heads, when that includes such a capable little head as yours, my dear, are infinitely better than one."

"Thank you," I replied, smiling, "I'll slip on my coat and come with you. Even if Mr. Durston is not in actual danger, we may just as well find out all we can about the symbol."

When we arrived at Scotland Yard, Mr. Bindold asked for Inspector Orless, with whom we had had dealings on several previous occasions. He listened very attentively to what we had to say, for, though at one time he had been inclined to regard my employer as something of a mountebank, the affair of the Mancroft Studio Murder had made him a little more deferential and evidently a little afraid at the mention of the professor's name.

"You say he found it in his pocket?" he asked at last.

"Yes," I replied. "He has no idea how it got there, but he had several times pictured the chromatic image of the same thing before he found the actual symbol in his possession."

"Well, I shouldn't worry about him, if I were you, miss," said the inspector kindly. "He knows how to take care of himself better than most. I wish I could recall the sign. But I feel sure I have never seen it before. I'll ask Fotheringham; he might know something about it."

Mr. Orless left the room and presently returned with a tall, shrewd-looking man, who gave one the impression of being a farmer with a taste for literature rather than a detective. Mr. Fotheringham was not the man to waste time.

"Where did you say you got this, miss?" he asked. "Ah! you don't know where it actually came from? That's a pity, a very great pity."

"You recognise it then?" I asked eagerly.

"Very nearly," he replied, "but not exactly. You remember when that fellow was murdered in the strangers' gallery at the House of

Commons three years ago? Well, he was holding in his hand a thing very like this. It was exactly the same shape, and the goblet was on it too, but with this difference: the snake was twisted round the stem and the glass was broken."

Arthur and I exchanged uneasy glances. We of course remembered the murder of the wealthy Spaniard in the House of Commons and we also both recalled the clever and stealthy nature of the murder. The man had simply collapsed on the floor, and when the doctors came to examine him they found a long steel pin under his shoulder blade. I began to be afraid.

"Was no one caught over that affair?" I asked.

"Not a soul, miss," the detective replied. "In fact, to tell you the truth there was no one whom we even suspected. Of course he was a foreigner, and perhaps if the police of his own country had been a little more wide awake we might have done something with it, but we never found out anything that was any good to us at all. My own idea about this charm was that it might be some sort of family crest; but we investigated that and found nothing there either. We never had a scent of the murderer, and we never even found out rightly who the murdered man was."

"Then," I said, "if this charm had anything to do with it, the sooner we find Mr. Durston and the closer we keep our eye on him the better."

"Yes, indeed," agreed Arthur readily. "Let us go home now, and if we get no news of him very soon, we will communicate with these gentlemen again. In the meantime we will find out whether he is at his club."

We drove out to Lorran House again; but, though we telephoned to his club, to the college, and to several other places where he might possibly have been, we could get no news of Mr. Durston. I decided to wait there till he returned, and I sent round a message to my cousin to tell her that I should not be home that night.

Arthur and I sat up till midnight, but still there was no sign of the professor.

"I remember my uncle doing something like this before," Mr. Bindold tried to reassure me. "He went out to post a letter one morning and returned about a week later, having been resting in an hotel up the river. He may have done something like that this time."

"I am quite positive he hasn't," I asserted. "He would either have left me with some work to go on with or else have told me I could have a holiday. I am sure he would never get up and walk out of the dome without a word, and then go away for three days' rest like that."

"But you don't suppose anything has happened to him yet, do you?" Arthur asked. "You seem to take the view that he has already met with some terrible fate."

"Goodness, my dear man," I cried, in exasperation, "should I be sitting here if I thought that? No; I simply think he is following up some clue, and I don't think it is safe, and frankly I am anxious."

"Well, until you know, you can do nothing," said Arthur emphatically, "so you had better go to bed and leave me to sit up."

I could see no use in the two of us sitting up, and as I might need all my strength in the morning, I took my companion's advice and turned in. But I could not sleep. As soon as I closed my eyes I saw the fateful symbol in front of me. And every time the vile, hideous snake twined up the stem of the goblet and crushed it in its venomous grip. I determined at last to concentrate my attention on something else and thus wipe out the strange impression. I thought of Mr. Durston and tried to picture to myself the face and figure of my friend. And as I did so I gave a sharp cry, for there before me I saw my dear employer beckoning to me with an expression of intense agony in his eyes. The sweat stood out upon his brow, his lips were the colour of lead, and, as I watched their painful, twisted movements, they seemed to say . . . Leslie . . . Leslie . . . Leslie . . .

I jumped out of bed to run to the dome. It was terribly cold, but somehow I must get in touch with my friend. I knocked at Arthur's door as I ran by. He was out in an instant, for he had not gone to bed. I told him to light the arcs in the dome and while he did so I ran back for a dressing-gown, which I threw over my shoulders. I was intensely interested. My whole being seemed changed, just as it had been on the night of my first visit to the dome. I

seemed to be possessed of endless strength and power. I rushed
on to the platform in the globe and, throwing myself into a chair, I
held my breath and waited for developments. I had not long to wait,
for almost immediately the black lozenge and the orange goblet
sprang up before me and then as suddenly it disappeared. In its
place there arose a great marble staircase, flanked on either side
by a dull grey mass. Gradually, out of the cloudy surround I began
to distinguish the movements of figures, and then suddenly I found
myself gazing into what appeared to be a huge reception hall in
some great palace. Leading up to the marble staircase was an avenue
of people in court dress and uniforms—a dazzling display of pomp.
That the scene was taking place in some foreign palace I had no
doubt, from the dresses I could see and from the general appearance of the individuals wearing them. Every eye was turned to the
great staircase. Evidently, I thought, they were expecting someone of the greatest importance. Here and there I perceived a slight,
restless movement in the crowd—a distinguished general leaned
down and whispered in the ear of the silver-haired diplomat beside
him; a self-conscious countess arranged her train with little, nervous twitches—but no eye strayed long from the staircase.

Presently I noticed a tall, thin lieutenant standing a little way
behind the others in front of a window, which seemed to open out
on to a balcony. His appearance caught my attention at once. He
was dark and good-looking, in a girlish sort of way, but he had the
face of an ascetic rather than a soldier. He held his hands behind
his back, and fidgeted from one foot to the other. Then, just as I
was speculating on the possible cause of the young soldier's nervousness, the women curtsied and the men bowed low. Walking
slowly down the staircase came six figures in uniform. I started
back with a cry of astonishment as I realised who they were, for I
was face to face with four of the crowned heads of Europe and two
princes of the royal blood. I understood the scene then, for who
had not read of the meeting of the kings at one of the most famous
historical palaces on the continent? The Imperial party walked
slowly down the avenue of courtiers, bowing to right and left, when
suddenly an immense figure rose in front of them, dimly outlined

but clearly recognisable. I clutched the arm of my chair and held my breath. It was Professor Durston. He lifted his hand in front of him. I turned my head in the direction which he indicated and saw that he was pointing directly at the young lieutenant. The officer leaned forward, his mouth open, his eyes staring and then, evidently with a tremendous effort, he flung his arms above his head. I shrank back in horror, for in his hands he held a bomb. I saw again the glittering eye and accusing finger of Mr. Durston, and then the bomb slipped from the assassin's hand and I saw no more. Before I could collect my wits, Arthur was standing on the platform beside me.

"Come, Leslie," he cried, "the police have telephoned for us. Orless thinks he knows where my uncle is."

"Where?" I asked excitedly, "where?"

"He has not said," Arthur answered; "but he thinks he knows and he says he may want you. The car is at the door. We are to meet him at Piccadilly Circus as soon as we can. Here is your coat."

I slipped into the coat he held out to me and thus, in dressing-gown and overcoat, my hair tumbling all over my shoulders, we dashed off into the night. We were certainly in danger more than once on the way; but it was early morning and the roads were clear and we did the journey in record time, without mishap. The two inspectors whom we had interviewed in the afternoon were waiting for us and opened the door of the car, even before we had stopped.

"Where is he?" I asked Inspector Orless, as he helped me to alight.

"That I don't know, miss," he replied, "but I think we can find him. He 'phoned us to follow a certain man and said that we should very likely meet in the course of the night. I gathered that Mr. Durston is probably following some other party who intends to meet the other man somewhere. He told me to 'phone you and ask you to come with us, and I may say you've been mighty quick about it."

"Who is the man you have to follow?" Arthur asked.

"Except that he is a music teacher at Camden Town, a foreigner of the name of Sovlov, we know nothing about him."

"Where is he now?" I interrupted.

"He left Camden Town and was walking down the Tottenham Court Road a few minutes ago," the inspector replied.

"Good heavens!" I exclaimed, "how do you know?"

"We have two men following him and another telephoning progress," he explained. "The police are never far from the telephone in London, even if it's only the fire alarm."

"And what do we do now?" I asked.

"I'm afraid we shall have to wait here for a few minutes till our man rings up again. Then he will tell us where it is we are wanted. Evidently the professor thinks we are on something big this evening."

Arthur chatted with Orless while I questioned Mr. Fotheringham about the orange goblet; but he could give me no further information and presently a plain clothes man ran across to us and told the inspector that we were wanted at the top of Wardour Street. We hurried up Windmill Street and along Shaftesbury Avenue till we came to the Queen's Theatre, where we halted to discuss our plans. I suggested that as I was almost in a state of *déshabillé* I should be least likely to arouse suspicion, and that I would go first, followed by Arthur and one of the inspectors. Mr. Orless would not hear of it.

"Certainly not," he said emphatically. "Miss Dalrayne, you must stop here until we send for you. I will leave someone with you and let you know when everything is safe."

"Did Mr. Durston send for me or did he not?" I demanded haughtily.

"Well, he certainly did, miss," Orless admitted; "but still I can't—"

"Very well, then," I said finally, "he sent for me and I am going to him."

"Better let her go," said Arthur quietly. "I'll keep an eye on her. If she's made up her mind to it she'll do it, whether you give her your permission or not."

"Oh! very well," said the policeman, shrugging his shoulders; "but I take no responsibility for the young lady's safety."

Accordingly I started off up Wardour Street, keeping in the shadow of the shops as well as I could. Presently I saw a man strolling towards me, and I began to sing a rough, music-hall song in a semi-intoxicated voice. The man passed very close to me and I recognised a Scotland Yard man, Foster, whom I had several times met before. I let him pass me to see if he would recognise me. As he failed to do so, however, I called him back.

"Where am I to go, Mr. Foster?" I said softly.

The detective turned sharply, with an exclamation of surprise.

"Miss Dalrayne!" he exclaimed. "What are you doing here?"

I told him hurriedly that his men were waiting at the end of the street and that I was the reconnoitring party, as it were, and I asked him where I should find Sovlov.

"The third alley on the right," he replied, "if you are quite determined to go."

I thanked him and strolled leisurely on, in case someone might have been watching us. When I reached the mouth of the alley I found another detective crouched in the shadow of a doorway. In response to my whispered questions, he pointed to a small door at the end of the passage. I walked straight up to it, affecting a slightly staggering gait, and still humming to myself. As I got to the doorway a big man, wearing a black Homburg hat, and dressed in a dark suit, stepped in front of me.

"Hullo," I leered at him, "fancy meeting you!"

He looked at me closely for a moment, and I was glad that the darkness hid my nervousness.

"Go away," he exclaimed angrily, at last; "you're drunk. Go away."

"Shan't go away," I retorted, "I live here and I'm not drunk. I think you're very rude," and I giggled foolishly.

The stranger muttered an oath and began to pull me along the alley. I saw my opportunity. The detective had stepped out of his hiding-place on hearing the disturbance. I let the tall man drag me along the passage, protesting volubly all the while until we reached the policeman. Then I suddenly exerted all my strength and pushed him heavily into the arms of my accomplice.

"Quick, seize him!" I cried, as loudly as I dared, and in almost less time than it takes to tell, the man was pinioned and gagged. I ran hastily through his pockets and found a small Yale key and a revolver, to both of which I helped myself. By this time the others had joined us and we held another hasty council of war, as a result of which I again made my way up the passage. At the door our captive had been guarding I paused for a moment and slipped off my great-coat. Then I tried the key in the lock. As I had expected, it turned and I pushed the door gently open.

"Is that you, Matteo?" came a voice in my ear. I did not stop to reply. Glancing up sharply I saw a dark figure standing inside, peering into my face in the gloom. With one swift movement I threw my coat over the man's head and pulled him towards me through the doorway. Stumbling in the confusion of the sudden surprise, he fell into the arms of the two inspectors. Then Mr. Orless filed his men silently inside the door, and Arthur and I wended our way down a corridor until we found ourselves outside another door, behind which I could hear the sound of voices. I saw a narrow shaft of light coming from the keyhole, and throwing myself on my knees I fixed my eyes upon a strange sight. I was looking into a big, un-distinguished-looking room; it might have been a hall in a public-house. In the middle of the room was a long table seated at which were a number of men wearing bright orange-coloured cloaks. The table was laid with a black cloth on the centre of which stood a great glass goblet of a slightly deeper colour than the cloaks. Round the stein of the goblet was coiled a long black adder. At the far end of the table sat a man who seemed to be the chief, and facing him, his arms pinioned behind his back, stood Professor Durston. The chief was speaking.

"So you know that you cannot have everything your way," he was saying, with a bitter sneer. "You know now that you have to contend with the only secret society which has ever been able to keep its existence secret—the Brotherhood of the Broken Cup. While the present-day psychology was yet unborn the Brothers of the Broken Cup held undisputed sway over the minds of thousands, and you have been the first to discover the secret of thought transmission and telepathic influence. You and your accursed science have gone further than we had dreamed of. You are the super-mesmerist, the all-conquering mind which rules all other minds. Therefore you must either join us or accept the fate my Brothers offer you. We warned you and you took no heed, and now to-night you have demonstrated your power to such a degree that you are too dangerous for us. But for you we should have been able to wipe out four of the crowned heads of Europe at one blow to-night, and you have caused us the loss of our dear brother, Lieutenant Gierstein. You, yourself, have pictured it to us and you admit it is so. For a life we take a life. Gentlemen, shall he live or shall he die?

I glanced round the room. There were some twenty or more of these men present, and at the question from their president they rose like one man and turned their cloaks about them, so that the orange colour was inside and the outside was black.

Then the president rose and copied their action with great precision.

"In the name of the Brotherhood of the Broken Cup—Death," he said. Then he leaned forward and touched the black adder with a long piece of wire. The hideous thing began to twine slowly round the stem of the goblet until its head was poised above the bowl. Then it seemed to draw its coils together sharply, and the stem of the goblet snapped and the glass fell to pieces. I waited for no more. I stepped aside and made way for the inspector. The whole thing was over in a moment. One of the policemen stepped forward, quietly unscrewed the hinges from the door and, giving it a sudden wrench, jerked it clear of the lock. The two inspectors and quite twenty policemen were inside the room holding their revolvers at the heads of the conspirators, almost before I could realise that the door was open.

I ran to Mr. Durston.

"I knew you'd come, my dear," he said, "I knew you'd come."

No. 6: Purple
THE MYSTERY OF THE PURPLE BINDING

"I shall start bullying you very soon," I said.

"You began that long ago, my dear," said Professor Durston, with a wan smile, "and I'm very glad you did. Otherwise I might not have been here to tell the tale."

"Now you mustn't talk like that," I said, "or I shall be very cross with you. You're tired, that's all. You've worked a great deal too hard for a long time and now you are paying for it."

"What do you say if we all go away and take a holiday together? Your cousin Doris, you, and Arthur and I?"

"I should love it," I cried. "Where shall we go?"

"You young people had better decide on that," he said, "and let me know your decision."

The professor undoubtedly did require a change and I must say I felt as if a good rest would do me no harm either. I had completed the typescript of his new textbook on Psychology, and also of the collected volume of lectures which was shortly to be published, and had indexed them both. There now only remained, so far as immediate work was concerned, the "Unbound Book." Professor Durston and I had gone through all the notes of his cases and decided as to which should be included and which omitted, and I had now only to tell the stories in a more popular form, devoid of technical phrases. It was one of the professor's most cherished ambitions to see the "Unbound Book" complete, because he considered his experiments in colour vibration and thought transference of more value than all his other work put together.

"Leslie," he said to me one day, "I want you, when you write the story of the 'Unbound Book,' to make it quite clear to everyone that I have absolutely and finally proved the practicability of thought visualisation. I want everybody to know that, with a careful training in colour vibration, thinking in colour, it is possible to convey or to receive any number of thought messages over any distance."

It was for this reason, therefore, that the episodes which I have already related have been specially included in the volume, and I think I may say that the professor himself would have approved the selection I have made of his cases, however much he might have criticised the manner of their telling.

I felt sure, when my employer spoke of our holiday that the finest thing in the world for him would be the final tabulating and binding of his experiments in colour vibration—the "Unbound Book." That the affair of the Broken Cup had told upon him, I was convinced. The old merry smile and springy step had left him, and he had become preoccupied and more easily depressed than I had ever seen him before. Hence my delight when he, himself, suggested a holiday. When Arthur Bindold came in to my room for a cup of tea that afternoon I hastened to tell him all about it.

"And you say he suggested it himself?" Arthur asked incredulously. "You're quite sure you didn't give him any help?"

"No," I asserted, "I never mentioned a word. Of course, we have often talked of the time when we should have a real rest, but I have never suggested it."

"Well, I think it's simply splendid," said Arthur emphatically. "I suppose your cousin will be willing?"

"Oh, yes! She'll be willing enough; besides, she can do her work pretty well anywhere, so she could come in any case."

"At the present moment, the same applies to me," he said.

"And I give you my word that I am not going to do anything at all the whole time I am away."

"Good!" exclaimed my companion, "I'm jolly glad to hear it. And, Leslie, when we really are away from all your psychological responsibilities, I shall want to remind you of a certain occasion when you said it would not always be all work. May I?"

I got up and strolled to the window.

"Yes," I said softly, "some day."

There were a great many things to be seen to before we could leave. Arthur took a furnished cottage in Devonshire and the housekeeper and one of the maids went down to get it in order, while Lorran House was left in charge of the cook. We were to have two months away from typewriters and lecture-rooms. But alas! we little knew what was in store for us.

Doris and I remained behind for a few days, as I had a number of things I had to finish and I did not want to feel that I had left anything undone. We returned to Lorran House after seeing them off from Paddington, and Doris went for a stroll while I went on with my work. I had not been long at the typewriter before I felt a curiously restless sensation. I felt as if I must get up and walk about, or do something. I tried to shake it off at first but it was of no avail. At last I found myself unable to resist the temptation and I jumped up from the table and left the room. I took a turn round the garden, but the feeling of uneasiness grew upon me, and I went indoors again. I decided to enter the dome, the great white globe which Mr. Durston had constructed in order to enable him to perfect the art of concentration. Many had been the experiments we had made there together, and I could not help smiling to myself as I stepped on to the platform, when I thought that the professor was really at last away on holiday, and I was left behind to commence some new experiment which might lead me, who knew whither?

I concentrated my attention upon the dazzling white walls of the globe and for the first time in the course of my experience they did not at any time appear to lose any of their brightness. Instead there suddenly sprang up across the vault, in brilliant purple lettering, the name of John Durston. I sat there fascinated as each letter appeared. Then, suddenly, a great hand of flame swept across and, seizing the letters, seemed to squeeze them into nothing.

I could not understand it. I had seen nothing of that sort before; there was no definite thought, no suggestion of a source from which the thought could have come. Purple was the colour we had chosen for the binding of the "Unbound Book," but what of that? I tried hard to visualise something further, but it was of no avail, so I gave it up and went back to the garden.

"Good afternoon, miss."

I turned round to find, to my surprise, a tall rather handsome man standing at my elbow.

"Good afternoon," I replied, and waited for him to explain his business.

"Is John Durston at home?"

I looked at him in astonishment. He was apparently a gentleman, but surely that was not the way to ask for the professor.

"Do you mean Professor Durston?" I asked frigidly.

"Very likely I do," he replied, with an insolent smile. "At any rate he is John Durston to me. Is he at home?"

"He is not at home," I replied coldly.

"Ah!" said my visitor, "I'm sorry."

"If you write, I shall forward any letters to him," I said.

"I have no wish to write to him, Miss Dalrayne," said the man quietly, and turned on his heel and walked away. He went round the path at the back of the kitchen while I stood and watched him. Then I turned and went into the house. I went into the study, intending to get the notes for the "Unbound Book" which I had left on a shelf; but when I got there they were nowhere to be seen. I hunted high and low for them, but they could not be found. I laid my hands on the carbon copies, but the actual script itself seemed to be missing. I thought of the man in the garden and wondered if he could possibly have anything to do with it. The windows were fastened and he certainly could not have come through the house. Eventually I gave up the search, persuading myself that the manuscript would turn up somewhere, and when Doris came in she assured me that I should find it somewhere where I had myself laid it.

"What do you make of the man in the garden?" I asked.

"I don't know what to make of him," she answered.

"I don't like the look of it," I said solemnly. "The three things happening together like that seems suspicious somehow."

"I suppose it was a real man," Doris asked scornfully, "and not a psychological gentleman?"

"No," I said, "he was real and very rude into the bargain."

"I wonder how he knew your name."

"He might get that from the tradespeople, or some of the servants at other houses in the road."

"It seems to me," said Doris, "rather like a burglary business."

"Why?" I asked.

"Well, isn't it obvious? The man comes and asks, 'Is Mr. Durston at home?' You say 'No,' and he says to himself, 'If there are no men in the house this is the place for me.'"

"But he didn't say, 'Mr. Durston,'" I pointed out. "That makes all the difference. He said, 'John Durston.'"

"Well, anyway, don't let's worry about it," my cousin concluded. "We are just going away on a holiday, and we don't want to spoil it in advance by imagining a whole lot of things which will probably never happen."

"All right," I agreed.

So we let the matter slide, but I felt very uneasy and apprehensive, although I could not have given a reason for it.

Two days later we left Lorran House, leaving Cooper to take care of it, and set out to join the others in Devonshire.

How glorious it was to be going on a holiday! I was looking forward immensely to seeing Mr. Durston and Arthur on the platform at the other end. I was looking forward to the drive from the station to the cottage like a schoolgirl.

So when we drew up at the station and Arthur was alone on the platform I was a little disappointed.

"Where's Mr. Durston?" I asked.

"He said he didn't think he'd come," said Arthur.

"Why?"

"He didn't say. He merely remarked that he thought he wouldn't meet the train but would wait for you at the cottage. He said he would potter about and not go far away, as the womenfolk have gone to some local function and they were very keen to see it."

I was hurt.

"Couldn't the stuffy old cottage have looked after itself for a bit?" I asked.

"Come, Leslie, dear," said Arthur, laughing, "you mustn't be grumpy with our blessed Uncle John, especially on your arrival."

So I promised Arthur that I would not let the professor see that I actually expected him at the station, and we spent the rest of the drive in excellent spirits.

Just as we were coming to the cottage I stood up in the trap and called out, but there was no reply.

"He's having an afternoon nap," said Doris.

"Or he's so intent on a book that he can't hear you."

"Or else," I suggested, "he's in one of his absent-minded fits, and has gone away for a stroll and taken the key with him."

And when we reached the house and found the doors locked and could get no reply at all, Arthur looked at me and laughed.

"That's just about what he has done," he said.

"Let's look round the garden," I suggested, "he may be dozing in the shade." But though we called many times and looked everywhere there was no trace of the professor.

"I don't in the least mind staying outside," said Doris at length, "but I am just dying to see the inside of the cottage. Let's see if we can get in through the window."

"Let's," I cried, and ran after Doris.

But I did not run far. I turned the corner and looked up at the house. There across the wall I saw the purple letters, 'John Durston,' and as I watched the flaming hand came again and swept them away.

"What is it?" Arthur asked running to my side.

"I'm afraid," I moaned.

"Afraid, Leslie? What of?"

"I'm afraid, Arthur, I'm afraid, I'm afraid!"

"Hush, my dearest," said Arthur, though neither he nor I noticed the endearment at the time. It was Doris who told us of it afterwards. "What are you afraid of?"

"Get into the house, Arthur," I cried in a hoarse voice.

Arthur did not stop to argue. He went straight up to the window into which we had been going to climb.

"My God!" he cried.

I stepped up behind him to the window, hardly knowing what I expected to see, yet fearing the worst.

He pointed to one side of the window and, peering in, I saw a hand holding fast on to the curtain, clutching it for support. We could not get the window open, but in a very few minutes we had burst in the back door. Arthur was first, and I followed close after him into the principal sitting-room. My dear Mr. Durston was lying, half propped against the wall, half supported by the curtain which he was clutching in his left hand; his eyes staring vacantly at the door in front of him. Suddenly I looked at his feet. There was a book of some sort there. Almost mechanically I stooped and picked it up. It was the "Unbound Book."

No. 7: Black
THE RAVEN OF DINSTONLEY

PART I

I stepped out of the tube at Leicester Square Tube Station and found Doris waiting for me under the clock.

"Come along, old girl," she remarked cheerfully as I approached; "I thought you were never coming."

"I'm not so very late," I protested. "Only ten minutes, and I've waited hours for you before now."

"What have you been doing?" my cousin asked. "Talking with Mr. Bindold, I suppose."

"No, I haven't," I declared. "I've been working and I wanted to finish what I was doing."

"Well, where shall we go?"

"Anywhere you like," I answered readily. "Why not the Café de la Croix?"

Doris agreed at once, and we turned up Charing Cross Road towards Soho.

The Café de la Croix is a little French Restaurant—one should really call it an eating-house—in a small turning out of Old Compton Street. Perhaps I should admit that we should have been ashamed to have entered its English equivalent; but the food was good, the place clean, and the customers amusing. We had been elbowed out of our favourite restaurants by the ever- increasing stream of suburban "Bohemians" "doing" Soho. The old days in which you ate what they had got with the comfortable knowledge that, whatever it was, it was certain to be good, had been replaced by more prosperous times of *tables d'hôte*—less than half the old quality at rather more than twice the old price. So we sought refuge with Madame Lalessan and though the *bœuf* was almost invariably *bouilli*, we were content to rub shoulders with the cheery artisans who frequented the place, and to make ourselves at home. On this occasion Doris and I intended to have a quiet little dinner together, and then go on to The Royalty Theatre to see Milestones. We dawdled over our coffee as we sat at our usual table in the tiny alcove.

"You know," said Doris eventually, "there's one thing I'm rather afraid of."

"And that is?" I asked.

"That you'll develop into a psychologist yourself, and become a stuffy old woman professor or something one of these days."

"You needn't be afraid of that," I laughed, "I'm not nearly clever enough."

"My dear Leslie," she replied, "if that is all that stops you, we may as well consider it a certainty. You are clever enough, that's just what worries me."

"I don't see what there is to worry about," I answered. "It would be very nice if I could, but of course I shall never leave Professor Durston."

"So long as you have to work, I hope you never will," said my cousin; "but I am rather afraid he may get you some position as assistant lecturer, or something of that sort."

"Of course, I could never do that," I replied, "because I don't know enough about the subject. But supposing I did, why should you be afraid about it?"

"Because it's not healthy, my dear. Oh! you needn't laugh; it's not. Here you are, a young, healthy, jolly, pretty girl, spending the entire day, week, year, working out mental vibrations, and filling your head with all sorts of wonderful things about centres of ideation. You must know that it isn't healthy."

"I'm very well," I protested, "and certainly I'm very happy. I give you my word I wouldn't change with any girl in London."

"I don't suppose you would," sighed Doris. "I admit that your work must be very interesting, if you're built that way, and have brains to understand it; and the professor and Mr. Bindold are both kindness itself to you, and you're very well paid. But I should like to see you doing something that any fool could do, and then you wouldn't wear yourself out, and you might have a little more spare time and spend it a little more rationally."

"What could be more rational than this?" I exclaimed.

"This is an exception," my cousin declared. "But you haven't been to a dance this year, and altogether you work too hard. What have you been doing to-day?"

"Correcting the proofs of Mr. Durston's book on Colour," I replied. "The concentration exercises took me rather longer to correct than I expected and that made me late. It is a splendid book, Doris. I am certain it will make a sensation."

"I'm sure I hope it will," said Doris dutifully.

"Just imagine what the world will be like," I cried eagerly, "a generation after concentration and mental control have been taught in the schools!"

"I don't know that I am very anxious to live in a world peopled with geniuses," she replied, with a touch of scorn.

"It is not a question of genius at all," I retorted. "Genius cannot be taught, although it can be developed. The effect will be far more valuable than if it did produce a race of mental giants in the sense you mean. Everything that is done will be done well and expeditiously; there will be no waste of power, no ability frittered away to no purpose; and if you can't see the value of universal mental organisation I give you up as hopeless."

"I quite agree up to a point," said my friend. "After that you must leave me behind. You seem to think that anyone can do anything by the simple process of giving the whole mind to that one thing and nothing else. Of course a great deal can be accomplished by determination. You can wake up at a certain time, if you make up your mind to it overnight. Any task can be done in half its ordinary time by setting yourself a programme and sticking to it like grim death. Where I don't follow you is in the purely psychological aspect of it. You say that if you train your mind to think in colours, you eventually read thought automatically, and even see, or, as you call it, visualise, actual events which are happening at a distance."

"But we've proved it," I exclaimed. "Go to Scotland Yard and ask them there what Professor Durston has done for them and see what they say. He has unravelled more mysteries and prevented more crimes than any man living, and that by the apparently impossible process of sitting at home and watching them happen. Naturally one expects the public to be sceptical. The inner and secret history of the great white dome would read to some people like the fanciful imaginings of a crank."

"I admit it sounds like that to me," said my cousin. "I find it very difficult to believe that one can sit and stare at a blank white space and then suddenly find yourself, as it were, miles and miles away watching something, some horrible tragedy of real life perhaps, enacted by people you have never heard of, in a place you have never seen."

"And yet we do it every day," I answered. "In one form or another we experiment daily. Concentration and colour thought can do very nearly everything. You admit that there must be something in chromatic vibration, and you know that concentration is the secret of all success. Take any walk of life you like! Think of Edison, of Napoleon. The only difference is that they have concentrated on a concrete subject, while we give our minds over entirely to the intangible."

"I wish you wouldn't say 'we' so often," said Doris plaintively. "I am quite sure it isn't healthy for a young, bright girl like you to give your mind over to the intangible, as you say."

I plunged into a long description of the colour theory in defence of my friend and master. I gave details of cases in which Professor Durston had proved himself capable of performing the most amazing feats of mental magic. I pointed out to her that the mind which was so trained as to be able to carry out these experiments must essentially be healthy, but I could not convince her, and at last she began to look worried.

"Oh! very well," I laughed at last; "have it your own way, dear. We are out to enjoy ourselves to-night. Let's forget about psychology till to-morrow."

I looked at my watch and then glanced guiltily at my friend.

"Do you know the time?" I asked. "It's a quarter to nine."

"Then we can't go to the Royalty tonight," said Doris. "Bother your stuffy old psychology."

"I'm dreadfully sorry," I apologised. "I had no idea it was so late, or I would have stopped."

"Oh, that's all right," she replied; for Doris was one of those comfortable people whom it is difficult to disappoint. "We can easily go there another night and, besides, you're really rather interesting when you get talking. I suppose I'm just a wee bit jealous that I'm not clever myself."

We called the "waitress," the elder Mademoiselle Lalessan, a snub-nosed urchin with her hair screwed up in a little pigtail, paid our bill, and, having said goodnight to 'maman' in very indifferent French, we strolled out into the street.

"There is something very fascinating about that place," said Doris. "It is hardly aristocratic, but I find it infinitely more attractive than the gaudy glitter of some of its high-born relatives."

"Yes," I agreed. "It is something to be able to enjoy the simple things in life. Now that I come to think of it I don't believe there is really anything I don't enjoy. I enjoy going out or stopping at home. I enjoy going to bed, and I even enjoy getting up!"

"That certainly sounds healthy enough," Doris laughed. "It is probably because you like your work, so it cuts both ways, and I won't say any more about it."

We turned down Frith Street into Shaftesbury Avenue, watching the strange procession of fellow creatures that is always to be seen in that thoroughfare. I suppose it is because it leads into such very different localities that Shaftesbury Avenue always strikes me as the most interesting street in London. It runs between Piccadilly and Oxford Street, Soho and Seven Dials. I suggested as much to my companion.

"Oh, I don't know," she replied. "I always think the most interesting street in London is the one you happen to be in at the time."

"Here's a picture palace!" I exclaimed suddenly. "Let's go to the pictures."

"Oh, good," said Doris willingly. We did not pay the slightest attention to the programme that was standing, in a big frame, outside the door, for we were both of us very easily pleased. As a matter of fact the programme was a very good one indeed. We took two shilling seats and thereby sated eighteen pence each on the evening's outing, a circumstance which, I must admit, did not detract from our enjoyment. Armed with a box of chocolates which we obtained from the attendant, we sat in a very comfortable circle and waited for the tail end of an American "comedy" to finish. Why British film producers seem to be incapable of competing with American "comics" I cannot for the life of me understand. I doubt very much whether we should have been much wiser, even if we had seen the film from the beginning. However, it came to an end at last, and was followed by a very interesting drama. Towards the end of the first part the film suddenly flickered and went out, leaving the screen a blank white space.

"Oh, what a shame," Doris exclaimed; "it was just beginning to be interesting."

We waited patiently with our eyes expectantly fixed on the sheet, but for two or three minutes nothing happened, except that the pianist went on playing with the greatest unconcern. It was what is called technically a 'break,' I believe. Presently a dark shadow fell on the sheet. I watched it, languidly until it gradually began to take shape. Slowly the picture grew before my eyes and I saw a great, black bird, chained to what appeared to be a stone step. Its head was thrust forward, and its eyes moved slowly from side to side. I was disgusted to notice that its left wing was clipped almost entirely away, and it seemed to be struggling painfully against its enforced captivity. I was very indignant to think that such cruelty could be perpetrated merely for the amusement of cinema-goers, and I could not even understand what part the wretched bird played in the drama. I turned to my companion intending to express my disgust, but at that moment Doris spoke.

"I wish they'd get on with it," she said crossly, "I'm getting tired of looking at an empty screen."

An empty screen! I looked at my friend and then at the sheet. The bird was gone; there was nothing but the blank white space.

"Haven't they started yet?" I asked weakly. "I haven't been looking. I was thinking of something else."

"No, nothing has happened at all," she answered. "Ah! here we are at last."

A round of applause greeted the picture as it was again thrown on the screen, but, for my part, I lost all interest in the drama. Where had the great black bird come from, and why hadn't Doris seen it? I knew at once that there could only be one explanation. Instinctively my mind had thrown itself into what the professor would have called a "receptive mood" the moment I fixed my attention on the white sheet. I had received a mind-message, and a very powerful one at that, for I had mistaken the image for an actual photograph. I did not follow the rest of the entertainment in the least. I tried to find some reason for the strange picture of the bird which had so mysteriously arisen before my eyes. I was tempted to tell Doris all about it at once, but I felt that it would be hardly fair. After all, we were supposed to be having a rest from work of every description, and I had very nearly spoiled her evening already by my enthusiasm at dinner-time. I tried to put the matter out of my mind and take an interest in the pictures, but it was impossible; and I waited patiently until my friend should announce her readiness to leave.

"The next is that stupid comedy thing," she said at last. "The one that was on when we came in. We don't want to see that, do we?"

"Goodness, no!" I exclaimed thankfully, and we hurriedly made our way out.

"Do you know, Leslie," my cousin exclaimed as we stepped into the street, "I feel that there's something in the air, some sort of . . . oh I don't know . . . only I have a restless feeling that something is going to happen."

"What sort of thing do you think?" I said.

"I haven't the least idea," she laughed; "but one does have these feelings sometimes."

"Yes," I agreed, "I often do, but I didn't think you did. Your temperament and mine are two very different things. When you feel at all moody it usually means that you are going to do something clever, some striking design or something. But with me it is often a sort of prescience of danger, or evil."

"That's just what I feel now," she replied, but her tone was light and did not fill me with any particular misgivings.

"I don't think there can be very much going to happen to us to-night," I answered. "If there were I should be very much more likely to feel uneasy than you."

"I wonder what could happen to us?" Doris mused.

"Getting run over seems the most probable," I exclaimed, as we stepped back on to the kerb just in time to avoid a passing taxi-cab.

"That would be so frightfully unromantic," my companion protested, "though I confess that it appears at first glance to be the only immediate possibility."

"We might be kidnapped," I suggested.

"I don't know that I wouldn't rather be run over after all," said Doris thoughtfully. "I think we'd better be content with a cup of coffee and a 'bus home."

Accordingly we made our way to a small coffee-shop at the back of Goodge Street station, kept by a Polish Jew of the name of Koplevski.

"I suppose you realise, my dear," said Doris as we strolled up the Tottenham Court Road, "that this is hardly the neighbourhood in which two young ladies would be expected to seek refreshment at this time?"

"Or any other time," I laughed. "But who cares? It is infinitely more respectable in some senses and certainly a very great deal more interesting than many of the fashionable quarters of the town. There is more real life and less artificiality in Koplevski's little coffee-den than in any of the first-class restaurants. It is curious that the most interesting and most human part of any great city is its foreign quarter. It doesn't matter in what country the city may be, it is always the same. In the foreign quarter you always seem to get down to the heart of things."

"I suppose it is the fact that the foreigner does not understand the language or the customs of the country that makes him so grateful for a little sympathy and so ready to extend sympathy to others," Doris remarked.

"The fact of being strangers in a strange land is a bond of brotherhood in itself," I answered, "and a very strong one too."

As I spoke we turned the corner into Goodge Street, and a man who was just in front of us stopped suddenly, with the result that we bumped into him before we could stop ourselves. He raised his hat with a charming smile and stepped out of our way.

"Nice-looking chap," I remarked to my friend. "Was he Spanish or Italian do you think?"

"I should think neither," Doris answered, "though it would be quite impossible to say definitely. There was a suggestion of Irish about him, I thought."

"Well, your judgement is worth a great deal more than mine," I replied; for the study of physiognomy was, of course, one of Doris's subjects in connection with her art work. "Anyway it was a striking face and a handsome one too."

We reached Koplevski's and, walking down to the far end of the long narrow room, we took the table next to the end. At the table beyond us four men were playing dominoes. They looked up casually as we sat down, and one of them started perceptibly. To my surprise I recognised the very man we had just been discussing. How had he got there before us? It would not take him a moment to plunge into a game of dominoes, for though he looked as if he had been there for hours, he possibly had only entered a couple of minutes before us. What surprised me was that he should have got there without passing us in the street, for that I was convinced he had not done. He smiled again as he noticed my surprise, raised his hat, and returned to his game without a word. Koplevski himself served us with our coffee and stood by our table chatting for a few minutes until the door opened and two new customers arrived. As they did so our acquaintance at the other table rose and came over to us.

"Excuse me," he said, in perfect English, "but you ladies are very likely feeling the draught here. If you will allow us, my friends

will be very pleased to change tables with you. We always reserve
the end table merely because it is the most comfortable in the room;
but we could not anticipate the honour of your presence this
evening."

It was only the carefully worded compliment that made me certain he was a foreigner. Simply dressed, with nothing conspicuous
about his appearance at all, it was impossible to hazard a guess at
his nationality; but Englishmen are too self-conscious to carry off
even so simple a situation with such an airy grace. I hastened to
assure him that we had not noticed the draught.

"We are very much obliged to you, monsieur," I replied; "but
neither my friend nor I have felt the draught in the least, and we
would not think of moving you from your usual place in any case."

To my astonishment he turned to his friends and said in a loud
voice, which made me wonder if some of them were deaf:

"The ladies are inconvenienced by the draught. We will give
them our table."

Either the man did not or would not understand me, and as his
party gathered up their dominoes and coffee cups in readiness for
the removal, there was nothing for us to do but to accept the invitation with as good a grace as possible. Doris and I thanked them
all profusely, but we were both at a loss to understand our new
friend's insistence. However, the change was certainly for the better, as we found ourselves warmer and also more conveniently
placed. We now commanded a view of the entire room, and we sat
there for nearly half an hour making idle conjectures as to the char-
acters, nationalities, and domestic affairs of our fellow customers.

"It would be very interesting to know the life histories of all
the men in this room," said Doris. "I wonder where they have all
come from, what sort of conditions they left behind, and why they
left. I daresay there are a lot of tiny tragedies mixed up here—perhaps some pretty big ones; who knows?"

"I expect the reasons of their coming to this country were mostly
domestic," I remarked. "Probably an aunt married an Englishman,
or an uncle came over to work for a London firm, and these came
to join them."

"Very likely you're right," my cousin replied; "but I prefer to look upon them as political refugees, or potential anarchists, or something of that sort. It makes them so much more interesting. Well, we have studied them all now, and it's getting late; we'd better be going."

"Yes," I agreed, "I don't suppose we shall learn very much more about them, if we stay here for ever, especially those two at the other end."

"Which two?" Doris asked.

"Those two that came in just before we moved tables. They are obviously Englishmen and—"

"And equally obviously of no special interest to us," added my companion, in which, as it proved, we showed our ignorance in an alarming degree.

We rose from the table, leaving, as was the custom of the place, two coppers on the table for "the woman who washed the cups," though that was none other than Madame Koplevski herself. As we did so our gallant cavalier among the domino players rose slowly from his seat and strolled towards the door. He was standing on the step as we went out and we exchanged a hearty "good-night" and hurried away. We had scarcely gone a dozen yards before I discovered I had left one of my gloves. I ran back to get it, only to find that I had tucked it in my waist. I turned to run back to Doris, who was strolling gently on, when I heard a clatter behind me. Turning round I saw one of the two Englishmen picking himself up from the pavement.

"You clumsy beast!" he exclaimed savagely, returning with a threatening air to the doorway. Then our foreign friend stepped out and stood in front of him.

"Ten thousand apologies, monsieur," he said. "I—"

"Get out of my way, imbecile," cried the other. "Don't stand there putting your hulking great carcass in everybody's way."

The Englishman made as if to push the domino player into the gutter, and advanced upon him with a menacing sweep of the arm.

"Monsieur will surely permit me to express my regrets," said the latter. "Monsieur moved so quickly, he came so unexpectedly, clumsy that I am, I had not time to move."

"Oh, all right, all right," said his victim. "Nobody but a blithering idiot would stand about in doorways for other people to fall over him. Now get out of my way."

But the foreigner was persistent. He had removed his hat with a sweeping bow, and now held it behind his back.

"Monsieur will please to understand . . ." he began, and it was then that I noticed he was signalling to me behind his back to go away. I did not wait for any more. I turned and ran to Doris.

"Come," I said, "quickly."

"What's all the trouble?" she asked, and as she spoke I heard the sound of hurrying footsteps behind us. Naturally we both stopped to ascertain what it was. The Englishman was pushing the foreigner along the pavement in our direction. We stopped to watch; on they came until they were almost on top of us, and then our cavalier made a determined stand.

"If monsieur does not accept my explanation, monsieur insults me, and I demand his apology."

"Don't be an ass, Charles," said the Englishman's companion. "Can't you see the man's a foreigner? Tell him you understand it was an accident, and you're sorry if you lost your temper."

To my intense amazement the domino-player, taking advantage of the diversion, turned his head quickly to me.

"For God's sake run, you little fool," he whispered over his shoulder. I took Doris by the arm, and together we ran round the corner and into the tube station.

"Whatever did he mean?" my companion asked. "Were they going to fight, do you think?"

"No," I said emphatically. "Our little foreigner was far too much of a cavalier to be mixed up in a vulgar street brawl. The other man, too, was most certainly a gentleman as far as birth goes."

"What was he doing in Koplevski's, then?" said Doris.

"What were we doing there, if it comes to that?" I replied. "I can't think why that man was so anxious to get rid of us. He might almost have been deliberately trying to keep the others back."

"Oh! nonsense," said Doris. "That great clumsy Englishman fell over him and he was trying to apologise, that was all. I don't see what our friend Charles has to complain about, because I nearly tripped over him on the way out. He was sitting with his feet out and I tumbled right on to him, only he warded me off with his hand."

"Did you?" I asked, "I didn't notice it."

"No, you were in front, and I shouldn't have thought about it again, only it just struck me that people who live in glass houses shouldn't throw stones."

We took the tube home and by the time we reached Hampstead we had almost forgotten the incident. We strolled up Heath Street to our flat admiring the beautiful moonlit night.

"What a pity we couldn't go for a walk on the heath," I said; "it looks perfectly lovely now."

"We're not going to do anything of the sort," said my companion emphatically. "We've done quite enough unconventional things for one evening, thank you."

When we reached the outside door of the flat we found it locked, and so we stood for a moment in the shadow while I got out my key. We had just stepped inside the doorway when a dark figure passed by, pausing for a moment outside.

"Mademoiselle will forgive me that I called her a little fool," said a voice, which we both recognised at once. I confess I was startled, and Doris and I looked at each other anxiously by the dim light which trickled down from the landing above. Then I seemed to regain my senses. I opened the door and ran out. About twenty yards away I saw a quickly receding figure.

"Come back," I called, and I must confess it was almost a scream. I admit that I was very nervous, for no girl likes being followed about. The foreigner came back and stood before us—for Doris had joined me—with his hat in his hand.

"Who are you?" I demanded angrily, "and why do you follow us about like this?"

"My name is Velpaux, Anatole Velpaux," he replied. "I followed you, mademoiselle, because I thought it was better that someone should see you safely home."

"Good gracious, man," I exclaimed, "we're not children. We're quite capable of looking after ourselves."

"That, of course, I am quite ready to believe," he replied; "but there are times when it is not advisable for two young ladies such as you to go about unescorted."

"Whatever are you talking about?" I asked, now thoroughly indignant. "When we require any assistance we shall ask for it."

"In that case," said M. Velpaux, "having rendered such assistance as I could, mademoiselle will no doubt be relieved if I say good-night." He bowed to us both and turned to go, but Doris called him back. Being the less excitable of the two she took a more sensible view of the air.

"One moment, Monsieur Velpaux," she said. "It is obvious that you mean us nothing but good. You do not look the sort of man who would follow us home merely for the amusement of finding out where we live, and you would have gone away before if we had not called you back."

"Yes, there is that," I admitted. "I am afraid I have done you an injustice."

"You must have been referring to some definite danger, or what you took to be a definite danger, this evening, and we should be glad to hear what it was."

I was glad Doris had taken the matter in hand, for, if the man had really come all the way out to Hampstead to see that we came to no harm, I had been exceedingly rude to him.

"You will remember," he answered, "that I met you at the corner of Goodge Street. I recognised you then as two ladies whom I had seen on one or two occasions in Koplevski's, although you do not appear to have recognised me. After you had gone on I saw that you were being followed by two men. I gathered that you were on your way to the café, and that they would probably follow you there. I ran up the alley and arrived at Koplevski's only a few minutes before you. Not long afterwards the two men entered, and I thought it desirable that you should change tables with us, in order that I might be better able to command any necessity that might arise. When you left I stood in the doorway and placed myself in the way of the first gentleman, who was rushing out after you, with results which mademoiselle here witnessed for herself."

I looked at Doris rather shamefacedly. It was clear that the man was perfectly genuine.

"And then I came round to the tube station and followed you here," Monsieur Velpaux concluded simply.

"But what—?" began Doris.

"It is not for me to suggest any reason why you should have been followed by these two men," he interrupted. "I merely put it that, in the circumstances, I thought it better that someone, anyone, should see that you arrived safely at your home."

I held out my hand.

"We are both very much obliged to you indeed, monsieur," I said, "and I hope that you will forgive me if I spoke foolishly without thinking."

"But no!" he laughed, "mademoiselle has nothing to reproach herself with. It was natural."

And with another low bow and a hurried glance up and down the street he was gone. Doris and I went upstairs to the flat.

"I say, Leslie," she said, "I wonder what our respective parents would think if they heard of this?"

"They won't," I replied emphatically; "but I'll admit we are a little careless in the way we go about. Since I went to Mr. Durston I have had such extraordinary confidence in my ability to take care of myself, that I never think where we are going, or what time it is, or any of the things one ought to remember according to convention."

"Well, I think we'd better be a little more careful in future," my cousin agreed. "After all, wandering about the Italian quarter at all hours of the night is hardly the wisest conduct for two youngsters such as we are. This ought to take us down a peg or two!"

"Yes!" I laughed. "It won't do us any harm. I confess I was a wee bit scared."

"Well, anyway, we'll turn in now. Put the kettle on and let us have a cup of cocoa," she suggested. "I'm tired."

"Are you?" I asked. "I think the business must have livened me up. I feel wide awake."

I put the kettle on, and Doris got the cocoa ready and cut some bread-and-butter.

"I should ask Mr. Durston what he thinks about our going round such places as Koplevski's and Lalessan's," said my companion. "He probably knows all about them, and he could tell us if there is any reason why we shouldn't go, except the obvious one that it isn't usual."

"I'll ask him when he comes back," I agreed. "Kettle's boiling," I added. I took the cup that she held out to me.

"Of course, I've been in some really dangerous places when we have been on business, and I'm not really afraid of anything happening to us. After all it's the twentieth century, you know, with its manifold complications of police and so forth."

"Oh, of course, I'm not a bit afraid either," she answered with a laugh. "Only if it really is so frightfully unusual, well, you know, a girl has to remember—"

And then, breaking off suddenly and abruptly in the middle of the sentence, Doris fell senseless at my feet.

PART II

I dropped the cup of cocoa in the fender, and jumped to Doris's assistance. At first I thought she had fainted, but when I had dashed a jugful of cold water in her face I seemed to realise instinctively that this was no ordinary faint. I ran to the next flat for help. The occupant—a young law student—came to the door in a dressing-gown and carpet slippers.

"My cousin is ill," I explained breathlessly. "Give me some brandy quickly, please, and run for a doctor."

It did not strike me at the time that I was ordering a total stranger about, and the young man did not demur in the least. He hurried quickly indoors, and returned in less than two minutes with a decanter in his hand and a Norfolk jacket in place of his dressing-gown. I took the brandy from him and ran back to my cousin. Mr. Figgis, as his name proved to be, rushed off to find a doctor, but before he did so he knocked up the people on the other side of the landing, and I was presently joined by a Mrs. Hatherlie, the charming young wife of an actor. I was grateful to Mr. Figgis for his forethought. Certainly one woman's help is worth more than that of two men in such circumstances. We had to force the brandy between Doris's teeth, but it only produced the faintest flicker of consciousness, and I began to be really alarmed about her and impatient for the arrival of the doctor.

"You mustn't be anxious, dear," said Mrs. Hatherlie kindly. "She will be all right presently, and the doctor can't be very long now. There is one just across the road."

Almost at that moment the doctor arrived. Unfortunately he was not the one who had attended me during my brief but unpleasant nervous breakdown. This was an older man, and he rather gave one the impression that the mere fact of his entering the room was a step on the way to recovery, and that therefore there was no need to hurry him. Of course, when those who are near and dear to us are in danger, we are naturally apt to be impatient and hasty in our judgements, and no doubt the doctor was a most capable man and one who would not waste a second if possible.

"What is it?" I asked anxiously. "Has she fainted?"

The doctor was looking puzzled; he did not reply to my question at all. He looked over his shoulder towards Mr. Figgis, who was standing in the corner waiting, I suppose, for further instructions.

"Fetch my assistant," he said, and without another word he returned to his patient. Mrs. Hatherlie took my hand and patted it, and I was very grateful for her sympathetic comfort. I knew that my cousin had not fainted, long before the doctor corroborated my suspicion by sending for his assistant. It does not take two doctors to bring a healthy girl out of a fainting fit. I felt that I was getting nervous and hysterical, and that I must do something. When Mr. Figgis returned with the doctor's colleague I called him aside.

"Is there anywhere that you can use a telephone about here at this time of night?" I asked.

"Yes," he replied, "the tube station is still open."

"You may telephone from the surgery," said the elder of the two medical men, without looking up. I gave our neighbour Mr. Bindold's number, and asked him to ring him up and ask him to come round immediately. Half an hour later, when he arrived, the doctors were still applying new methods in order to revive my poor friend.

"Arthur!" I cried, as I met him in the hall. "Thank heaven you have come; I should have broken down in another moment."

"What's the matter, Leslie?" he asked anxiously. "I was afraid you were ill or hurt or something."

"It's Doris. She was standing talking to me an hour ago, and she suddenly fell down unconscious and she has not come round yet."

"Don't be frightened, dear," he replied. "She'll be all right very soon. It is probably just a bad fainting fit."

"I'm sure it's not," I insisted; "I'm sure it's not. It is something very much worse than that."

"What are you afraid of?" Arthur asked.

"I don't know in the least," I admitted distractedly. "There is something really wrong I am sure. Good heavens!" I cried, suddenly remembering.

"What is it?"

"Doris said this evening that she had a feeling something was going to happen to her. She said she had a sort of instinct that there was some danger near her."

Arthur linked his arm through mine.

"Come and rest a little, Leslie," he suggested gently. "Everything will be all right very shortly. Evidently Doris was not feeling very well this evening. One often has these depressed fits, imagining all sorts of things are going to happen, but then the illness is the cause of the depression and not vice versa."

"She wasn't at all depressed," I insisted. "She was perfectly well and very bright, and I was never more surprised in my life than when she went over."

"Well, you'd better come and rest," he repeated, "or we shall have you going over next." He led me into our little den, and pulled an easy chair in front of the fire and pushed me gently into it.

"What have you been doing to-night?" he asked.

"Nothing in the least strenuous," I replied; "nothing that could have made Doris ill. We had dinner at the Café de la Croix and then went to the pictures."

"Has she been overworking lately?"

"No," I answered, "not recently. She has not been quite so busy as usual for the past few weeks."

"And she isn't worried about anything?"

"Oh dear no! Doris never worries about anything," I assured him. "This is not just an ordinary illness, Arthur, I am quite certain of that."

"Well, you stop here, dear, while I go and speak to the doctor," he said, as he left the room. In a few moments he came back with a very different expression on his face; but I was relieved to notice that it was more of acute interest than of anxiety.

"Where do you say you dined, Leslie?" he asked.

"Lalessan's," I replied. "You know, that little place I took you to one Sunday evening, just off Old Compton Street."

"Was the food all right?"

"Quite," I answered. "I'm sure that can't have upset her. We went on to Koplevski's after the pictures and had a cup of coffee, but that was quite all right too. Mine was just the same as usual, and Doris did not complain of anything."

"Well," said Arthur, "the doctors suspect poisoning."

"Poisoning?" I cried.

"Yes," he answered. "They both seem to regard it as a case of attempted suicide."

"Attempted suicide! Doris attempt suicide!" I jumped up from my chair in indignation. "If they can't do better than talk rubbish like that," I cried, "you had better send them away, and let us get a real doctor to her."

"Come, come, my dear Leslie," Mr. Bindold said quietly, "sit down and be sensible, like a good girl. They can only go by the symptoms they see. They don't know Doris as you do. In their opinion she has either tried to poison herself and failed, or else she has been very heavily drugged—dangerously so."

At the word "dangerous" I jumped up and ran into the bedroom, and was just entering the door when I heard one of the doctors call my name.

"Yes," I answered, "here I am. Is she better?"

"She is delirious, which means that we have relieved the pressure to some extent. I want you to listen carefully to every word she says, and try to see if there is any significance in it so far as you know. This may possibly be of the greatest importance."

The assistant was sitting by the bed with a notebook and pencil in his hand. Doris's slim hand was clutching nervously at the coverlet, and she was tossing restlessly in a high fever. Arthur came into the room and stood behind me, his hand resting reassuringly on my shoulder. Presently Doris's lips began to move.

"Speak to her," said the doctor.

I knelt beside her and took her hand in mine.

"Doris darling," I said softly, "it is I, Leslie. Speak to me, dear, speak to me."

"Let the poor beast go," she cried suddenly, sitting up in bed. "Let it go."

"Do you know what she means?" the doctor asked. I shook my head. The strange words conveyed nothing to me.

"Don't you know, dear?" I urged again. "It is Leslie, Leslie."

"It's black," she murmured, sobbing gently. "Oh! so black. Why don't you leave it alone."

"What is black, darling?" I asked. "Tell Leslie what it is."

It was no use. For some minutes I kept repeating my name into my dear friend's ear, but there was not a sign of recognition in her beautiful eyes.

"Doris, wake up!" I called suddenly in a loud voice, and to our astonishment she sat bolt upright at the words.

"Hullo, Leslie!" she exclaimed, "what time is it? I suppose monsieur will permit me to express my regrets."

Before I could say a word she fell back and lost consciousness again. I turned to the doctor's assistant.

"Her last phrase was one we overheard this evening," I explained, and the young man nodded his head solemnly and made a note of the fact.

We all spoke to my poor cousin in turns; but we could do nothing with her, and for several hours we sat there in the hope that she would open her eyes again. The doctor went away at last, and left his assistant in charge.

"Come, dear," said Arthur. "Run and slip into a dressing-gown, and I will make you a cup of tea, or whatever you prefer, and get you something to eat."

"I couldn't eat," I protested.

"You must, Leslie," he replied. "Do as you're told, like a good girl, or you will break down. Doris will come round before morning, but if you feel you must sit with her then make yourself comfortable, or as comfortable as you possibly can."

Although I had declined his offer to get me something to eat, I was very glad of it when it came, and when I had drunk a cup of tea and Arthur had propped me up in an arm-chair by the side of my cousin's bed I felt better able to cope with the situation. It was not till after dawn that Doris spoke again, and when she did she startled us all.

"You're burning a hole through my arm," she whimpered. "Leave me alone. It burns, it burns."

The young medico jumped to his feet in an instant.

"Which arm?" he demanded excitedly, but Doris did not reply.

"Which arm, Doris?" I repeated, as she did not speak. "Tell Leslie which arm."

"My left arm," she replied faintly. "They are burning a hole through it. Stop them; it hurts."

The doctor caught her hand and quickly pushing back the sleeve ran over her arm with deft fingers, examining it carefully all the time.

"I can see nothing," he said at last, and began to pinch the arm gently, first in one place and then another, his eyes fixed intently on her face.

"Oh! it hurts," said Doris again, in a voice scarcely audible. The doctor leaned over and looked carefully at her arm at the point where his finger had been pressing.

"My God!" he exclaimed, suddenly, and turned to me with a face as white as a sheet, his eyes literally dancing with suppressed excitement. I jumped to my feet.

"What is it?" I cried.

"A magnifying glass, quickly," he said, in a voice that shook. Doris had a large magnifying glass, which she kept among her drawing implements. I had returned with it in a second. The doctor turned the arm over and examined it through the glass, just on the inside of the elbow joint. Suddenly he dropped the glass and slipped his hand in his pocket.

"A bowl," he said curtly, and taking a pencil and card from his waistcoat pocket he wrote down a couple of words and handed the card to Arthur.

"Give that to my partner at once," he said, and then, taking the bowl which I handed him, he took a sharp instrument from his bag and severed one of the veins in Doris's wrist. I stood by with a towel, feeling utterly miserable and unspeakably helpless.

"Speak to her again," he said at last. "Ask her what has happened."

I leaned over the bed and repeated the question several times. At the fifth time Doris opened her eyes.

"It is all right, dear," she sighed. "I'm better now, it burned me with its beak."

I looked at the doctor helplessly. What could the poor girl mean? What was this mysterious burning? What was it that was black? And what could she possibly mean by the strange words, "it burned me with its beak"? I had not long to ponder over it for the doctor spoke to me abruptly.

"Make a note of it!" he said sharply. I picked up his notebook humbly and did as I was told. Arthur and the senior partner returned at that moment. The face of the latter was completely transformed. He was all energy and vitality. He gave one the impression that he had just made a marvellous discovery, which he found it impossible to believe.

"This is preposterous, Cunliffe," he exclaimed, almost before he had entered the room. "You must be dreaming."

"It is a fact," said the young man simply.

"But never in my life . . . my dear fellow, there have only been two cases recorded in Europe."

"Look yourself," was the only reply. I must say I admired the calm and deliberate way in which Doctor Cunliffe went about his work, as soon as he had recovered from his obvious surprise. He did not stop to discuss the matter with his partner. He tied up Doris's wrist rapidly and then prepared the articles which he required for his further treatment, with hands which moved with masterly precision.

"Don't you agree with me, Walters?" he asked without looking up.

"It seems to fit," the other admitted grudgingly, as he forced open Doris's mouth and prepared to examine it.

"You're right!" he exclaimed an instant later. "By heaven! you're right! Quickly, man, we're only just in time."

I stood anxiously looking on, my hand almost unconsciously resting in Arthur's while the two doctors set to work. Doctor Walters made up for his previous scepticism by an amazing activity. In one swift movement he took off his coat and slung it across the room. In another he rolled up his shirt sleeves; in another he placed his arm under Doris's head and held her up while he swiftly propped up the pillows. I felt it was useless to try and help them; I should only have been in the way. I stood there helpless, but ready, watching my dearest friend, perhaps dying before my eyes, and then for an hour or more not a word was spoken, while the doctors worked unceasingly. I could not follow their treatment at all. For one thing my brain seemed numbed, and I was hardly conscious even of the fact that Arthur lifted me gently into a chair. While one of the medical men was rubbing Doris's feet, the other seemed to be scraping her teeth with a flat knife. Then they would shake her or slap her arms and then, apparently, massage the muscles of her neck. Several times they poured some medicine down her throat, and twice they gave her a hypodermic injection.

Then, at last, after what seemed to me to be years of waiting, for I had not taken my eyes from her face, Doris stirred and sighed softly. The two doctors stood up and looked at each other, a strange light in their eyes, and then they solemnly shook hands across the bed. I shivered from head to foot in the nervous reaction, as I gathered the significance of their silent handshake. It told me more

eloquently than any words could possibly have done how near my
dear cousin had been to the shadow of death. I began to cry quietly, as I realised how devotedly these two men had striven to ward
off that grim spectre, and I began to understand for the first time
how much we owe to these men, who dedicate their lives to the
alleviation of suffering and the shepherding of human life. They
did not even yet relax their watch. In a moment they returned to
their work with the same vigour, the same strained attention as
before.

The clock in our little den had struck six when Doris spoke,
and when they heard the sound of her voice again the two doctors
looked once more into each other's eyes with a smile of gratifica-
tion, almost triumph.

"It was black and it burned me with its beak, and if monsieur
will not accept my apology he insults me," she murmured.

Dr. Cunliffe called me to the bedside with a look. I took my
cousin's hand and bent over her.

"It is Leslie," I said again. "Tell me what is worrying you, dear."
But she did not recognise me yet, though presently she spoke again
in a dreamy, far-off manner.

"I think it was a raven," she said.

A raven! I stirred strangely at the word. What did it convey to
me? Surely I, too, had had some dream of a raven, or I had seen
one somewhere.

"It burned me with its beak," the thin, tired voice went on. "Yes,
it burned me. Clumsy that I am, I had not time to move."

"What can she mean?" I cried, turning to the doctors.

"Does it convey nothing to you at all?" the elder asked.

"Nothing that means anything," I replied. "The last part of the
sentence was part of the same conversation which I mentioned
before. We overheard it on our way home to-night."

"It does not concern anything which could possibly be of any
importance to the patient?" he queried.

"Not in the least," I answered emphatically. "We simply overheard a Frenchman, I think he was, and an Englishman having an
argument, and she is repeating the former's phrases."

"That is of no consequence, then," said Doctor Cunliffe. "Can you think what she means by the raven?"

"No," I said, "and yet I seem to remember something about one, but I can't bring it to mind."

"Ask her what it was like and what it did to her."

"Doris," I said, taking her hand again, "what was the raven like, dear?"

"It must have been a raven, it was so black," she said softly after I had repeated the question several times.

"What was it like, dearest?"

"It burned me with its beak. I wanted to let it go because it was chained up."

I started back with a loud cry. The three men ran to me at once, but I pushed Arthur's hand away. In an instant I remembered my strange vision in the picture palace. I had seen an image of a raven which must have been a mental picture. Doris had not seen it then. What terrible significance could the chained bird hold for us that Doris should be stricken down like this? I bent over Doris and almost shouted into her ear in my fright.

"Its wings," I cried. "Its wings! Did you notice them? Doris! did you notice its wings?"

Doris turned over restlessly.

"One of its wings was clipped," she murmured.

Of course, the whole thing might be capable of the simplest explanation. Almost subconsciously I tried to persuade myself, even then, that there might possibly be nothing very sinister in the strange affair at all. And yet I found myself struggling in the icy grip of a weird, intangible terror. I felt that I was confronted with some terrible danger, at the very nature of which I could not even guess.

Doctor Cunliffe lifted me to my feet and held a glass of brandy to my lips.

"All right, my dear," he said soothingly, "don't be alarmed, you'll be all right in a moment."

I gulped the brandy hurriedly, desperately grasping at anything which would help me to regain control of my nerves, and rid my brain of that terrible, numb, aching feeling of cramp.

"Yes, I shall be all right," I replied breathlessly; "I've got to be all right."

Arthur took my hands in his, and I held to him as hard as I could; and thus in a short time I recovered some of my confidence in myself.

"Tell us what is the matter, dear," he said quietly at last.

"I don't know," I confessed weakly. "That is what I am afraid of. It is nothing really, and yet it frightens me."

"What is this raven you spoke of?" asked Dr. Walters.

"It—well—please don't laugh at me," I replied. "But there was no raven really. It was— Well, you won't understand—"

"We shall understand, my dear," said the old man kindly. "Don't be afraid of telling us anything. It might be of the greatest importance. It might mean the difference between life and death."

"I had better tell you the whole story from the beginning," I suggested.

"I am secretary to Mr. John Durston," I began presently, and the two medicos exchanged an interested glance. I thought I would explain my connection with Mr. Durston at the outset, so that they would understand how I came to visualise the image of the raven. I must admit too that I was afraid of being laughed at, and I knew that no man of science, physician or what not, would laugh at anything connected with the magic name of John Durston.

"This image was absolutely unforced," the younger of them asked when I told them of the picture on the screen.

"Yes," I replied, "absolutely. I was simply dreaming, waiting idly for the show to go on again."

"You had not, so far as you remember, seen a picture of a raven in captivity during the day?"

"No," I answered, "I am sure I had not."

"Try and remember, my dear," urged Dr. Walters. "You see, it is possible that both you and your cousin may have seen a picture in a shop window, or even a captive raven in a house, without either of you taking any particular notice of it at the time."

I thought hard for a few minutes, but I could recall no such thing. I needed no convincing that the image was purely mental, that I had received the vibrations circulating from some other mind.

"Have you heard my uncle speak of a raven, or any other black bird?" Arthur asked.

"No," I said, "never."

"You are quite sure no such thing has ever occurred in any of your experiments, Leslie?"

But I was positive that this was something new, some strange sinister symbol that had come into our lives for the first time that evening.

"Do you think that my cousin's ramblings can have any real importance?" I asked.

"They might have," Dr. Cunliffe admitted. "They might help us to discover the cause of her attack and in the event of—well, of anything happening to her, they might prove of the greatest importance, although I am thankful to say that I am sure she is well on the road to recovery."

"You are not sure of the cause then?" I asked with a sense of disappointment, for I thought from their manner that they had already diagnosed poor Doris's sudden illness.

"The cause, but not the source," he replied. "At least I think we have discovered the cause, although it seems improbable."

"What is it?" I asked interestedly.

"Before I tell you what I think it is," he replied, "let me ask you a few questions. In the first place, where were you a couple of hours before the attack came on?"

"In the picture palace, I think," I replied. "We went from there to a little café off Goodge Street, Koplevski's, and sat there for about an hour altogether. Then we came home."

"Did anything unusual happen this evening?"

"Well, yes," I admitted, "though it can't have anything to do with Doris's illness."

"Never mind," said Arthur, "tell us about it, Leslie."

I told them the story of our young French friend, Monsieur Velpaux, and the two Englishmen.

"You say he effectually prevented them from following you?" asked Doctor Cunliffe with a gleam of acute interest in his handsome grey eyes.

"Certainly," I said. "They were still arguing in the street when we got into the tube station."

"Can you suggest any reason for their wanting to follow you?"

"Well," I began, "only—"

"Apart from the fact, excuse my putting it bluntly, apart from the fact that you were two pretty girls, whose acquaintance they desired to make," he replied. "Can you think of any other reason?"

"None at all," I answered, for indeed I could imagine no earthly reason for the strange behaviour of the two men in the café.

"Have you assisted Mr. Durston in any other capacity than that of secretary?"

"I help him in all sorts of ways, however and whenever I can," I replied.

"Do you mean, does she help my uncle in the active and physical part of his experiments?" Arthur asked, and Doctor Cunliffe nodded his head. "Yes, she does. She has been of the greatest practical assistance to him in his criminal investigations."

"But even then," I interposed, "I don't see how that could be the cause of Doris being taken ill."

"She was not taken ill," said the doctor quietly.

"Not what?" I exclaimed. "But we—"

"Had your cousin died there would have been an inquest," he replied solemnly, "and, had there been an inquest, I should have attended and urged the jury to return a verdict of murder against some person or persons unknown."

I jumped to my feet.

"Murder?" I cried. "Impossible!"

"Almost a certainty," said Dr. Walters over his shoulder, for he had not left Doris's side for an instant.

"But I don't understand," I repeated. "How can anyone have tried to murder her? Why should anyone want to murder her? I was with her all the evening, and she was perfectly well up to the very moment she fell at my feet."

"All of which helps to confirm our theory," the physician replied with a smile. "You may think that what I am about to tell you is impossible. It is one of nature's fairytales. Seventeen or eighteen years ago a French scientist, one of the most able men of his day, was exploring Africa, on a scientific expedition. One day, in the middle of the jungle, he and his party came suddenly upon the body, or rather the remains, of a man. The scientist in his own account describes that moment as the greatest in his life, for there, at his feet, lying in what appeared to be a pool of water, lay a dead man, *almost entirely dissolved*. When the Frenchman recovered from his astonishment he set about examining this remarkable phenomenon. The process of liquefaction was not complete, and was still progressing slowly. He was absolutely at a loss to account for this extraordinary state of affairs, because he had never even heard of anything of the sort before. He subjected the liquid to a great many tests, but all to no purpose. He was so much absorbed in the scientific aspect of his discovery, that he did not for some time notice a curious insect which was lying in the pool of water. However, he recovered this and received his second shock, for the insect was one which was previously unknown. When every other test, every other theory, had proved useless, he began to see if he could connect the strange insect with the dissolving man. The insect itself was, as he put it, something like a cross between a snake and a butterfly, about six inches long. He experimented with this beast for some time, and, having satisfied himself that it was supplied with poison glands, he did his best to make it poison a rabbit. It was only after repeated efforts that he discovered the way in which he could make the insect sufficiently angry to use its poison, but one morning he succeeded, and three days later there was nothing left of the rabbit but skin—and water."

"Good heavens!" I exclaimed; "is that really true?"

"Yes," he replied. "It is known as the le Mauzielle Fly, called, of course, after the celebrated scientist who discovered it. Now, Miss Dalrayne, you may or may not believe me, but your cousin was bitten by one of these insects."

"But how is that possible?" I asked, refusing to believe my ears. "I don't see where it could have come from. I don't understand—are there any in this country?"

"There used to be one at the Royal College of Surgeons," he answered; "but I do not think there is one in Europe to-day, except the one that stung Miss Doris."

"It seems ridiculous," I exclaimed, and hurriedly apologised. "I don't mean that; I beg your pardon. It seems impossible. Have there been any other cases?"

"There were two cases recorded in Europe, whose symptoms coincide with those reported by le Mauzielle, but they occurred before his great discovery. They were, naturally, the cause of a great deal of speculation among scientists of the day, but they were not fortunate enough to find the insect."

"And you really mean," I gasped, "that the poison of this insect dissolves bone and—and—all that?"

"Everything except hair, so far as we have been able to discover," he replied.

"But you mentioned murder," I reminded him, suddenly returning to the case in point.

"I said that," he answered, "because it requires a great deal of patient effort to make the animal angry enough to use its poison. That is why I regarded it as probably a deliberate attempt upon your cousin's life. You have not, of course, seen this insect or anything that might account for the attack?"

"No, I haven't," I assured him. "I feel convinced that she could not have been bitten in that way. If she had been she would surely have noticed something at the time; and an insect six inches long must have been seen by one or other of us."

"Yes," the doctor admitted, "I imagine she would have felt the sting, and felt it pretty acutely. I may say I have no practical experience of the poison; but I have read a good deal about it because, of course, it is of extreme interest."

"Are you sure that the symptoms are accurate?"

"Absolutely," he replied emphatically. "If we had not taken it in time, the teeth would already have begun to dissolve. We were not a moment too soon. From le Mauzielle's account once the dissolution has set in nothing in the world can save the life. I believe that in another hour your cousin's teeth would have begun to melt."

"Good heavens," I exclaimed as I glanced at poor Doris, with a sigh of heartfelt thankfulness that the hideous danger was past.

"When does the patient die?" I asked.

"Oh, quite early, I am glad to say," Doctor Cunliffe replied. "The animals so far experimented on have usually never regained consciousness after the first attack, which is usually immediately preceded by a tired feeling, illustrated in animals by a disinclination to move."

"Why! Doris remarked that she was tired almost at the moment she fell, and it is very unusual for her to complain of tiredness."

"That is one further symptom, although I have every confidence that the diagnosis, however extraordinary it may seem, is correct. It could not possibly be anything else. Look!"

He leaned over and taking Doris's poor limp arm in his hand, turned it over.

"You see that small round black mark? That always arrives a few hours after the bite. It will probably remain for years and may be a permanent disfigurement."

I went over the strange affair in my mind. Could there by any means have been one of these ghastly insects in the picture theatre? It was dark there and consequently it might not have been seen by either of us. What a merciful thing it was that Fate should have sent us a young doctor who was prepared to believe the almost impossible! How many, even if the idea had ever entered their heads, would have dismissed it in a moment as utterly ridiculous? And then my darling would have—but I could not bear to think of that. I felt a gentle pressure on my shoulder and looking up I found Arthur standing over me.

"Now, if you'll get the doctor some breakfast, and have some yourself, I'll come back and join you presently."

"Where are you going?" I asked.

"To see if the free library is open," he replied, and before I could speak again he was gone.

I bent over Doris and looked lovingly at the beautiful, familiar features now clothed in a deep and peaceful sleep.

"I am glad you told me that death comes early," I sighed. "How awful it would be to think of that poor fellow lying all alone there in the jungle, slowly . . . ugh! Did le Mauzielle ever find out who he was or anything about him?"

"Oh! yes!" the doctor answered. "I've forgotten the man's name, but he was out big-game hunting with the Earl of Dinstonley. They got cut off from the rest of their party, and eventually the earl came back and reported that his friend had been taken very ill and died in the jungle. Dinstonley was picked up by a missionary party some weeks afterwards, and then came straight home."

"I don't seem to have heard of the Earl of Dinstonley," I said. "I don't know very much about the peerage."

"No, one never sees his name in the papers; but he was not the earl at that time. As far as I remember, he and his companion were both second cousins of the then earl. I have only read the case in le Mauzielle's treatise, and I don't remember much about that."

"Enough to have saved a very dear and valuable life," I remarked gratefully. "Now I'll get you some breakfast."

"None for me, thanks," Dr. Walters interposed. "I must be getting across. I think you had better stay a little longer, Cunliffe, just in case anything happens. I will attend to your duties for you, and you had better take this young lady under your entire charge. You know a great deal more about this than I do," he added, and I thought it was exceedingly handsome of a senior partner to make such a graceful admission.

"I should like a clean up," Dr. Cunliffe confessed, with a laugh, and after he had had a final look at his patient I showed him into our tiny bathroom, and set about cooking the ham and eggs of which he must have been sadly in need. I lighted the fire and tidied up our little den, and made the sickroom as straight as possible and got a fire in there too.

"You seem to be what the Americans would call a hustler, Miss Dalrayne," said Dr. Cunliffe as he rejoined me.

"Sit down and have your breakfast while it's hot," I replied, with a laugh.

"I wandered into the studio, at least I suppose it is the studio," he said.

"It isn't really one, but we turned it into the nearest approach to it we could manage when we came back."

"If I may say so there is some very delightful work there. Do you do that as well as your work with the professor?" he asked.

"I? Good gracious, no!" I laughed. "The patient is our artist."

"Indeed?" he exclaimed with a look of frank surprise on his clean-cut, clever face.

"Why be so astonished?" I asked.

"I—er—well, I ought not to be astonished," he mumbled awkwardly; "but to tell you the truth I—well, I have never associated a beautiful girl with—er—with such remarkable talent before."

I laughed quietly.

"Please don't laugh at me," he pleaded, "I must confess that most of my time has been spent among books and what we call 'accidents.' It was exceedingly rude of me to doubt your cousin's ability."

"I wasn't exactly laughing at that," I replied.

"What were you laughing at, then?" he asked a trifle anxiously.

"I don't think I'll tell," I replied; "it wouldn't be fair."

"But it might be kinder," he urged.

"You will probably think me conceited," I suggested, "which would serve me right. I don't set up to be a beauty, but you certainly don't seem to think much of my looks if you accuse me of doing clever things merely because you don't associate them with good-looking people."

"I am exceedingly sorry," he stammered, "I'm afraid I express myself very clumsily."

"Please don't look so embarrassed," I pleaded, "or I shall feel sorry I told you."

And so by mutual, tacit consent we changed the subject; but I had taken a fancy to the quiet, shy, obviously clever young doctor, a fancy which has never left me to this day. Arthur joined us a few minutes afterwards.

"Ah! here you are," I greeted him.

"It won't take me five minutes to get you some breakfast, and meanwhile sit down, Arthur, and have a cup of coffee. You must be famished."

Without a word Arthur tossed a bit of paper in front of me.

"I am not an artist, Leslie," he said. "That is a very rough sketch, and in any case I don't think it is likely to be of any use to us at all."

I picked up the paper and started back with a cry of surprise.

"Where did you get this? "I asked.

"I copied it out of a book in the free library," he answered.

"What is it, Miss Dalrayne?" asked the doctor, who had risen from the table.

"It is the raven," I exclaimed, hardly believing my eyes. "The very raven I saw, exactly right in pose and position. The chain and everything are right."

"Then this is what Miss Doris was talking about?"

"It must be," I said. "Arthur, why do you say this will probably be of no use to us?"

"Oh! because I got it out of a book of heraldry," he replied. "I looked up all the encyclopaedias they had and books on birds, and then it just struck me that I might find a design which would convey or recall something to you in a book on heraldry. So I looked it up and that is it."

"What is it exactly?" Doctor Cunliffe asked, with a look of extreme interest.

Arthur threw himself into a chair, with an expression of weariness and disappointment.

"It's only a crest—the crest of the Earl of Dinstonley," he replied.

PART III

Doctor Cunliffe was the first to speak. "This is extraordinary," he exclaimed. "The most extraordinary thing I have ever heard!"

Arthur jumped up at once.

"What do you mean?" he cried. "What's extraordinary? I thought it would be of no use at all."

"It may be of the greatest use, Arthur," I replied. "The doctor will tell you how."

"Let me get this right," said Mr. Bindold, as Doctor Cunliffe concluded a concise and graphic narrative. "You say that Dinstonley, or whatever his name was at the time, was the first man in the world to witness the action of this poison insect?"

"I don't go so far as to say that he was the first to witness the symptoms," the doctor replied, "but I do say that he was the first man we know of who came in contact with this extraordinary poison. Of course, wherever the insect has existed there have probably been cases of death arising from its bite, but the first case known to science was that of Dinstonley's companion. He himself therefore was the man who first, in the knowledge of present-day medical history, came in contact with the le Mauzielle fly."

"Did he himself know that his friend died from the bite of this insect?" I asked.

"I really don't remember what le Mauzielle said about that," Dr. Cunliffe replied, "but I should think it very improbable."

"The amazing part of it is that Leslie should have seen the image, and that Doris should have been bitten by the insect, both in the same evening."

"Doris must have seen the image too," I pointed out. "She connected them very closely in her mind, for she said that the raven had burned her arm with its beak."

"Still, that only adds to the complexity of it," Arthur remarked; "for the remarkable thing is that Dinstonley and the raven and the le Mauzielle fly have all cropped up together on the same evening."

"I don't profess to understand," the doctor admitted.

"What a pity Mr. Durston is not here," I said. "He would have been able to suggest something."

"Is he far away? Could you wire for him?"

"No, he's gone to Lausanne," I replied, "to the International Psychological Congress. He's chairman this year."

"Well, I don't know what to make of it," Arthur admitted, "but as he is not here we must get on as well as we can without him. I will make a few enquiries, though whether they will be of any use seems very doubtful.

"I am entirely at your service, Miss Dalrayne," said Dr. Cunliffe. "I must admit that, to my mind, the simplest thing would be to regard the whole thing as a most remarkable coincidence. What good any enquiries can do I cannot see, but I am quite prepared to do anything in my power to assist you and Miss Doris."

"Thank you, doctor," I replied simply, "but I confess that I cannot see where we are to commence our enquiries. If Mr. Durston were here, it would be different, because he can usually tell the reasons for the association of apparently unconnected subjects."

"Well," said Arthur definitely, "I am going to find the Earl of Dinstonley and ask him if he can make any suggestions, and we must do all we can to discover the insect and capture it before it does any more harm."

"Yes," I agreed, "it is extremely improbable that everyone would be so fortunate as to secure a doctor who would be able to save the life of the patient."

At that moment there was a ring at the doorbell—a deliberate, prolonged ring.

"See if it's the baker," I said to Arthur, "and, if it is, call me."

To my surprise I heard an exclamation of astonishment from Mr. Bindold, and a moment later the door opened and Professor Durston burst into the room.

"You!" I cried. "Oh! I am so glad. Whatever brought you back? I thought you weren't coming for another week."

The professor took my hands in his and looked into my eyes with a strange anxiety, which told me at once that he was not sure about something.

"What is it?" I asked, fearing that he had bad news for me.

"Nothing," he said, with a sigh of relief; "nothing, thank God. I was afraid I should find you—find you ill."

"I am very well," I answered; "but Doris is ill."

"Doris!" he exclaimed, "since when?"

"Last night," I replied. "It was very sudden and it is an extraordinary affair altogether. She suddenly fell at my feet, and Doctor Cunliffe here has been with her ever since."

I was astonished to see the sudden change in Mr. Durston's expression, his face turned a deathly grey.

"What is the matter? Is she—how is she now?"

"She is sleeping now, I am thankful to say," said the young physician.

"You mean that the danger is over?" the professor asked.

"Yes," replied the other. "There is no danger now; I am confident of that."

Mr. Durston looked at the doctor closely, and then suddenly laid his hand on his shoulder.

"Thank God you were here," he said devoutly. "Where is she?"

Followed by Arthur and the doctor I led him into Doris's room. The poor girl was still fast asleep, but the expression on her face was peaceful and contented, and I had no doubts at all about her recovery.

"Give me a dressing-gown," said the professor abruptly.

I handed him my own and, holding it in his hand, he advanced to the bed and laid his other on my cousin's forehead.

"Doris, my dear," he said in a low voice, so low that it was almost a whisper. "Wake up! Wake up!"

Doris stirred and rubbed the back of her hand across her eyes.

"Who's that?" she asked, in a sleepy voice. Mr. Durston beckoned to me with a finger, and I stepped to the bedside. Then he turned to Dr. Cunliffe.

"What did you think was the matter?" he asked. "Tell me in two words."

"Le Mauzielle," said the doctor quietly.

"Thank God you thought so," Mr. Durston replied, "but you are wrong."

"Wrong," cried Dr. Cunliffe, "how do you mean?"

"I am glad you thought so because you saved the child's life, but you are wrong all the same."

"Then what was the matter with her?" the other asked incredulously.

"Nothing at all," the professor answered.

The physician looked from one to the other of us in bewilderment. I could not follow the drift of my employer's remark and waited for him to explain, and the old, strange feeling of the presence of some unfathomable danger returned with renewed force.

"Speak to her, Leslie!" said the professor. "Tell her it is time to get up."

"Doris," I whispered into my friend's ear, "Doris, darling, it's time to get up. Breakfast, old girl."

My cousin rubbed her eyes and, much to my surprise, sprang out of bed.

"Oh, good gracious!" she cried as she saw the room full of people, "what are you all doing here?"

"Come to wish you good morning, my dear," said the professor, wrapping the dressing-gown round her.

"Leslie, dear," she asked, her eyes growing rounder and wider, "what is it? What does this mean?"

I put my arms round her and kissed her, and tried to assure her that everything was all right.

"You weren't very well last night, dear," I explained. "Dr. Cunliffe came in to see how you are and Mr. Durston and Arthur called for me. That is how we all came together like this."

"I wasn't very well?" she asked. "I don't remember being ill. I had a horrible nightmare, but I am quite well."

The doctor looked nervously at his patient.

"She ought not to be standing about," he said anxiously. "She must be weak at least."

"Yes, I do feel rather weak," Doris admitted, and the professor helped her gently on to the bed.

"I am convinced that what I said was right," said Cunliffe.

"Where was the—er—where was it?" Mr. Durston asked.

In answer to the question the doctor stepped forward and took Doris by the hand. He pushed the sleeve from her arm.

"Here," he said, and suddenly stepped back. "Good heavens! it's gone."

"There is nothing the matter with her at all, I can assure you of that. Of course, she must feel weak, and you will no doubt advise her to stay in bed; but, otherwise, she is as well as you or I."

The young physician looked so disappointed that his wonderful discovery had been discredited that I felt sorry the professor had spoken of the matter. But Mr. Durston came to the rescue at once. He stepped forward and laid his hand on the doctor's shoulder.

"My dear boy," he said, "you have saved her life. If you had not thought of le Mauzielle she would be dead by now. You were right and so am I; but I ask you not to demand an explanation until I have the whole matter weighed in my own mind."

After that I prepared a warm egg and milk for my cousin; we put her back to bed, and then adjourned to the den, in order that the professor might learn the whole strange story from the beginning.

"Leslie," said Mr. Durston, as I concluded, "we have dealt with some strange cases, and we have had some unusual adventures, but I think this is the most mysterious of all."

"Can you suggest anything?" I asked.

"No," he replied thoughtfully, "not yet. But in time, my dear, we may get to the bottom of the matter. Was there anything in this book of heraldry, Arthur, giving a history of the crest? Any reason offered for its adoption?"

"No," said Mr. Bindold, "nothing at all. Of course, I have not gone into the matter thoroughly. I simply availed myself of the resources of our local library, which are not very great."

"But you haven't told me," I pointed out, "why you have come back or anything about that part of it."

"I came back because I had a feeling that someone had designs upon your life, my dear Leslie. I cannot tell you how relieved I was to find you here and well."

"On *my* life!" I exclaimed, "but why?"

"Ah! that I cannot tell. But you, who know me, know by what means I knew that there was something amiss. It is a remarkable thing that I should have realised the possibility of the le Mauzielle fly without in the least visualising the raven."

"Did you know that Doris was being poisoned, then?" I asked.

"No," he replied thoughtfully, "I only knew that there was an evil influence at work against you, and that in some way it was connected with that terrible insect. Fortunately as soon as I visualised the fly I recognised it, for when I was a student I was very much struck by the case."

"Well, anyway," I remarked, with a sigh of relief, "it's all over now, and we can go to bed and have some sleep."

"You must certainly do that," he replied, "but it is not all over, I am afraid. We have a great deal to do first. Still, you need not worry about it. Go to bed, my dear, and have the rest you have so well earned, and leave us to get on with the case."

"Certainly not," I protested. "You've never left me out of a case yet, and I'm not going to be left out of this."

"Very well, Leslie," the professor replied. "You shall be with us, little girl, but you must certainly have a rest before you do anything. So you had better go to bed now. I have one or two enquiries to make, as I want to get the whole facts of the le Mauzielle fly at my finger tips before we go any further. I shall want your help too, Arthur; so we will come back for Leslie when we have finished."

"I shall be ready whenever you come," I promised. "But do you think I ought to leave Doris just yet?"

"Well we can see about that later, anyway," said Mr. Durston. "Come along, my boy. Now be sure you go to bed, Leslie."

I gave them my word that I would turn in at once, and the doctor having had a final look at his patient went away with the others, promising to come back later in the day. I found Doris asleep, so I slipped into bed without disturbing her and was very soon fast asleep. It was Doris who woke me some hours later.

"Leslie," she asked, "are you awake?"

"Yes," I murmured. "What is it? Isn't that the front door bell?"

I sat up in bed and listened. There could be no doubt about it, so I sprang out of bed and slipped into a dressing-gown and went to the door. It was Mr. Durston and Arthur.

"Come in, please," I said, "and excuse my garb."

"How long will it take you to dress and get ready to come on a journey with us?" the professor asked abruptly, and I noted a look of stern business in his eye.

"Three minutes," I said; "but I can't very well leave Doris all by herself in the flat."

"Well, I forgot that," said Mr. Durston impatiently. "Arthur, run out and fetch that young doctor, he might be able to help us out of that difficulty."

As it happened the doctor could and would help us, for he sent over his housekeeper to sit with my cousin while he went out to find one of his nurses.

"Well?" I asked as I settled myself in the taxi which was waiting at the door, "where are you taking me to now?"

"Paddington," said the professor.

"And then?"

"Well, then we are going down to Herefordshire to a quiet little country village. We shall find the most comfortable inn and stop there the night."

"That all sounds very pleasant," I laughed, "but what is it for, and what do we do to-morrow?"

"To-morrow we go to Dinstonley Castle; at least we think it will be to-morrow."

"Dinstonley Castle!" I exclaimed. "We seem to be getting straight to the point, as usual!"

"Yes," Arthur agreed. "We are not going to waste a minute. We are going to call on the earl. In fact, it may be necessary to call on his lordship to-night."

I glanced ruefully at my little suit-case. "I wish you'd told me about this before I packed," I laughed.

Three hours later we stepped out of the train at the little country station, which I will call Crenderton, and found it impossible to get a fly to take us to the village, which was, of course, nearly three miles away. But it was a beautiful evening and we enjoyed the walk through the lovely old lanes. At last we came to a charming old English village, and it struck me as strange that we should have come to such a peaceful place on a mission connected with anything so tragic as my cousin's sudden attack.

"Are you prepared to take your chance in the matter of accommodation, Leslie?" the professor asked.

"Anything that suits you will suit me," I replied with a laugh. "That looks like an inn along the road. Isn't that a signpost?"

I could just see a post bearing a swinging sign-board looming out of the dusk a little way ahead of us, and when we came to it we found painted on the board, "The Dinstonley Raven." We stopped and looked at each other.

"This is ominous," Arthur exclaimed.

"But of course it is very natural, and if we went to the home village of the Duke of Endlymore, we should probably find a house called 'The Endlymore Goat,' which is the somewhat unaristocratic emblem of that family."

"Anyway, we'll see what they can do for us," said Mr. Durston, and we entered the quaint old courtyard. It was a delightful spot altogether. I was charmed with its low doors and long smoky rafters, for we found ourselves in a sort of serving bar the moment we stepped into the house. A lout of a potman looked up from the pewter he was putting away on a shelf and gave us a suspicious stare for some moments.

"Is the landlord about?" Mr. Bindold asked, for he always took charge of what he called the commonplace side of our expeditions.

"I am the landlord," said a voice behind us. "What can I do for you, sir?" And we turned to see a tall, pleasant-looking man stepping through a low doorway in the panelling.

"We want three bedrooms for to-night," Arthur replied.

"Very good, sir," mine host answered, in a tone which suggested that thirty bedrooms would have been at our disposal had we desired them. "Put these gentlemen's things in number 3 and number 7, and tell Matilda to show this lady into the countess's room."

Later in the evening, when we had finished our dinner and were sitting idly chatting, the landlord came in to see if we had everything we required, and I noticed that Mr. Durston wanted to encourage him to talk. Accordingly I treated him to the sweetest smile I could muster and asked him:

"Why do you call the room I am sleeping in the countess's room?"

"Well, you see, miss," he began, "it's an old tradition in these parts that once upon a time, maybe a couple of hundred years ago, they was having a high old time at the castle, and they do say that my lord had invited some woman friend of his that my lady didn't exactly approve of and so her ladyship came down here for the night."

"I see," said I. "They must have been pretty merry times in those days."

"They must indeed, miss," he answered, "very different from what they are now, very," and he shook his head sadly.

"Still I suppose there are plenty of people about the castle nowadays," said Arthur.

"Plenty of people!" snorted mine host, with fine scorn. "Why, there's nobody, sir—at least not what you could call anybody. Why, I should be ashamed to run the Raven on the staff they keep at the castle. There are hardly half a dozen servants about the place."

"But why is that?" I asked. "Is the earl poor?"

"Bless you no, miss! Not poor; mean if you like, or a trifle crazy perhaps, but not poor! He must be a bit touched, I think. There isn't a man in the village that has spoken to him, and he never entertains though he very often goes away for weeks at a time, and perhaps he gets all the amusement he wants while he's away. Still, it isn't fair on local trade, not by no manner of means."

"Is he at home now?" I asked carelessly.

"That I couldn't say for certain, miss," he replied. "I was told he went up to London last week and he may have gone to America for all I know. They say he often goes there."

We could gather no further information from the landlord and, although I should have liked to have listened to his gossip of local history, it was not helping us in the least, so we gave him to understand as soon as we could that we did not require to know anything further, and he went away.

"I think I'll go and have a cigar quietly," said Mr. Durston presently, "I'll just go for a stroll along the road."

"Don't be very long," I called after him, and Arthur and I were left alone.

"I wonder what this all means?" Arthur mused. "You usually have a marvellous intuition about things, Leslie; what do you think of it?"

"I don't know what to think of it," I replied. "I have long since given up being astonished at these things. I am in good hands, for nothing will happen to me that Mr. Durston can prevent, so why should I worry?

"Aren't you ever afraid?" he asked.

"I think I can honestly say I am never afraid when I know what the danger is. If it is a material danger I don't think it would worry me much."

"My uncle is firmly convinced that someone tried to murder you yesterday and nothing will persuade him otherwise."

"But why should they want to murder me? And in any case it was poor Doris that was the victim, if there was anything of that sort about."

"Still, you must promise me that you will take care of yourself, won't you? I must say I can't tell you how much I admire your pluck, Leslie. Most girls would be frightened out of their wits, but it doesn't seem to worry you in the least."

"Because I have such complete confidence in your uncle," I replied. "If I had not, I might be afraid. As it is I am not afraid of anything." I lifted my liqueur glass and smiled at Arthur. "Here's very good health and long life to us all."

And, even as I spoke, the glass split into a thousand pieces, and the bits spattered the walls all round the room.

PART IV

Arthur and I jumped to our feet instantly, and I noticed that blood was pouring from his ear, where he must have been struck by a flying splinter of glass.

"What was that?" he cried.

We looked round the room, but we could see nothing that in any way accounted for the remarkable occurrence. Suddenly Arthur pointed to the panelling behind us. I walked over and looked at it carefully. There could be no doubt what had happened, and evidently the same thought struck us both at the same time, for Arthur suddenly jumped forward and placed himself between me and the window. For the panelling had been splintered by the passage of a bullet. Before we could speak again the door opened and Mr. Durston entered.

"Come," he said. "Don't make a noise, and appear as if you were just going out to look at the stars, but follow me quickly."

It was clear that he knew nothing of the silent shot which had so nearly found its mark, and we did not enlighten him at that time. We walked leisurely into the great square hall and then strolled out into the courtyard. We turned into the street and walked slowly along for some minutes.

"Now, run," said Mr. Durston suddenly, as soon as we were out of sight of the inn. We ran in silence till we came to a lane, which was flanked on either side by a great wall. Presently we saw a small gate in the wall and, crouching along the shadow on the other side, we hid behind a tree. Mr. Durston stole over presently and tried the gate and found to our relief that it was open. Then, at a signal, Arthur and I followed him across, and together we slipped through into the castle grounds. Crossing the open ground to the castle was out of the question if we wished to avoid detection, and we had to make a long and tiring detour. I had not dared to speak a word, or I would have asked Mr. Durston the object of our clandestine visit. I did not tell him either of the fulfilment of his fears, the attempt on my life, and to tell the truth, so many things had happened during the last two days that I was not particularly worried about it. I left myself entirely in the hands of fate and hoped for the best.

"Look!" whispered Arthur shortly.

We turned and looked in the direction he indicated, and I saw the silhouette of a tall man, creeping stealthily, evidently looking now and then from right to left to see if he were being watched.

"Who can that be?" I asked.

"Hush!" said Mr. Durston, "don't make a noise. We shall soon find out, but we must not run the slightest risk of being discovered ourselves."

The man, whoever he was, did not take long to cross the ground, for, in a moment or two, his shadow was swallowed up in the darkness below the castle wall. Dinstonley Castle, though I never saw it by daylight, was at any rate a very imposing place in the semi-moonlight. I should have liked to have explored it, examined all its quaint turrets and ramparts, but we had all our time fully occupied the night we were there, and by the morning we had returned to town. We had been waiting about a quarter of an hour when Mr. Durston touched my hand and motioned to me to follow him, and then we hurried across to the other side of a great lawn and found ourselves on a terrace outside the main entrance to the castle.

"Now," said Mr. Durston, "let us call upon the earl."

"Do you think he will be likely to see us?" I asked. "If he is such a peculiar man, we shall have to devise some exceptional means of getting at him."

"I think I can manage that," the professor replied, and at that moment we saw the man who had been so stealthily making his way across the grass coming towards us with the same fox-like tread. "Stand by, Arthur," whispered the professor. Arthur slipped in front of me and I noticed that he had a revolver in his hand. It was the first time I had known him carry one. I wondered what it could all mean, but there was no chance to ask questions then. The man came closer and closer. Mr. Durston hid in the shadow of the wall until the stranger was only a yard or two off, then suddenly he spoke.

"Hullo, Jafforman," said the professor, in a short, sharp voice. The figure in the shadow jumped back as if it had been shot.

"Hullo, Charlie Jafforman," said the professor again. The man stood just where he was, and I could see that he was trembling like a leaf. I was surprised and not a little disgusted that a big, strong fellow, such as he was, could be such a coward. At last he spoke.

"Are you there?" he asked in a trembling voice.

"I am here, Charlie," said the professor. "Where did you expect me to be?"

Suddenly the man pulled himself together with an evident effort.

"Good God," he muttered to himself, "there *is* someone there. Who are you? Come out of it. Who are you, I say?"

I had never seen such a sudden change in any man. He had suddenly been transformed from a cringing, whining coward, to a fierce, overbearing animal almost shrieking with rage. I could only see him silhouetted against the sky, but I knew that if I could discern his features they must have proved an interesting study.

"Who are *you?*" Arthur asked, and I believe it was part of a prearranged plan that he should take up the conversation at this point.

"I am the Earl of Dinstonley," the shadow replied. "Now, tell me who you are, and what you are doing here, or I'll knock your brains out."

"I don't think you will," said Arthur quietly, springing forward and pointing his revolver in the face of the earl. Then he drew an electric torch from his pocket and shone it on the earl's face.

"Good heavens!" I cried in astonishment, for there before me, his hands above his head, the muzzle of Mr. Bindold's revolver within a few inches of his head, stood the man who had tripped over Monsieur Velpaux coming out of Koplevski's the previous night.

The professor walked up to him, and took a revolver from his pocket.

"Now, sir," he said, "you will kindly lead the way. I have something to say to you, which had better be said elsewhere. If you make the slightest attempt to escape there are two of us here to shoot you."

Then began a strange procession along the terrace by the faint light of the moon. The prisoner leading the way, followed by Arthur, Mr. Durston, and myself, must have made a curious picture against the deep grey walls of the castle. We had turned off the terrace and were walking down a steep path leading to what was evidently a side door. Suddenly there was a shout from Arthur, followed by a dull thud. Then the air was pierced by the shrill scream of a great bird and a huge black shape fluttered past our faces and flew off shrieking into the night. When we obtained lights and assistance it was found that the earl had flung himself headfirst into a disused moat and broken his neck. The reader will remember the story of the suicide, but I am enabled now to give, for the first time, the truth of the matter. In a confession which was found by Inspector Orless, Mr. Durston, and myself, in a secret hiding-place in one of the castle towers, the pitiful truth was unmasked. The confession began with the words, "I, Charles Warsley Jafforman, falsely calling myself Earl of Dinstonley," and little more need be told of the story. He had been alone, lost in the jungle, with his cousin the heir to the earldom, when the latter was suddenly taken ill. Jafforman was quite sure in his confession that it was a case of fever, and he accused himself of having murdered his cousin. He seems to have suffered years of agonising remorse afterwards, because he believed that his cousin had slowly dissolved. He did not know that death had come during the first few hours, so that he must immediately have run away and left his friend to die or get better. It was not, of course, until le Mauzielle came back with his wonderful story that he knew the truth, and then this image of his victim, as he put it, "melting to death," began to haunt him incessantly. Later he grew to be so horribly afraid that his secret would be found out, that he almost developed into a murderer himself. Indeed it was only that Fate was against him that saved him from that crime.

As we journeyed back in the train after an exceedingly trying and tiring experience, I asked Mr. Durston for an explanation of the whole affair.

"Well, you know most of it, my dear," he said. "What part do you want to know about?"

"Well, in the first place," I asked, "why was Jafforman so anxious to harm you and Doris and me?"

"It was only you and me, Leslie," he replied, "not Doris at all. He thought that you were Doris."

"But what on earth had I done to the poor wretch?" I asked in bewilderment.

"You had done nothing, but I had. He tried to hurt me, but he was afraid of failing, afraid of being discovered, and afraid, too, of what might happen to him if he only partially succeeded."

"But did you know the man?" I asked.

"I only met him once, and then I made a remark which was the cause of all the danger which has since arisen. They told me that the earl, as they called him, would never hear the word le Mauzielle mentioned in his presence, that he had such a regard for the memory of his poor cousin that he could not bear to look at a map of Africa, and the mention of big-game was like a red rag to a bull with him. Now, I must admit that I had no suspicion whatever about him, I was not in the least interested in him; but I considered it rank hypocrisy for a man to talk like that when he had not even had sufficient regard for his friend to bury him. He seems to have come back with the story that his friend died of fever. Then le Mauzielle finds the man. What I wanted to know was, why hadn't he buried this poor chap for whom he had so much regard? I did not think sufficiently over the affair to be suspicious, but that point struck me at once, and so when I met Jafforman less than a fortnight ago, quite casually, in a friend's club, I pointed out to the earl, as he then appeared to be, that science would have suffered a terrible loss if he had had time to stay and bury his dead cousin."

"I see," I remarked thoughtfully. "And he wanted to harm me, because he found out in the intervening week that you and I are very good friends, and that if he did me an injury you would probably be too busy doing your own typewriting to worry about him!"

"Don't put it that way, my dear, please," he urged. "Anyway, let us be thankful that he has not succeeded in hurting any of us."

"Thankful indeed!" I murmured fervently. "Tell me," I asked later, "what was really the matter with Doris, and why did we see the raven? Because Doris must have seen it too."

"You saw the raven because he always saw it, because he had the idea that he had eternally disgraced the Dinstonleys, of which family he was a member; don't forget that the captive raven of their crest was burnt into his brain. He tells you in his confession that the raven seemed to him to be always striving to break away from its captivity, which shows you what agonies the poor devil must have suffered."

"And Doris's illness?" I asked.

"I am surprised at you asking a question like that, Leslie," the professor replied reproachfully. "You have gone so far into the phenomena of thought transference and its amazing powers, that I thought you would have realised the cause of her illness. You have seen cases in which, by simply telling the patient he has a certain disease, he can be made to develop the symptoms of the disease. So in this case, strange as it may seem, this man, haunted by the memory of this ghastly poison, even accidentally and unknowingly hypnotised Doris into believing that she had been poisoned, and into developing the very symptoms which were his constant night-mare."

When we got back to the flat, I found Doris sitting by the fire in the den, while young Doctor Cunliffe, who had spent most of his time hitherto among books and hospitals, was sitting beside her vigorously buttering her toast.

"Hullo! darling," she cried as I entered, "has it all come right in the end?"

"Yes, dear old thing," I said, as I bent down and kissed her, "I think it will all come right in the end."

No. 8: Violet
THE HERMIT OF WOLDERSMEAD

"I wonder what I should do without you!" said Professor Durston one sweltering afternoon in August, as I folded up the proofs which I was correcting.

"Put an advertisement in *The Daily Telegraph* and get some-one else as quick as you could," I laughed.

"I think I should have to retire," he replied kindly. "I could never work with anyone else, and I know I could certainly never find such a capable and clever assistant, to say nothing of such a charming little friend. You've absolutely spoilt me, Leslie, my dear. You never seem to tire of your work, and even in this broiling weather you never complain."

"Having tea on the lawn, in your beautiful old garden, is hardly the sort of thing that would make one complain," I protested. "Have another cup? And anyway," I added, "we've finished for to-day, and I am not going to bother about any more colour studies, or crimi-nals, or anything at all."

The trim parlour-maid came across the lawn at the moment to the chestnut tree under which we were sitting, and handed the pro-fessor a card.

"I'm afraid you've spoken too soon," said Mr. Durston, as he looked at the name. "But of course you can please yourself whether you go or stay, my dear. Show him out here, Cooper."

"Who is it?" I asked.

"Orless," was the reply.

"I'm afraid I did speak too soon," I agreed, for a visit from the new Chief Inspector of the Criminal Investigation Department certainly suggested some further discussion on the subject of crime. The inspector crossed the lawn with a tired, languid step, which seemed strangely unsuited to him.

"Well, Orless," said the professor as he rose to greet him, "you look as if you were in need of a little refreshment, my dear fellow. Leslie can give you a cup of tea, or would you prefer something else?"

"How do you do, Miss Dalrayne?" said the detective, turning to me. "A cup of tea will do splendidly, if you'll be so kind."

Well," said Mr. Durston, in a few minutes, after we had all agreed that the heat was well-nigh unbearable, "it is perfectly obvious that you have not come out here in this weather to ask the time or anything of that sort. Let's hear about it. Leslie can go, if you prefer it."

"Oh, dear me, no," laughed the other. "If she will stay, I should like her to hear anything I have to say."

I confess that I felt a little thrill of pride at the implied compliment as I picked up my shorthand notebook and a pencil, and prepared to make any notes that I might think necessary or advisable.

"In the first place, as a preface to a curious story," the inspector began, "I should like to ask you a few questions."

"Fire away, my dear fellow," said the professor genially; "I daresay we shall be able to answer them between us."

"Well, then, I want to try and understand something, a mere outline will do, of your colour theory. I know, of course, all about your criminal work, but I don't understand the amazing psychical experiments by which you arrive at some of your conclusions. I admit that at one time I thought that you were an exceptionally clever and useful man, with something like a bee in your bonnet. I hope you won't think I mean that in any patronising sense. I know you are absolutely pre-eminent in the world of psychology, and when I said 'useful' I meant useful in the matter of criminal investigation. Since that affair in the Mancroft Studios I have withdrawn that opinion altogether, and I am now quite prepared to accept pretty well anything you may decide on, without in the least pretending to understand how you arrive at your decision."

"Tell me exactly what it is you want to know about the colour theory?" Mr. Durston asked.

"I take it that your theory presupposes that every mind thinks in colour waves and vibrations, and that certain colours are good and others bad. You say, I believe, that by training yourself to think in colour you have made your mind capable of receiving colour vibrations from other minds, and of visualising their thoughts, just as if they were actually happening?"

"As a bare outline you are putting it very clearly, Orless," said the professor.

"Now, then," the detective went on, in a more hopeful voice, "just suppose that I am in excellent health, no liver or anything of that sort, and that I suddenly saw everything round me turn green, green, or blue, or yellow, for a few seconds, or even a fraction of a second, would that be of any interest to you, or would you say it was merely a case for the doctor?"

The professor looked at his visitor with an expression of curious interest.

"It might be of the greatest interest, the very greatest interest," he said quietly.

Mr. Orless lay back in his rattan chair with something like a sigh of relief as he said:

"Then I'll tell you the story. To begin with, you have read about the murder of young Sir Ian Minnachan at his coming-of-age party? You have? Good; but, if you don't mind, I'll just run over the details of the crime. You know what newspaper reporters are, especially in the dog days. Well, Minnachan was shot on the night of his twenty-first birthday and the murderer has completely disappeared. He has got clean away and left not the slightest clue of any description. It happened in this way. He was staying at his family place in Inverness-shire—the Minnachans are a very old Highland family—with his mother and a large house-party. The coming-of-age was a very important event in the history of the glen, and was quite a county affair. The young baronet was a favourite and, of course, all the young people for miles around were there with their people. The invitations included all the professional men in the district and their families, and the crofters and keepers and shepherds and gillies were invited to watch the festivities. I mention this for the reason that you must know that the whole of the castle grounds were smothered in guests. Minnachan Castle is an exceptionally beautiful spot, and with its elaborate illuminations, which were fitted up for the occasion, it must have been a magnificent sight. It appears that every heir to the title has to stand on a certain Stone in the grounds and make a speech on his twenty-first birthday, the idea being, apparently, to show that the house is founded on a rock, or something of that sort. They had the pipers there and a band from Glasgow, and a dance was in progress on the lawn when the hour came for the young baronet to return thanks. They escorted him amid terrific cheering, the pipes playing and everyone making a great deal of noise, to this Stone. Of course his appearance on the Stone was the signal for a renewed outburst and he waited for them to let him say a few words. Then, to the horrified amazement of everyone present, he suddenly fell forward on his face, shot through the lungs."

"Poor fellow," I murmured.

"Poor fellow, indeed," the inspector replied, "and you may guess that it was a very terrible blow to his family and a grave shock for all present. The suddenness of the tragedy struck everyone with awe. Nobody could for the moment believe their own eyes. At first it was thought that the excitement had overtaxed a weak heart. This happened exactly a week ago, and we have not the slightest clue. The poor lad himself was unable to give any help before he expired. He lingered for a couple of hours and the three doctors who were among the party did everything in their power to save him; but it was hopeless from the start. There were two detectives present from the Glasgow police—the birthday presents were many of them exceedingly valuable—but they were unable to fix anything."

"From what direction was he shot?" I asked; "not from the direction of the house, I suppose?"

"No; judging by the wound, he was shot from some place in the grounds immediately opposite the house," said Mr. Orless. "But then, he was standing on this Stone turning all ways to the people, and it is quite impossible to say which way he was looking when he was actually struck. That, of course, complicates matters a good deal."

"No one seems to have heard the report," Mr. Durston remarked.

"Not a soul," sighed the inspector. "The report was evidently drowned in the noise of the bagpipes and the cheering and shouting that were all going on at the time."

"And the weapon?" I asked, making a note of the previous point.

"That is interesting," the other replied. "He was shot with a big-game rifle."

"That didn't by any chance come from the gun-room at the castle, I suppose?"

"No, my dear young lady, unfortunately it did not. But it was not till I got there myself that the point arose. If the men on the spot had been as quick to note these little points as you are, they might have landed on something which would have given them a clue."

"All this, my dear fellow," said the professor, "is very interesting, but it has no immediate connection with my colour theory. What is the point of the story?"

The detective sat forward in his chair, a new light of interest in his tired eyes.

"Ah! yes," he said. "That brings me to the point. I was staying in a little Highland village about forty miles away when I heard of this affair, and needless to say I got to Minnachan Castle as soon as I possibly could. I interviewed some dozens of the people present and it was only when I saw Lady Muriel Aldencote that I was repaid for my trouble. She told me something which at first seemed curious, but not of the slightest value. The poor girl was very distressed, she and Sir Ian had been great chums since childhood, and I think the family expected and hoped for an engagement when they were both old enough. I had the usual difficulty in getting a

coherent narrative from her, but she told me that the poor boy had
several times during the evening complained of his eyesight. He
said to her on one occasion, early in the afternoon, that he thought
there was something the matter with his eyes. Then, in the evening,
she noticed that he was wearing a very worried look and he said to
her, in reply to her anxious enquiry, that he thought he must be
going either blind or mad. She asked what made him say so, and
he replied that he kept on seeing great flashes of violet sheet-light-
ning. He was quite sure that nobody else saw it, because nobody
remarked on it. She told him it was all imagination and that it was
probably 'nerves,' brought on by the excitement of the festivities.
Now, I personally thought that she was probably quite right, but,
womanlike, she was difficult to convince, and I believe she is firmly
of the opinion that the violet lightning and the tragedy are closely
connected. I was struck by the fact that the doctors and the boy's
mother, who were with him at the end, all state that one of the last
things he was able to say was: 'It's violet, everything . . .
everything's violet.' They put it down to the ramblings of delirium,
with the exception of young Lady Muriel, and she insisted that
therein lay the clue to the mystery. Needless to say I was very busy,
having a great many enquiries to make and various things to attend to—the possible means of the murderer's escape for one—and
I paid little attention to it, except for making the usual note. However, the next morning I was standing in the grounds talking to
the very capable young fellow they sent up from Glasgow, when
suddenly, to my utter astonishment, there was a sharp flash of vivid
violet, which completely covered the whole landscape. I was staggered for the moment, and then I asked Maclaren if he had noticed anything unusual. He assured me he had not, and asked me
if anything was the matter. I had no wish to encumber him with
anything which could possibly lead him off the object of his visit,
and I told him there was nothing. I spent several valuable hours
trying to find some feasible and natural explanation, and eventually
gave it up and made up my mind that it was a curious hallucination, put into my head by Lady Muriel's insistence."

"Where were you standing at this time, Orless?" asked the professor. "Anywhere near the spot where the boy was murdered?"

"No," replied the detective, "a very considerable distance away. Why do you ask?"

"It would have been interesting if you had been standing by this Stone you speak of," said Mr. Durston.

"You don't seem to think this all moonshine, then, eh? I admit I was a little afraid of being laughed at. Do you really think there may be some connection between the two?"

"I don't think at all, my dear Orless," said the professor quietly, "I know."

"I'm very glad of that, very glad indeed," the Scotland Yard man replied, "and I'll tell you why. Two days after the murder I was recalled by wire over a very important diplomatic matter which had just cropped up. The Minnachan murder had nothing to do with it, and I had merely offered my services because I happened to be on the spot. I found I required all my energy and brain-power in connection with this affair, and so I left the murder in the very capable hands of the Glasgow police and forgot all about it. That may seem impossible, but you know what this business is; you simply have to concentrate on one thing to the exclusion of everything else, and I needn't tell you anything about the value of concentration."

"I don't think you could tell him much," I laughed.

"Well?" asked Mr. Durston, a trifle impatiently; "go on."

"This morning," continued Mr. Orless, "I worked as hard as I have ever done, in spite of the heat, on a problem which was entirely unconnected with Minnachan or any other murder. I was walking up Whitehall, my head full of intricate details and figures, when I heard the sound of distant bagpipes. I turned to see if there was a Scottish battalion on the march anywhere near, and then, quite suddenly, the same violet flash broke across everything in sight. It was some minutes before I could bring myself to realise that there were no highlanders and no bagpipes anywhere about."

The professor and I exchanged a hurried glance. There could be no question as to the sincerity of the narrator. If there was anyone in the world unlikely to be attacked by nervous hallucination it was Chief Inspector Orless.

"And that," concluded the detective, lying back in his chair and preparing to light a cigarette, "that is my story. What do you think of it?"

Mr. Durston rose to his feet and rang the small bell which stood on the tea-table.

"Cooper," he said when the maid appeared, "bring me a Bradshaw. Orless, my dear fellow, Leslie and I are going to Minnachan Castle."

The detective sprang up and held out his hand.

"Splendid!" he cried. "Splendid! You've taken a weight off my mind."

It was a perfect morning when we arrived at Castle Minnachan station, and I could not help wishing that our mission had been one of a less tragic nature, for the sun shone beautifully and there were just sufficient clouds to take away the appearance of desolate barrenness from the rugged Highland scenery. It was rather a surprise to us that Mr. Hamish Minnachan met us as we stepped off the train.

"Professor Durston?" he asked as my companion alighted.

"This is my assistant, Miss Leslie Dalrayne," said the professor when the stranger had introduced himself. "I suppose Orless must have telegraphed you."

"He did," replied the other, "and I was very relieved to get the wire. This is no ordinary affair, Mr. Durston, and is, to my mind, beyond the scope of the ordinary policeman."

"The ordinary policeman, as you call him, is exceedingly difficult to beat at his own game," said the professor. "But, of course, there are occasions on which one is able to render them a little assistance."

"I devoutly hope this may be one of them," said Mr. Minnachan solemnly. "But before we start to discuss the matter, what about breakfast? You must be famished."

We both confessed that we were certainly hungry, for we had not waited for dinner the previous evening. After Mr. Orless left we had just time to catch the 7.20 from King's Cross, which brought us to Castle Minnachan a little after eight in the morning.

A tall footman relieved me of my suitcase and a quarter of an hour later we drew up in front of the main entrance to the castle in a sixty horse-power Napier car. I bathed and changed and was shown into a small morning-room to find the professor and Mr. Minnachan awaiting me.

"Mr. Minnachan was Sir Ian's uncle, Leslie," said the former. "I have just been making a few enquiries about the succession. The heir is a younger brother Robert, aged fifteen, so that point can be of no use to us."

"You were present on the occasion of the tragedy, of course, Mr. Minnachan?" I asked.

"I was," he replied. "In fact, I was standing within a few feet of the poor boy at the moment he fell."

"And yet you heard no report and you have no idea where the shot came from?"

"No, I don't think anyone heard the slightest sound, and the only conclusion I can come to, as to the direction of the murderer, is based on the assumption that, whoever he was, he was not one of the guests and that he got clear away."

"You mean that there are only certain directions in which he could have escaped unseen?" I asked as I sat down to my breakfast.

"Precisely," he replied. "The shot cannot have come from the house, because that is the one direction in which we are certain the boy was not looking at the time. I will show you afterwards what I mean."

"You can think of nothing whatever that could serve, even for the purpose of investigation, as a motive for the murder?" my friend asked.

"Nothing, my dear sir, absolutely nothing," our host replied emphatically. "Picture to yourself a mere boy, always a bright, cheerful and conspicuously healthy lad, full of life and spirits and a general favourite with everybody, suddenly murdered, and ask me for a motive! I can give you no suggestion even; it must have been the work of a madman."

"Accident is impossible in the circumstances," murmured the professor to himself.

"Quite out of the question," said Mr. Minnachan. "It must have been a cool and calculated murder, however impossible, or rather, however unreasonable, that may seem."

"Supposing the murderer escaped," I asked; "how could he get away without being seen and where could he get to?"

"There is the train in the first place, but that is out of the question, too, because no one could have reached the station between the time of the murder and the time the last train left. I cannot understand how the murderer can have got away at all, considering the detectives did not lose a minute in commencing the search."

"Perhaps he didn't get away," I suggested. "I think in similar circumstances I should not have made any attempt."

"What would you have done?" asked our host with an expression of interest.

"I should have made my way straight into the middle of the crowd, and eventually I should have found an opportunity of condoling with one of the family, yourself for example. You could not possibly know everyone there that night, even by sight. I might have been staying with the doctor from the next village, and have come under the comprehensive invitation 'and friends.'"

"There is certainly that possibility, Leslie," Mr. Durston agreed; "but you forget that houses are few and far between, scattered up and down the glens, and if you were, as you put it, staying with the doctor in the next village, everyone for miles around would have known about it, and the mere fact that you were a stranger, as you are supposing, would place you to some extent under the suspicion of local gossip."

"The man may be hiding in the hills," said Mr. Minnachan. "We have a search-party out now, every available gillie and shepherd in the neighbourhood, to say nothing of many volunteers, have been searching ever since the tragedy. There again we are not likely to get much further, because, as the police point out, even if he had a secure hiding-place, which is quite possible, he could not live for a week without coming in for food."

"Which is a foolish line of argument," I interrupted. "Don't you think that, if your life depended on your escape and you had committed what must have been a well-thought-out crime, you would have prepared a stock of provisions which would enable you to lie low for some time?"

"When you put it like that, Miss Dalrayne," he answered, "I must say I agree with you. There seems to be no end to the possibilities, but we cannot get a single probability to work on."

Mr. Minnachan put his head on his hands and sighed deeply. He was a tall, handsome man of about fifty, exceedingly well preserved, and he evidently felt the loss of his nephew, from feelings of personal affection as well as from a merely family point of view.

"Come," he said at last, "if you are ready I will show you round the grounds."

We followed him out on to the lawn, and he took us to the Minnachan Stone. It was a granite rock about four feet high and about eight feet by five, nearly flat on the top. As Inspector Orless had said, the eldest of the Minnachans greeted the tenantry from this Stone on his twenty-first birthday, to symbolise the fact that the family and the clan were founded on a rock. The Stone stood only a few feet from the outer wall of the castle, and it was impossible for the shot to have been fired from that direction. Some distance away on the left was a wall dividing the lawns from the kitchen gardens; that again was put out of court by the fact that there was no means of exit for the murderer. Directly opposite the castle there was a deep lake over a mile long and two hundred yards across at its narrowest point; beyond that were two other lakes running almost parallel with the first.

"You see," said Mr. Minnachan finally, "the man must have escaped by the apparently unlikely means of walking down the drive. He could not climb the old wall, he would not surely walk into the castle, and he would not swim the chain of three lochs that you see here."

"Any boats?" asked Mr. Durston.

"There is one boat on the first loch," the other replied; "but that had not been moved, and in any case he could not get over the other two except by swimming. I confess that I thought it possible he might have done this; but it would take him some considerable time and he stood a chance of being found by the detectives, who by that time were out on the hunt. I think possibly Miss Dalrayne's theory may be correct after all, and that the criminal simply walked in among the crowd."

"With his gun under his arm?" Mr. Durston asked.

"I forgot that," I admitted. "But there is the possibility that he threw it into the loch."

"Well, I suppose that has been searched," the professor remarked.

"Yes," said Mr. Minnachan, "it has, and nothing has been found. The police hunted high and low for the weapon and found nothing at all. In fact, they haven't a clue."

"Supposing the man to have got away, clean out of the district; you say it would be a physical impossibility for him to have done so by train?"

"Certainly. We are all agreed on that point. There is only one way to the station and that is round the road. It is about seven miles, though as the crow flies it is hardly one. These lochs intervene and it is impossible to go that way."

"A bicycle might have done it in the twenty minutes that elapsed," Mr. Durston pointed out.

"Yes, but nothing went down the road at all," Mr. Minnachan replied, "and a bicycle could not travel this road in the dark without a light. We have a custom at all our family celebrations, weddings and so forth, that everyone who is on Minnachan land shall be welcome. We have two men on the road to invite any passing stranger to come in and join with us."

"Good heavens!" exclaimed Mr. Durston. "Did anyone accept the invitation on this occasion?"

"Not a soul," the other replied. "It appears in the light of recent events to be a dangerous custom, but it has this advantage; we had two men who were to all intents and purposes guarding the road."

"Was the train up to time that night?" I asked.

"That I couldn't tell you, Miss Dalrayne. I very foolishly did not think of asking. No doubt the detective made enquiries though."

At Mr. Durston's request we were driven back to the station immediately.

"You seem to favour the railway, Leslie," he said.

"Yes," I admitted, "I do. It seems absurd of me to argue in the face of an apparent impossibility, but I have a feeling that the murderer must have gone away by the train. I want to find out if a luggage-train went down the line at any time that night. There are so many hills, on this railway that it might easily have been going slowly enough at some spot for a man to climb on board."

But when we reached the station and interviewed the station-master—"collector," as they call him in the Highlands—I was doomed to disappointment. No luggage-train had gone through that night at all.

"As for the night mail," he said, "well, there were only two passengers from this station. One was an old woman, a Mrs. McKellaich, going to Glasgow to see her son who is taken badly. The other was Mr. Porter."

"Who is Mr. Porter?" I asked.

"He is a gentleman well known in these parts," the station-master replied. "He takes a great many photographs in the Highlands every summer; has done now for a number of years. He comes along with his camera as regular as a clock. I have some of them here, if you'd like to see them. They are very beautiful pictures many of them. Come in, miss, and I'll show them to you."

We followed the collector into his little room, rather begrudging the waste of valuable time, but I think we both felt that we might learn something from the railway official that might put us on the track of a stranger arriving in the district, even if we could not trace him going away.

"This is one he sent me some months ago," the station-master said, handing me a very beautiful photograph of Ben MacDhuie under snow. It was a carbon enlargement, and was really, as the man had said, a very beautiful picture indeed. "And this," he added, "is the letter he sent with it."

I took the letter from his hand and dropped it, with a startled exclamation.

"What is it, miss?" cried the stationmaster, while Mr. Durston sprang to my side.

"Nothing," I said, "nothing, thank you. I am not feeling very well. I think I'll get outside in the fresh air."

The professor put his arm round me and almost carried me out on to the platform. The collector went away at a run, to see if he could find me some brandy.

"It's all right," I said as soon as he was out of earshot. "It was the violet flash."

Mr. Durston left me to recover from my "faintness," and questioned the man cautiously about his friend, Mr. Porter. On the night of the tragedy the photographer had arrived in time to have a few minutes' chat with his friend the collector. He arrived on foot carrying his big camera and his tripod case, so, as the professor said to me, it seemed impossible that he could have any connection with the crime. We motored back to the castle, not altogether in the best of spirits, and sought Mr. Minnachan.

"Know anybody of the name of Porter?" Mr. Durston asked.

"No," he said, "nobody at all."

We sat out on the terrace and waited while our host attended to his correspondence, the post having just arrived. I was seated beside the small table and I glanced idly at the newspaper which was lying there. On top of the paper lay an envelope addressed to Hamish G. McV. Minnachan, Esq., at Minnachan Castle, Inverness-shire. I jumped to my feet.

"Mr. Minnachan," I cried, "who is this from? Please tell me at once."

My host looked rather surprised at my excitement, but he glanced at the envelope to which I pointed and smiled.

"I'm afraid it is only a letter from a cousin, Miss Dalrayne," he said.

"It is a letter from the man Porter," I declared emphatically.

I was certain the writing was the same.

Mr. Durston leaned forward and picked it up. Then he brushed his hand across his eyes.

"Good heavens, Leslie," he cried, "you are right, it is the violet flash."

Mr. Minnachan jumped to his feet with a cry.

"What do you mean?" he gasped.

Mr. Durston laid a hand on his arm and pressed him into his seat.

"Tell us all about this man," he said.

"There is not much to tell," Mr. Minnachan replied. "I have not seen him for years. He quarrelled with the family. He was my grandfather's favourite, and the old man left him some seventy thousand pounds in a will which was afterwards disputed by Ian's father. The will was set aside, and Shiel Minnachan was ruined by the costs of the litigation. I think he had run through everything he had and mortgaged his expectations under the will. When the will was set aside he disappeared entirely for a time, and then it was discovered that he was living the life of a hermit, at Wolders-mead, in Surrey. He had just enough saved from the wreck to live on, I believe. Needless to say there was no love lost between him and my brother and myself after the case, and I have not seen him since. He writes now to say how sorry he is to hear of poor Ian's tragic death."

"Leslie, my dear," said Mr. Durston immediately, "unless I have forgotten the facts we got from our friend the stationmaster, we have just time to catch the evening train."

Early next morning we reached London again and sought out Arthur. While we rested he made some enquiries and procured a large-scale ordnance map, by which we were able to locate the exact position of the hermit's cottage. Then we motored down to Woldersmead. But there again we were doomed to disappointment. We made careful and tactful enquiries, only to be met on all sides with the very last evidence we expected to hear. The hermit had not slept away from home for many months. Every night at a quarter past eleven he went to bed. He was so regular in his time that the people in a neighbouring cottage invariably set their clock by the appearance of the light in his bedroom window. We could learn nothing that would help us in the least.

"It is late to pay calls," said the professor, "but I am going to have a look at this hermit."

Accordingly we went up to the cottage, and following the lead of my companion, I tip-toed up the garden path as noiselessly as possible. We had almost reached the door when, suddenly, the sitting-room light went out. A minute or so later a light appeared in the bedroom above. I looked at my luminous wrist-watch . . . it was a quarter past eleven. Mr. Durston suddenly knocked loudly on the door. There was no reply. He knocked again. At that moment I saw a shadow creeping round the corner of the house.

"Look out!" I cried and sprang forward in time to knock up a pistol that was aimed at the professor. I saw Arthur draw his revolver and felt myself hurled against the wall, and then I knew no more.

Three weeks later I was sitting on the lawn at Lorran House with Arthur and the professor, who had read me Shiel Minnachan's confession, which he had given to the police after his arrest. It seems that he swore vengeance on Ian's father and made all his plans to murder the boy on his twenty-first birthday. The father meanwhile died, but Shiel went on with his hideous plot. He made his plans carefully. He got to be known, under a slight disguise, by the name of Porter, an enthusiastic photographer, and thus prepared the way for his escape, for when the police found his photographic materials they discovered a duplicate camera case and tripod bag which contained a wonderfully made folding canvas boat and a rifle. In the cellar of his cottage they found a wonderful mass of electric fittings and accumulators. There was a clock which worked in conjunction with a contact breaker, so that every night at a certain time the light in the sitting-room was switched on and then at a later hour it was replaced by the bedroom light. Thus he had arranged his alibi. But he reckoned without Professor Durston, for little did he think that his crime would be recorded in the "Unbound Book."

"And now he is awaiting trial," said Arthur. "Do you know, Leslie, that I too am waiting to know my fate? Oh, you needn't look surprised. You've known for a long time. I did not mean to speak yet, but I cannot bear to see you running these risks. You might have been killed. Won't you let me take care of you, Leslie?"

And that, as I told Doris afterwards, was really all that happened.

THE "UNBOUND BOOK"

I could not understand it. Everything seemed to be quite impossible; how could anything have happened to my dear Mr. Durston? What right had Fate to treat me in this way? I stood aimlessly gazing at the dear face before me. Arthur knelt down and lifted Mr. Durston gently in his arms and, as he did so, I seemed to hear a faint far-off chuckle, like the laugh of a fiend.

"Is he really—" I began, but could not finish the sentence.

"Dead," said Arthur in a hoarse low voice. He held his ear against his uncle's chest, and once more solemnly nodded his head. Then again, hovering above the prostrate figure I saw the purple letters "John Durston," and even as I saw them my dear friend stirred. I literally flung myself at his feet.

"Uncle dearest!" I cried, "are you all right? Tell me you are all right."

I held my arms round him, and he turned his head towards me but he did not speak.

"It's Leslie, dear," I cried anxiously, "Leslie, Leslie!"

Arthur by this time was holding a glass of brandy to Mr. Durston's lips, and soon he spoke, though only in a gentle whisper.

"Broken Cup," he murmured.

I jumped to my feet. What could he mean? Had we not closed the episode of the Broken Cup? I saw that he wished to say something more and again placed my ear to his mouth.

"Too many," he said slowly and painfully. "Too many—to one—not strong enough—getting—old man."

"How are they molesting you, dear?" I asked.

"Too many—too many—vibrations—my brain not—not strong enough to withstand—"

But before he told me what it was he was not strong enough to withstand he lost consciousness again. Meanwhile Arthur and Doris had sent out for the local doctor and Doris had wired to Jack Cunliffe to come down at once. We got Mr. Durston to bed and the doctor came. He was almost rude to us when we told him that Mr. Durston had been apparently dead, and that his eyes were glazed and his heart still. I made up my mind that we would get on as best we could without him until Doctor Cunliffe arrived.

"Could you make any sense of what he said to you?" Arthur asked when I had a second to spare from the bedside.

"He mentioned the Broken Cup," I said. "That was all, except that there were too many of them and that he was not strong enough to withstand their vibrations."

"They swore revenge, you know," said Arthur thoughtfully, "and he admitted himself that they had gone very much upon his lines. In that case it seems possible that they might be a source of very real danger to his health without ever coming near him in person."

"Yes," I admitted sadly. "That is just what I am afraid of. If they would come in person, it would be simple, for then some of us could deal with them. But they don't and they won't."

"Are you sure?" he asked.

"It seems unlikely that they should run into danger again, considering what happened to their gang last time they ran against Mr. Durston. Those that are left are not likely to want to follow their companions to penal servitude."

"What, of course, is the remarkable thing is that you were obviously terrified before you knew that there was anything wrong."

"Not before I knew," I corrected him, "before I saw with my own eyes."

"But for that and the fact that I have never seen a state of coma so closely resembling death, I should be inclined to put it down as a fairly ordinary attack."

"Did you see that book that I picked up from beside him?" I asked.

"Yes," he replied. "What was it?"

"It was the 'Unbound Book,'" I answered.

"But I didn't think it had come back from the binders yet," he remarked.

"It has only just gone to the binders," I replied significantly.

"Then I don't understand—"

"Arthur," I said solemnly, "I do understand. I think I have managed to see the drift of this. Someone is trying to torture your uncle to death. He knows; he said, 'The Broken Cup,' and he is right. They are having their revenge. They are the only community in the world trained in concentration and thought-transference. They would have had the world at their feet, but that Mr. Durston was too strong for them. Now he is tired and run down and they are proving too strong for him."

"What do you suggest, Leslie?" Arthur asked.

"That I don't know yet," I replied. "I want to be sure of my facts, and when I am sure of them, then, Arthur, we will cut psychology and leave their minds alone, and go for the men."

"How do you mean they are torturing him to death?" asked Arthur. "Do you mean by mental suggestion or what?"

"No," I answered, "it is not only that. That is where the wickedness of the whole thing comes in. It was some intangible mental fear that possessed the professor and yet it was a real, solid, tangible book which he held in his hand. They knew how much store he set upon the 'Unbound Book'; they knew how much he was longing to get it finished and bound up, and they knew too just when was the earliest possible date it could return from the binders. They therefore put a duplicate before him quite suddenly, long before the real thing could be ready, and he probably thought he was going mad."

"What a hideous business, Leslie," Arthur exclaimed. "It is a terrible thing this extraordinary power of visualisation."

"Used in the wrong way it is," I agreed, "hideous!"

Suddenly a voice cried out through the house

"John Durston, come to us."

Arthur and I looked at each other in horror-stricken anxiety. What could it mean?

"John Durston, come to us," the strange uncanny voice cried again; but before the sentence was half begun Arthur and I were both out on the landing in search of its source. We searched the house high and low, but there was nobody to be found. It must be a human voice. I was convinced of that. I had never heard it before, so far as I could remember. I ran back to Mr. Durston's bedside. He was lying still, as pale as death, but there was no sign of distress upon his face now.

When Doctor Cunliffe arrived he took the first opportunity to interrogate me as to any sudden shock that the professor might have had, but, of course, I was unable to help him much. Together we bent over his bed and together we started back suddenly. I felt the doctor's hand fix my wrist in a grip of iron.

"What is it?" I asked in a whisper of sheer fear.

"Hush," he said gently. "Watch!"

I fixed my eyes on the face of my dear master and there I saw the most amazing sight I have ever seen in my life. I saw his eyes shine with a deep yellow glare, and then a faint, misty plume of purple fire seemed to curl upwards from his face and disappear through the ceiling.

"Extraordinary!" the physician exclaimed, "extraordinary!"

But we neither of us knew what it meant. I tried to fix my mind upon the symbol of the Broken Cup, endeavouring to counteract any influence which they might be applying, but it was of no use. I could do nothing. Till bedtime I sat beside Mr. Durston, praying fervently that he might soon recover consciousness at least. I leaned over and laid my hand on his forehead. It was very hot. I moistened a cloth with water and put the jug beside the bed. Then I sat in the dark for fear a light should disturb him, he always hated a light when he wanted to sleep. I had been sitting there for nearly an hour when suddenly I felt a cold, clammy hand upon my face. I cannot tell what made me think of it, but I suddenly dashed the jug that stood beside me, upwards and outwards with all my force and at the same time I must have screamed. There was a dull thud and a muttered oath. I heard the door open and suddenly the room was lighted up with a bright purple flash. I could not see what was going on, but presently Doris managed to bring in a lamp. It was then that I saw the last of the Brotherhood of the Broken Cup, standing, trussed up between Arthur and Dr. Cunliffe. And they dragged him out of the room with scant ceremony and handed him over to the police.

That is the true story of Professor's Durston's "breakdown." There have been many wild rumours about. He was ill for nearly three months, but when he recovered he had not lost a particle of his magnificent intelligence. The only difference is that he will never speak of colour vibrations or of anything appertaining to them. Since our marriage he has lived with Arthur and me, and, although I might not have believed it before, we all find it quite easy to be gloriously happy without ever making the slightest reference to the "Unbound Book."

FROM WHOSE BOURNE

ROBERT BARR

1

"My dear," said William Brenton to his wife, "do you think I shall be missed if I go upstairs for a while? I am not feeling at all well."

"Oh, I'm so sorry, Will," replied Alice, looking concerned; "I will tell them you are indisposed."

"No, don't do that," was the answer; "they are having a very good time, and I suppose the dancing will begin shortly; so I don't think they will miss me. If I feel better I will be down in an hour or two; if not, I shall go to bed. Now, dear, don't worry; but have a good time with the rest of them."

William Brenton went quietly upstairs to his room, and sat down in the darkness in a rocking chair. Remaining there a few minutes, and not feeling any better, he slowly undressed and went to bed. Faint echoes reached him of laughter and song; finally, music began, and he felt, rather than heard, the pulsation of dancing feet. Once, when the music had ceased for a time, Alice tiptoed into the room, and said in a quiet voice—

"How are you feeling, Will? any better?"

"A little," he answered drowsily. "Don't worry about me; I shall drop off to sleep presently, and shall be all right in the morning. Good night."

He still heard in a dreamy sort of way the music, the dancing, the laughter; and gradually there came oblivion, which finally merged into a dream, the most strange and vivid vision he had ever experienced. It seemed to him that he sat again in the rocking chair

near the bed. Although he knew the room was dark, he had no difficulty in seeing everything perfectly. He heard, now quite plainly,
the music and dancing downstairs, but what gave a ghastly significance to his dream was the sight of his own person on the bed. The
eyes were half open, and the face was drawn and rigid. The colour
of the face was the white, greyish tint of death.

"This is a nightmare," said Brenton to himself; "I must try and
wake myself." But he seemed powerless to do this, and he sat there
looking at his own body while the night wore on. Once he rose and
went to the side of the bed. He seemed to have reached it merely
by wishing himself there, and he passed his hand over the face,
but no feeling of touch was communicated to him. He hoped his
wife would come and rouse him from this fearful semblance of a
dream, and, wishing this, he found himself standing at her side,
amidst the throng downstairs, who were now merrily saying good-
bye. Brenton tried to speak to his wife, but although he was conscious of speaking, she did not seem to hear him, or know he was
there.

The party had been one given on Christmas Eve, and as it was
now two o'clock in the morning, the departing guests were wishing
Mrs. Brenton a merry Christmas. Finally, the door closed on the
last of the revellers, and Mrs. Brenton stood for a moment giving
instructions to the sleepy servants; then, with a tired sigh, she
turned and went upstairs, Brenton walking by her side until they
came to the darkened room, which she entered on tiptoe.

"Now," said Brenton to himself, "she will arouse me from this
appalling dream." It was not that there was anything dreadful in
the dream itself, but the clearness with which he saw everything,
and the fact that his mind was perfectly wide awake, gave him an
uneasiness which he found impossible to shake off.

In the dim light from the hall his wife prepared to retire. The
horrible thought struck Brenton that she imagined he was sleeping soundly, and was anxious not to awaken him—for of course
she could have no realization of the nightmare he was in—so once
again he tried to communicate with her. He spoke her name over
and over again, but she proceeded quietly with her preparations

for the night. At last she crept in at the other side of the bed, and in a few moments was asleep. Once more Brenton struggled to awake, but with no effect. He heard the clock strike three, and then four, and then five, but there was no apparent change in his dream. He feared that he might be in a trance, from which, perhaps, he would not awake until it was too late. Grey daylight began to brighten the window, and he noticed that snow was quietly falling outside, the flakes noiselessly beating against the window pane. Every one slept late that morning, but at last he heard the preparations for breakfast going on downstairs—the light clatter of china on the table, the rattle of the grate; and, as he thought of these things, he found himself in the dining-room, and saw the trim little maid, who still yawned every now and then, laying the plates in their places. He went upstairs again, and stood watching the sleeping face of his wife. Once she raised her hand above her head, and he thought she was going to awake; ultimately her eyes opened, and she gazed for a time at the ceiling, seemingly trying to recollect the events of the day before.

"Will," she said dreamily, "are you still asleep?"

There was no answer from the rigid figure at the front of the bed. After a few moments she placed her hand quietly over the sleeper's face. As she did so, her startled eyes showed that she had received a shock. Instantly she sat upright in bed, and looked for one brief second on the face of the sleeper beside her; then, with a shriek that pierced the stillness of the room, she sprang to the floor.

"Will! Will!" she cried, "speak to me! What is the matter with you? Oh, my God! my God!" she cried, staggering back from the bed. Then, with shriek after shriek, she ran blindly through the hall to the stairway, and there fell fainting on the floor.

2

William Brenton knelt beside the fallen lady, and tried to soothe and comfort her, but it was evident that she was insensible.

"It is useless," said a voice by his side.

Brenton looked up suddenly, and saw standing beside him a stranger. Wondering for a moment how he got there, and thinking that after all it was a dream, he said—

"What is useless? She is not dead."

"No," answered the stranger, "but *you* are."

"I am what?" cried Brenton.

"You are what the material world calls dead, although in reality you have just begun to live."

"And who are you?" asked Brenton. "And how did you get in here?"

The other smiled.

"How did *you* get in here?" he said, repeating Brenton's words.

"I? Why, this is my own house."

"Was, you mean."

"I mean that it is. I am in my own house. This lady is my wife."

"*Was*," said the other.

"I do not understand you," cried Brenton, very much annoyed. "But, in any case, your presence and your remarks are out of place here."

"My dear sir," said the other, "I merely wish to aid you and to explain to you anything that you may desire to know about your new condition. You are now free from the incumbrance of your body. You have already had some experience of the additional powers which that riddance has given you. You have also, I am afraid, had an inkling of the fact that the spiritual condition has its limitations. If you desire to communicate with those whom you have left, I would strongly advise you to postpone the attempt, and to leave this place, where you will experience only pain and anxiety. Come with me, and learn something of your changed circumstances."

"I am in a dream," said Brenton, "and you are part of it. I went to sleep last night, and am still dreaming. This is a nightmare and it will soon be over."

"You are saying that," said the other, "merely to convince yourself. It is now becoming apparent to you that this is not a dream. If dreams exist, it was a dream which you left, but you have now become awake. If you really think it is a dream, then do as I tell you—come with me and leave it, because you must admit that this part of the dream is at least very unpleasant."

"It is not very pleasant," assented Brenton. As he spoke the bewildered servants came rushing up the stairs, picked up their fallen mistress, and laid her on a sofa. They rubbed her hands and dashed water in her face. She opened her eyes, and then closed them again with a shudder.

"Sarah," she cried, "have I been dreaming, or is your master dead?"

The two girls turned pale at this, and the elder of them went boldly into the room which her mistress had just left. She was evidently a young woman who had herself under good control, but she came out sobbing, with her apron to her eyes.

"Come, come," said the man who stood beside Brenton, "haven't you had enough of this? Come with me; you can return to this house if you wish;" and together they passed out of the room into the crisp air of Christmas morning. But, although Brenton knew it must be cold, he had no feeling of either cold or warmth.

"There are a number of us," said the stranger to Brenton, "who take turns at watching the sick-bed when a man is about to die, and when his spirit leaves his body, we are there to explain, or comfort, or console. Your death was so sudden that we had no warning of it. You did not feel ill before last night, did you?"

"No," replied Brenton. "I felt perfectly well, until after dinner last night."

"Did you leave your affairs in reasonably good order?"

"Yes," said Brenton, trying to recollect. "I think they will find everything perfectly straight."

"Tell me a little of your history, if you do not mind," inquired the other; "it will help me in trying to initiate you into our new order of things here."

"Well," replied Brenton, and he wondered at himself for falling so easily into the other's assumption that he was a dead man, "I was what they call on the earth in reasonably good circumstances. My estate should be worth $100,000. I had $75,000 insurance on my life, and if all that is paid, it should net my widow not far from a couple of hundred thousand."

"How long have you been married?" said the other.

"Only about six months. I was married last July, and we went for a trip abroad. We were married quietly, and left almost immediately afterwards, so we thought, on our return, it would not be a bad plan to give a Christmas Eve dinner, and invite some of our friends. That," he said, hesitating a moment, "was last night. Shortly after dinner, I began to feel rather ill, and went upstairs to rest for a while; and if what you say is true, the first thing I knew I found myself dead."

"Alive," corrected the other.

"Well, alive, though at present I feel I belong more to the world I have left than I do to the world I appear to be in. I must confess, although you are a very plausible gentleman to talk to, that I expect at any moment to wake and find this to have been one of the most horrible nightmares that I ever had the ill luck to encounter."

The other smiled.

"There is very little danger of your waking up, as you call it. Now, I will tell you the great trouble we have with people when they first come to the spirit-land, and that is to induce them to forget entirely the world they have relinquished. Men whose families are in poor circumstances, or men whose affairs are in a disordered state, find it very difficult to keep from trying to set things right again. They have the feeling that they can console or comfort those whom they have left behind them, and it is often a long time before they are convinced that their efforts are entirely futile, as well as very distressing for themselves."

"Is there, then," asked Brenton, "no communication between this world and the one that I have given up?"

The other paused for a moment before he replied.

"I should hardly like to say," he answered, "that there is *no* communication between one world and the other; but the communication that exists is so slight and unsatisfactory, that if you are sensible you will see things with the eyes of those who have very much more experience in this world than you have. Of course, you can go back there as much as you like; there will be no interference and no hindrance. But when you see things going wrong, when you see a mistake about to be made, it is an appalling thing to stand there helpless, unable to influence those you love, or to point out a palpable error, and convince them that your clearer sight sees it as such. Of course, I understand that it must be very difficult for a man who is newly married, to entirely abandon the one who has loved him, and whom he loves. But I assure you that if you follow the life of one who is as young and handsome as your wife, you will find some one else supplying the consolations you are unable to bestow. Such a mission may lead you to a church where she is married to her second husband. I regret to say that even the most imperturbable spirits are ruffled when such an incident occurs. The wise men are those who appreciate and understand that they are in an entirely new world, with new powers and new limitations, and who govern themselves accordingly from the first, as they will certainly do later on."

"My dear sir," said Brenton, somewhat offended, "if what you say is true, and I am really a dead man—"

"Alive," corrected the other.

"Well, alive, then. I may tell you that my wife's heart is broken. She will never marry again."

"Of course, that is a subject of which you know a great deal more than I do. I all the more strongly advise you never to see her again. It is impossible for you to offer any consolation, and the sight of her grief and misery will only result in unhappiness for yourself. Therefore, take my advice. I have given it very often, and I assure you those who did not take it expressed their regret afterwards. Hold entirely aloof from anything relating to your former life."

Brenton was silent for some moments; finally he said—

"I presume your advice is well meant; but if things are as you state, then I may as well say, first as last, that I do not intend to accept it."

"Very well," said the other; "it is an experience that many prefer to go through for themselves."

"Do you have names in this spirit-land?" asked Brenton, seemingly desirous of changing the subject.

"Yes," was the answer; "we are known by names that we have used in the preparatory school below. My name is Ferris."

"And if I wish to find you here, how do I set about it?"

"The wish is sufficient," answered Ferris. "Merely wish to be with me, and you *are* with me."

"Good gracious!" cried Brenton, "is locomotion so easy as that?"

"Locomotion is very easy. I do not think anything could be easier than it is, and I do not think there could be any improvement in that matter."

"Are there matters here, then, that you think could be improved?"

"As to that I shall not say. Perhaps you will be able to give your own opinion before you have lived here much longer."

"Taking it all in all," said Brenton, "do you think the spirit-land is to be preferred to the one we have left?"

"I like it better," said Ferris, "although I presume there are some who do not. There are many advantages; and then, again, there are many—well, I would not say disadvantages, but still some people consider them such. We are free from the pangs of hunger or cold, and have therefore no need of money, and there is no necessity for the rush and the worry of the world below."

"And how about heaven and hell?" said Brenton. "Are those localities all a myth? Is there nothing of punishment and nothing of reward in this spirit-land?"

There was no answer to this, and when Brenton looked around he found that his companion had departed.

3

William Brenton pondered long on the situation. He would have known better how to act if he could have been perfectly certain that he was not still the victim of a dream. However, of one thing there was no doubt—namely, that it was particularly harrowing to see what he had seen in his own house. If it were true that he was dead, he said to himself, was not the plan outlined for him by Ferris very much the wiser course to adopt? He stood now in one of the streets of the city so familiar to him. People passed and repassed him—men and women whom he had known in life—but nobody appeared to see him. He resolved, if possible, to solve the problem uppermost in his mind, and learn whether or not he could communicate with an inhabitant of the world he had left. He paused for a moment to consider the best method of doing this. Then he remembered one of his most confidential friends and advisers, and at once wished himself at his office. He found the office closed, but went in to wait for his friend. Occupying the time in thinking over his strange situation, he waited long, and only when the bells began to ring did he remember it was Christmas forenoon, and that his friend would not be at the office that day. The next moment he wished himself at his friend's house, but he was as unsuccessful as at the office; the friend was not at home. The household, however, was in great commotion, and, listening to what was said, he found that the subject of conversation was his own death, and he learned that his friend had gone to the Brenton residence as soon as he heard the startling news of Christmas morning.

Once more Brenton paused, and did not know what to do. He went again into the street. Everything seemed to lead him toward his own home. Although he had told Ferris that he did not intend to take his advice, yet as a sensible man he saw that the admonition was well worth considering, and if he could once become convinced that there was no communication possible between himself and those he had left; if he could give them no comfort and no cheer; if he could see the things which they did not see, and yet be unable to give them warning, he realized that he would merely be adding to his own misery, without alleviating the troubles of others.

He wished he knew where to find Ferris, so that he might have another talk with him. The man impressed him as being exceedingly sensible. No sooner, however, had he wished for the company of Mr. Ferris than he found himself beside that gentleman.

"By George!" he said in astonishment, "you are just the man I wanted to see."

"Exactly," said Ferris; "that is the reason you do see me."

"I have been thinking over what you said," continued the other, "and it strikes me that after all your advice is sensible."

"Thank you," replied Ferris, with something like a smile on his face.

"But there is one thing I want to be perfectly certain about. I want to know whether it is not possible for me to communicate with my friends. Nothing will settle that doubt in my mind except actual experience."

"And have you not had experience enough?" asked Ferris.

"Well," replied the other, hesitating, "I have had some experience, but it seems to me that, if I encounter an old friend, I could somehow make myself felt by him."

"In that case," answered Ferris, "if nothing will convince you but an actual experiment, why don't you go to some of your old friends and try what you can do with them?"

"I have just been to the office and to the residence of one of my old friends. I found at his residence that he had gone to my"— Brenton paused for a moment—"former home. Everything seems to lead me there, and yet, if I take your advice, I must avoid that place of all others."

"I would at present, if I were you," said Ferris. "Still, why not try it with any of the passers-by?"

Brenton looked around him. People were passing and repassing where the two stood talking with each other. "Merry Christmas" was the word on all lips. Finally Brenton said, with a look of uncertainty on his face—

"My dear fellow, I can't talk to any of these people. I don't know them."

Ferris laughed at this, and replied—

"I don't think you will shock them very much; just try it."

"Ah, here's a friend of mine. You wait a moment, and I will accost him." Approaching him, Brenton held out his hand and spoke, but the traveller paid no attention. He passed by as one who had seen or heard nothing.

"I assure you," said Ferris, as he noticed the look of disappointment on the other's face, "you will meet with a similar experience, however much you try. You know the old saying about one not being able to have his cake and eat it too. You can't have the privileges of this world and those of the world you left as well. I think, taking it all in all, you should rest content, although it always hurts those who have left the other world not to be able to communicate with their friends, and at least assure them of their present welfare."

"It does seem to me," replied Brenton, "that would be a great consolation, both for those who are here and those who are left."

"Well, I don't know about that," answered the other. "After all, what does life in the other world amount to? It is merely a preparation for this. It is of so short a space, as compared with the life we live here, that it is hardly worth while to interfere with it one way or another. By the time you are as long here as I have been, you will realize the truth of this."

"Perhaps I shall," said Brenton, with a sigh; "but, meanwhile, what am I to do with myself? I feel like the man who has been all his life in active business, and who suddenly resolves to enjoy himself doing nothing. That sort of thing seems to kill a great number of men, especially if they put off taking a rest until too late, as most of us do."

"Well," said Ferris, "there is no necessity of your being idle here, I assure you. But before you lay out any work for yourself, let me ask you if there is not some interesting part of the world that you would like to visit?"

"Certainly; I have seen very little of the world. That is one of my regrets at leaving it."

"Bless me," said the other, "you haven't left it."

"Why, I thought you said I was a dead man?"

"On the contrary," replied his companion, "I have several times insisted that you have just begun to live. Now where shall we spend the day?"

"How would London do?"

"I don't think it would do; London is apt to be a little gloomy at this time of the year. But what do you say to Naples, or Japan, or, if you don't wish to go out of the United States, Yellowstone Park?"

"Can we reach any of those places before the day is over?" asked Brenton, dubiously.

"Well, I will soon show you how we manage all that. Just wish to accompany me, and I will take you the rest of the way."

"How would Venice do?" said Brenton. "I didn't see half as much of that city as I wanted to."

"Very well," replied his companion, "Venice it is;" and the American city in which they stood faded away from them, and before Brenton could make up his mind exactly what was happening, he found himself walking with his comrade in St. Mark's Square.

"Well, for rapid transit," said Brenton, "this beats anything I've ever had any idea of; but it increases the feeling that I am in a dream."

"You'll soon get used to it," answered Ferris; "and, when you do, the cumbersome methods of travel in the world itself will show themselves in their right light. Hello!" he cried, "here's a man whom I should like you to meet. By the way, I either don't know your name or I have forgotten it."

"William Brenton," answered the other.

"Mr. Speed, I want to introduce you to Mr. Brenton."

"Ah," said Speed, cordially, "a new-comer. One of your victims, Ferris?"

"Say one of his pupils, rather," answered Brenton.

"Well, it is pretty much the same thing," said Speed. "How long have you been with us, and how do you like the country?"

"You see, Mr. Brenton," interrupted Ferris, "John Speed was a newspaper man, and he must ask strangers how they like the country. He has inquired so often while interviewing foreigners for his paper that now he cannot abandon his old phrase. Mr. Brenton has been with us but a short time," continued Ferris, "and so you know, Speed, you can hardly expect him to answer your inevitable question."

"What part of the country are you from?" asked Speed.

"Cincinnati," answered Brenton, feeling almost as if he were an American tourist doing the continent of Europe.

"Cincinnati, eh? Well, I congratulate you. I do not know any place in America that I would sooner die in, as they call it, than Cincinnati. You see, I am a Chicago man myself."

Brenton did not like the jocular familiarity of the newspaper man, and found himself rather astonished to learn that in the spirit-world there were likes and dislikes, just as on earth.

"Chicago is a very enterprising city," he said, in a non-committal way.

"Chicago, my dear sir," said Speed, earnestly, "is *the* city. You will see that Chicago is going to be the great city of the world before you are a hundred years older. By the way, Ferris," said the Chicago man, suddenly recollecting something, "I have got Sommers over here with me."

"Ah!" said Ferris; "doing him any good?"

"Well, precious little, as far as I can see."

"Perhaps it would interest Mr. Brenton to meet him," said Ferris. "I think, Brenton, you asked me a while ago if there was any hell here, or any punishment. Mr. Speed can show you a man in hell."

"Really?" asked Brenton.

"Yes," said Speed; "I think if ever a man was in misery, he is. The trouble with Sommers was this. He—well, he died of delirium tremens, and so, of course, you know what the matter was.

Sommers had drunk Chicago whisky for thirty-five years straight along, and never added to it the additional horror of Chicago water. You see what his condition became, both physical and mental. Many people tried to reform Sommers, because he was really a brilliant man; but it was no use. Thirst had become a disease with him, and from the mental part of that disease, although his physical yearning is now gone of course, he suffers. Sommers would give his whole future for one glass of good old Kentucky whisky. He sees it on the counters, he sees men drink it, and he stands beside them in agony. That's why I brought him over here. I thought that he wouldn't see the colour of whisky as it sparkles in the glass; but now he is in the Café Quadra watching men drink. You may see him sitting there with all the agony of unsatisfied desire gleaming from his face."

"And what do you do with a man like that?" asked Brenton.

"Do? Well, to tell the truth, there is nothing *to* do. I took him away from Chicago, hoping to ease his trouble a little; but it has had no effect."

"It will come out all right by-and-by," said Ferris, who noticed the pained look on Brenton's face. "It is the period of probation that he has to pass through. It will wear off. He merely goes through the agonies he would have suffered on earth if he had suddenly been deprived of his favourite intoxicant."

"Well," said Speed, "you won't come with me, then? All right, good-bye. I hope to see you again, Mr. Brenton," and with that they separated.

Brenton spent two or three days in Venice, but all the time the old home hunger was upon him. He yearned for news of Cincinnati. He wanted to be back, and several times the wish brought him there, but he instantly returned. At last he said to Ferris—

"I am tired. I must go home. I have *got* to see how things are going."

"I wouldn't if I were you," replied Ferris.

"No, I know you wouldn't. Your temperament is indifferent. I would rather be miserable with knowledge than happy in ignorance. Good-bye."

It was evening when he found himself in Cincinnati. The weather was bright and clear, and apparently cold. Men's feet crisped on the frozen pavement, and the streets had that welcome, familiar look which they always have to the returned traveller when he reaches the city he calls his home. The newsboys were rushing through the streets yelling their papers at the top of their voices. He heard them, but paid little attention.

"All about the murder! Latest edition! All about the poison case!"

He felt that he must have a glimpse at a paper, and, entering the office of an hotel where a man was reading one, he glanced over his shoulder at the page before him, and was horror-stricken to see the words in startling headlines—

THE BRENTON MURDER.
The Autopsy shows that Morphine was the Poison used.
Enough found to have killed a Dozen Men.
Mrs. Brenton arrested for Committing the Horrible Deed.

4

For a moment Brenton was so bewildered and amazed at the awful headlines which he read, that he could hardly realize what had taken place. The fact that he had been poisoned, although it gave him a strange sensation, did not claim his attention as much as might have been thought. Curiously enough he was more shocked at finding himself, as it were, the talk of the town, the central figure of a great newspaper sensation. But the thing that horrified him was the fact that his wife had been arrested for his murder. His first impulse was to go to her at once, but he next thought it better to read what the paper said about the matter, so as to become possessed of all the facts. The headlines, he said to himself, often exaggerated things, and there was a possibility that the body of the article would not bear out the naming announcement above it. But as he read on and on, the situation seemed to become more and more appalling. He saw that his friends had been suspicious of his sudden death, and had insisted on a post-mortem examination. That examination had been conducted by three of the most eminent physicians of Cincinnati, and the three doctors had practically agreed that the deceased, in the language of the verdict, had come to his death through morphia poisoning, and the coroner's jury had brought in a verdict that "the said William Brenton had been poisoned by some person unknown." Then the article went on to state how suspicion had gradually fastened itself upon his wife, and at last her arrest had been ordered. The arrest had taken place that day.

After reading this, Brenton was in an agony of mind. He pictured his dainty and beautiful wife in a stone cell in the city prison. He foresaw the horrors of the public trial, and the deep grief and pain which the newspaper comments on the case would cause to a woman educated and refined. Of course, Brenton had not the slightest doubt in his own mind about the result of the trial. His wife would be triumphantly acquitted; but, all the same, the terrible suspense which she must suffer in the meanwhile would not be compensated for by the final verdict of the jury.

Brenton at once went to the jail, and wandered through that gloomy building, searching for his wife. At last he found her, but it was in a very comfortable room in the sheriff's residence. The terror and the trials of the last few days had aged her perceptibly, and it cut Brenton to the heart to think that he stood there before her, and could not by any means say a soothing word that she would understand. That she had wept many bitter tears since the terrible Christmas morning was evident; there were dark circles under her beautiful eyes that told of sleepless nights. She sat in a comfortable armchair, facing the window; and looked steadily out at the dreary winter scene with eyes that apparently saw nothing. Her hands lay idly on her lap, and now and then she caught her breath in a way that was half a sob and half a gasp.

Presently the sheriff himself entered the room.

"Mrs. Brenton," he said, "there is a gentleman here who wishes to see you. Mr. Roland, he tells me his name is, an old friend of yours. Do you care to see any one?"

The lady turned her head slowly round, and looked at the sheriff for a moment, seemingly not understanding what he said. Finally she answered, dreamily—

"Roland? Oh, Stephen! Yes, I shall be very glad to see him. Ask him to come in, please."

The next moment Stephen Roland entered, and somehow the fact that he had come to console Mrs. Brenton did not at all please the invisible man who stood between them.

"My dear Mrs. Brenton," began Roland, "I hope you are feeling better to-day? Keep up your courage, and be brave. It is only for a very short time. I have retained the noted criminal lawyers, Benham and Brown, for the defence. You could not possibly have better men."

At the word "criminal" Mrs. Brenton shuddered.

"Alice," continued Roland, sitting down near her, and drawing his chair closer to her, "tell me that you will not lose your courage. I want you to be brave, for the sake of your friends."

He took her listless hand in his own, and she did not withdraw it.

Brenton felt passing over him the pangs of impotent rage, as he saw this act on the part of Roland.

Roland had been an unsuccessful suitor for the hand which he now held in his own, and Brenton thought it the worst possible taste, to say the least, that he should take advantage now of her terrible situation to ingratiate himself into her favour.

The nearest approach to a quarrel that Brenton and his wife had had during their short six months of wedded life was on the subject of the man who now held her hand in his own. It made Brenton impatient to think that a woman with all her boasted insight into character, her instincts as to what was right and what was wrong, had such little real intuition that she did not see into the character of the man whom they were discussing; but a woman never thinks it a crime for a man to have been in love with her, whatever opinion of that man her husband may hold.

"It is awful! awful! awful!" murmured the poor lady, as the tears again rose to her eyes.

"Of course it is," said Roland; "it is particularly awful that they should accuse you, of all persons in the world, of this so-called crime. For my part I do not believe that he was poisoned at all, but we will soon straighten things out. Benham and Brown will give up everything and devote their whole attention to this case until it is finished. Everything will be done that money or friends can do, and all that we ask is that you keep up your courage, and do not be downcast with the seeming awfulness of the situation."

Mrs. Brenton wept silently, but made no reply. It was evident, however, that she was consoled by the words and the presence of her visitor. Strange as it may appear, this fact enraged Brenton, although he had gone there for the very purpose of cheering and comforting his wife. All the bitterness he had felt before against his former rival was revived, and his rage was the more agonizing because it was inarticulate. Then there flashed over him Ferris's sinister advice to leave things alone in the world that he had left. He felt that he could stand this no longer, and the next instant he found himself again in the wintry streets of Cincinnati.

The name of the lawyers, Benham and Brown, kept repeating itself in his mind, and he resolved to go to their office and hear, if he could, what preparations were being made for the defence of a woman whom he knew to be innocent. He found, when he got to the office of these noted lawyers, that the two principals were locked in their private room; and going there, he found them discussing the case with the coolness and impersonal feeling that noted lawyers have even when speaking of issues that involve life or death.

"Yes," Benham was saying, "I think that, unless anything new turns up, that is the best line of defence we can adopt."

"What do you think might turn up?" asked Brown.

"Well, you can never tell in these cases. They may find something else—they may find the poison, for instance, or the package that contained it. Perhaps a druggist will remember having sold it to this woman, and then, of course, we shall have to change our plans. I need not say that it is strictly necessary in this case to give out no opinions whatever to newspaper men. The papers will be full of rumours, and it is just as well if we can keep our line of defence hidden until the time for action comes."

"Still," said Brown, who was the younger partner, "it is as well to keep in with the newspaper fellows; they'll be here as soon as they find we have taken charge of the defence."

"Well, I have no doubt you can deal with them in such a way as to give them something to write up, and yet not disclose anything we do not wish known."

"I think you can trust me to do that," said Brown, with a self-satisfied air.

"I shall leave that part of the matter entirely in your hands," replied Benham. "It is better not to duplicate or mix matters, and if any newspaper man comes to see me I will refer him to you. I will say I know nothing of the case whatever."

"Very well," answered Brown. "Now, between ourselves, what do you think of the case?"

"Oh, it will make a great sensation. I think it will probably be one of the most talked-of cases that we have ever been connected with."

"Yes, but what do you think of her guilt or innocence?"

"As to that," said Benham, calmly, "I haven't the slightest doubt. She murdered him."

As he said this, Brenton, forgetting himself for a moment, sprang forward as if to strangle the lawyer. The statement Benham had made seemed the most appalling piece of treachery. That men should take a woman's money for defending her, and actually engage in a case when they believed their client guilty, appeared to Brenton simply infamous.

"I agree with you," said Brown. "Of course she was the only one to benefit by his death. The simple fool willed everything to her, and she knew it; and his doing so is the more astounding when you remember he was quite well aware that she had a former lover whom she would gladly have married if he had been as rich as Brenton. The supreme idiocy of some men as far as their wives are concerned is something awful."

"Yes," answered Benham, "it is. But I tell you, Brown, she is no ordinary woman. The very conception of that murder had a stroke of originality about it that I very much admire. I do not remember anything like it in the annals of crime. It is the true way in which a murder should be committed. The very publicity of the occasion was a safeguard. Think of poisoning a man at a dinner that he has given himself, in the midst of a score of friends. I tell you that there was a dash of bravery about it that commands my admiration."

"Do you imagine Roland had anything to do with it?"

"Well, I had my doubts about that at first, but I think he is innocent, although from what I know of the man he will not hesitate to share the proceeds of the crime. You mark my words, they will be married within a year from now if she is acquitted. I believe Roland knows her to be guilty."

"I thought as much," said Brown, "by his actions here, and by some remarks he let drop. Anyhow, our credit in the affair will be all the greater if we succeed in getting her off. Yes," he continued, rising and pushing back his chair, "Madam Brenton is a murderess."

5

Brenton found himself once more in the streets of Cincinnati, in a state of mind that can hardly be described. Rage and grief struggled for the mastery, and added to the tumult of these passions was the uncertainty as to what he should do, or what he *could* do. He could hardly ask the advice of Ferris again, for his whole trouble arose from his neglect of the counsel that gentleman had already given him. In his new sphere he did not know where to turn. He found himself wondering whether in the spirit-land there was any firm of lawyers who could advise him, and he remembered then how singularly ignorant he was regarding the conditions of existence in the world to which he now belonged. However, he felt that he must consult with somebody, and Ferris was the only one to whom he could turn. A moment later he was face to face with him.

"Mr. Ferris," he said, "I am in the most grievous trouble, and I come to you in the hope that, if you cannot help me, you can at least advise me what to do."

"If your trouble has come," answered Ferris, with a shade of irony in his voice, "through following the advice that I have already given you, I shall endeavour, as well as I am able, to help you out of it."

"You know very well," cried Brenton, hotly, "that my whole trouble has occurred through neglecting your advice, or, at least, through deliberately not following it. I *could* not follow it."

"Very well, then," said Ferris, "I am not surprised that you are in a difficulty. You must remember that such a crisis is an old story with us here."

"But, my dear sir," said Brenton, "look at the appalling condition of things, the knowledge of which has just come to me. It seems I was poisoned, but of course that doesn't matter. I feel no resentment against the wretch who did it. But the terrible thing is that my wife has been arrested for the crime, and I have just learned that her own lawyers actually believe her guilty."

"That fact," said Ferris, calmly, "will not interfere with their eloquent pleading when the case comes to trial."

Brenton glared at the man who was taking things so coolly, and who proved himself so unsympathetic; but an instant after he realized the futility of quarrelling with the only person who could give him advice, so he continued, with what patience he could command—

"The situation is this: My wife has been arrested for the crime of murdering me. She is now in the custody of the sheriff. Her trouble and anxiety of mind are fearful to contemplate."

"My dear sir," said Ferris, "there is no reason why you or anybody else should contemplate it."

"How can you talk in that cold-blooded way?" cried Brenton, indignantly. "Could you see *your* wife, or any one *you* held dear, incarcerated for a dreadful crime, and yet remain calm and collected, as you now appear to be when you hear of another's misfortune?"

"My dear fellow," said Ferris, "of course it is not to be expected that one who has had so little experience with this existence should have any sense of proportion. You appear to be speaking quite seriously. You do not seem at all to comprehend the utter triviality of all this."

"Good gracious!" cried Brenton, "do you call it a trivial thing that a woman is in danger of her life for a crime which she never committed?"

"If she is innocent," said the other, in no way moved by the indignation of his comrade, "surely that state of things will be brought out in the courts, and no great harm will be done, even looking at things from the standpoint of the world you have left. But I want you to get into the habit of looking at things from the standpoint of this world, and not of the other. Suppose that what you would call the worst should happen—suppose she is hanged—what then?"

Brenton stood simply speechless with indignation at this brutal remark.

"If you will just look at things correctly," continued Ferris, imperturbably, "you will see that there is probably a moment of anguish, perhaps not even that moment, and then your wife is here with you in the land of spirits. I am sure that is a consummation devoutly to be wished. Even a man in your state of mind must see the reasonableness of this. Now, looking at the question in what you would call its most serious aspect, see how little it amounts to. It isn't worth a moment's thought, whichever way it goes."

"You think nothing, then, of the disgrace of such a death—of the bitter injustice of it?"

"When you were in the world did you ever see a child cry over a broken toy? Did the sight pain you to any extent? Did you not know that a new toy could be purchased that would quite obliterate all thoughts of the other? Did the simple griefs of childhood carry any deep and lasting consternation to the mind of a grown-up man? Of course it did not. You are sensible enough to know that. Well, we here in this world look on the pain and struggles and trials of people in the world you have left, just as an aged man looks on the tribulations of children over a broken doll. That is all it really amounts to. That is what I mean when I say that you have not yet got your sense of proportion. Any grief and misery there is in the world you have left is of such an ephemeral, transient nature, that when we think for a moment of the free, untrammelled, and painless life there is beyond, those petty troubles sink into insignificance. My dear fellow, be sensible, take my advice. I have really a strong interest in you, and I advise you, entirely for your own welfare, to forget all about it. Very soon you will have something much more important to do than lingering around the world you have left. If your wife comes amongst us I am sure you will be glad to welcome her, and to teach her the things that you will have already found out of your new life. If she does not appear, then you will know that, even from the old-world standpoint, things have gone what you would call 'all right.' Let these trivial matters go, and attend to the vastly more important concerns that will soon engage your attention here."

Ferris talked earnestly, and it was evident, even to Brenton, that he meant what he said. It was hard to find a pretext for a quarrel with a man at once so calm and so perfectly sure of himself.

"We will not talk any more about it," said Brenton. "I presume people here agree to differ, just as they did in the world we have both left."

"Certainly, certainly," answered Ferris. "Of course, you have just heard my opinion; but you will find myriads of others who do not share it with me. You will meet a great many who are interested in the subject of communication with the world they have left. You will, of course, excuse me when I say that I consider such endeavours not worth talking about."

"Do you know any one who is interested in that sort of thing? and can you give me an introduction to him?"

"Oh! for that matter," said Ferris, "you have had an introduction to one of the most enthusiastic investigators of the subject. I refer to Mr. John Speed, late of Chicago."

"Ah!" said Brenton, rather dubiously. "I must confess that I was not very favourably impressed with Mr. Speed. Probably I did him an injustice."

"You certainly did," said Ferris. "You will find Speed a man well worth knowing, even if he does waste himself on such futile projects as a scheme for communicating with a community so evanescent as that of Chicago. You will like Speed better the more you know him. He really is very philanthropic, and has Sommers on his hands just now. From what he said after you left Venice, I imagine he does not entertain the same feeling toward you as you do toward him. I would see Speed if I were you."

"I will think about it," said Brenton, as they separated.

To know that a man thinks well of a person is no detriment to further acquaintance with that man, even if the first impressions have not been favourable; and after Ferris told Brenton that Speed had thought well of him, Brenton found less difficulty in seeking the Chicago enthusiast.

"I have been in a good deal of trouble," Brenton said to Speed, "and have been talking to Ferris about it. I regret to say that he gave me very little encouragement, and did not seem at all to appreciate my feelings in the matter."

"Oh, you mustn't mind Ferris," said Speed. "He is a first-rate fellow, but he is as cold and unsympathetic as—well, suppose we say as an oyster. His great hobby is non-intercourse with the world we have left. Now, in that I don't agree with him, and there are thousands who don't agree with him. I admit that there are cases where a man is more unhappy if he frequents the old world than he would be if he left it alone. But then there are other cases where just the reverse is true. Take my own experience, for example; I take a peculiar pleasure in rambling around Chicago. I admit that it is a grievance to me, as an old newspaper man, to see the number of scoops I could have on my esteemed contemporaries, but—"

"Scoop? What is that?" asked Brenton, mystified.

"Why, a scoop is a beat, you know."

"Yes, but I don't know. What is a beat?"

"A beat or a scoop, my dear fellow, is the getting of a piece of news that your contemporary does not obtain. You never were in the newspaper business? Well, sir, you missed it. Greatest business in the world. You know everything that is going on long before anybody else does, and the way you can reward your friends and jump with both feet on your enemies is one of the delights of existence down there."

"Well, what I wanted to ask you was this," said Brenton. "You have made a speciality of finding out whether there could be any communication between one of us, for instance, and one who is an inhabitant of the other world. Is such communication possible?"

"I have certainly devoted some time to it, but I can't say that my success has been flattering. My efforts have been mostly in the line of news. I have come on some startling information which my facilities here gave me access to, and I confess I have tried my best to put some of the boys on to it. But there is a link loose somewhere. Now, what is your trouble? Do you want to get a message to anybody?"

"My trouble is this," said Brenton, briefly, "I am here because a few days ago I was poisoned."

"George Washington!" cried the other, "you don't say so! Have the newspapers got on to the fact?"

"I regret to say that they have."

"What an item that would have been if one paper had got hold of it and the others hadn't! I suppose they all got on to it at the same time?"

"About that," said Brenton, "I don't know, and I must confess that I do not care very much. But here is the trouble—my wife has been arrested for my murder, and she is as innocent as I am."

"Sure of that?"

"*Sure* of it?" cried the other indignantly. "Of course I am sure of it."

"Then who is the guilty person?"

"Ah, that," said Brenton, "I do not yet know."

"Then how can you be sure she is not guilty?"

"If you talk like that," exclaimed Brenton, "I have nothing more to say."

"Now, don't get offended, I beg of you. I am merely looking at this from a newspaper standpoint, you know. You must remember it is not you who will decide the matter, but a jury of your very stupid fellow-countrymen. Now, you can never tell what a jury *will* do, except that it will do something idiotic. Therefore, it seems to me that the very first step to be taken is to find out who the guilty party is. Don't you see the force of that?"

"Yes, I do."

"Very well, then. Now, what were the circumstances of this crime? who was to profit by your death?"

Brenton winced at this.

"I see how it is," said the other, "and I understand why you don't answer. Now—you'll excuse me if I am frank—your wife was the one who benefited most by your death, was she not?"

"No," cried the other indignantly, "she was not the one. That is what the lawyers said. Why in the world should she want to poison me, when she had all my wealth at her command as it was?"

"Yes, that's a strong point," said Speed. "You were a reasonably good husband, I suppose? Rather generous with the cash?"

"Generous?" cried the other. "My wife always had everything she wanted."

"Ah, well, there was no—you'll excuse me, I am sure—no former lover in the case, was there?"

Again Brenton winced, and he thought of Roland sitting beside his wife with her hand in his.

"I see," said Speed; "you needn't answer. Now what were the circumstances, again?"

"They were these: At a dinner which I gave, where some twenty or twenty-five of my friends were assembled, poison, it appears, was put into my cup of coffee. That is all I know of it."

"Who poured out that cup of coffee?"

"My wife did."

"Ah! Now, I don't for a moment say she is guilty, remember; but you must admit that, to a stupid jury, the case *might* look rather bad against her."

"Well, granted that it does, there is all the more need that I should come to her assistance if possible."

"Certainly, certainly!" said Speed. "Now, I'll tell you what we have to do. We must get, if possible, one of the very brightest Chicago reporters on the track of this thing, and we have to get him on the track of it early. Come with me to Chicago. We will try an experiment, and I am sure you will lend your mind entirely to the effort. We must act in conjunction in this affair, and you are just the man I've been wanting, some one who is earnest and who has something at stake in the matter. We may fail entirely, but I think it's worth the trying. Will you come?"

"Certainly," said Brenton; "and I cannot tell you how much I appreciate your interest and sympathy."

Arriving at a brown stone building on the corner of two of the principal streets in Chicago, Brenton and Speed ascended quickly to one of the top floors. It was nearly midnight, and two upper stories of the huge dark building were brilliantly lighted, as was shown on the outside by the long rows of glittering windows. They entered a room where a man was seated at a table, with coat and vest thrown off, and his hat set well back on his head. Cold as it was outside, it was warm in this man's room, and the room was blue with smoke. A black corn-cob pipe was in his teeth, and the man was writing away as if for dear life, on sheets of coarse white copy paper, stopping now and then to fill up his pipe or to relight it after it had gone out.

"There," said Speed, waving his hand towards the writer with a certain air of proprietary pride, "there sits one of the very cleverest men on the Chicago press. That fellow, sir, is gifted with a nose for news which has no equal in America. He will ferret out a case that he once starts on with an unerringness that would charm you. Yes, sir, I got him his present situation on this paper, and I can tell you it was a good one."

"He must have been a warm friend of yours?" said Brenton, indifferently, as if he did not take much interest in the eulogy.

"Quite the contrary," said Speed. "He was a warm enemy, made it mighty warm for *me* sometimes. He was on an opposition paper, but I tell you, although I was no chicken in newspaper business, that man would scoop the daylight out of me any time he tried. So, to get rid of opposition, I got the managing editor to appoint him to a place on our paper; and I tell you, he has never regretted it. Yes, sir, there sits George Stratton, a man who knows his business. Now," he said, "let us concentrate our attention on him. First let us see whether, by putting our whole minds to it, we can make any impression on *his* mind whatever. You see how busily he is engaged. He is thoroughly absorbed in his work. That is George all over. Whatever his assignment is, George throws himself right into it, and thinks of nothing else until it is finished. *Now* then."

In that dingy, well-lighted room George Stratton sat busily pencilling out the lines that were to appear in next morning's paper. He was evidently very much engrossed in his task, as Speed had said. If he had looked about him, which he did not, he would have said that he was entirely alone. All at once his attention seemed to waver, and he passed his hand over his brow, while perplexity came into his face. Then he noticed that his pipe was out, and, knocking the ashes from it by rapping the bowl on the side of the table, he filled it with an absent-mindedness unusual with him. Again he turned to his writing, and again he passed his hand over his brow. Suddenly, without any apparent cause, he looked first to the right and then to the left of him. Once more he tried to write, but, noticing his pipe was out, he struck another match and nervously puffed away, until clouds of blue smoke rose around him. There was a look of annoyance and perplexity in his face as he bent resolutely to his writing. The door opened, and a man appeared on the threshold.

"Anything more about the convention, George?" he said.

"Yes; I am just finishing this. Sort of pen pictures, you know."

"Perhaps you can let me have what you have done. I'll fix it up."

"All right," said Stratton, bunching up the manuscript in front of him, and handing it to the city editor.

That functionary looked at the number of pages, and then at the writer.

"Much more of this, George?" he said. "We'll be a little short of room in the morning, you know."

"Well," said the other, sitting back in his chair, "it is pretty good stuff that. Folks always like the pen pictures of men engaged in the skirmish better than the reports of what most of them say."

"Yes," said the city editor, "that's so."

"Still," said Stratton, "we could cut it off at the last page. Just let me see the last two pages, will you?"

These were handed to him, and, running his eye through them, he drew his knife across one of the pages, and put at the bottom the cabalistic mark which indicated the end of the copy.

"There! I think I will let it go at that. Old Rickenbeck don't amount to much, anyhow. We'll let him go."

"All right," said the city editor. "I think we won't want anything more to-night."

Stratton put his hands behind his head, with his fingers interlaced, and leaned back in his chair, placing his heels upon the table before him. A thought-reader, looking at his face, could almost have followed the theme that occupied his mind. Suddenly bringing his feet down with a crash to the floor, he rose and went into the city editor's room.

"See here," he said. "Have you looked into that Cincinnati case at all?"

"What Cincinnati case?" asked the local editor, looking up.

"Why, that woman who is up for poisoning her husband."

"Oh yes; we had something of it in the despatches this morning. It's rather out of the local line, you know."

"Yes, I know it is. But it isn't out of the paper's line. I tell you that case is going to make a sensation. She's pretty as a picture. Been married only six months, and it seems to be a dead sure thing that she poisoned her husband. That trial's going to make racy reading, especially if they bring in a verdict of guilty."

The city editor looked interested.

"Want to go down there, George?"

"Well, do you know, I think it'll pay."

"Let me see, this is the last day of the convention, isn't it? And Clark comes back from his vacation to-morrow. Well, if you think it's worth it, take a trip down there, and look the ground over, and give us a special article that we can use on the first day of the trial."

"I'll do it," said George.

Speed looked at Brenton.

"What would old Ferris say *now*, eh?"

6

Next morning George Stratton was on the railway train speeding towards Cincinnati. As he handed to the conductor his mileage book, he did not say to him, lightly transposing the old couplet—

"Here, railroad man, take thrice thy fee,
For spirits twain do ride with me."

George Stratton was a practical man, and knew nothing of spirits, except those which were in a small flask in his natty little valise.

When he reached Cincinnati, he made straight for the residence of the sheriff. He felt that his first duty was to become friends with such an important official. Besides this, he wished to have an interview with the prisoner. He had arranged in his mind, on the way there, just how he would write a preliminary article that would whet the appetite of the readers of the Chicago *Argus* for any further developments that might occur during and after the trial. He would write the whole thing in the form of a story.

First, there would be a sketch of the life of Mrs. Brenton and her husband. This would be number one, and above it would be the Roman numeral I. Under the heading II. would be a history of the crime. Under III. what had occurred afterwards—the incidents that had led suspicion towards the unfortunate woman, and that sort of thing. Under the numeral IV. would be his interview with the prisoner, if he were fortunate enough to get one. Under V. he would give the general opinion of Cincinnati on the crime, and on

the guilt or innocence of Mrs. Brenton. This article he already saw
in his mind's eye occupying nearly half a page of the *Argus*. All
would be in leaded type, and written in a style and manner that
would attract attention, for he felt that he was first on the ground,
and would not have the usual rush in preparing his copy which
had been the bane of his life. It would give the *Argus* practically
the lead in this case, which he was convinced would become one of
national importance.

The sheriff received him courteously, and, looking at the card
he presented, saw the name Chicago *Argus* in the corner. Then he
stood visibly on his guard—an attitude assumed by all wise offi-
cials when they find themselves brought face to face with a newspaper man; for they know, however carefully an article may be prepared, it will likely contain some unfortunate overlooked phrase
which may have a damaging effect in a future political campaign.

"I wanted to see you," began Stratton, coming straight to the
point, "in reference to the Brenton murder."

"I may say at once," replied the sheriff, "that if you wish an
interview with the prisoner, it is utterly impossible, because her
lawyers, Benham and Brown, have positively forbidden her to see
a newspaper man."

"That shows," said Stratton, "they are wise men who understand their business. Nevertheless, I wish to have an interview with
Mrs. Brenton. But what I wanted to say to you is this: I believe the
case will be very much talked about, and that before many weeks
are over. Of course you know the standing the *Argus* has in newspaper circles. What it says will have an influence, even over the
Cincinnati press. I think you will admit that. Now a great many
newspaper men consider an official their natural enemy. I do not;
at least, I do not until I am forced to. Any reference that I may
make to you I am more than willing to submit to you before it goes
to Chicago. I will give you my word, if you want it, that nothing
will be said referring to your official position, or to yourself personally, that you do not see before it appears in print. Of course
you will be up for re-election. I never met a sheriff who wasn't."

The sheriff smiled at this, and did not deny it.

"Very well. Now, I may tell you my belief is that this case is going to have a powerful influence on your re-election. Here is a young and pretty woman who is to be tried for a terrible crime. Whether she is guilty or innocent, public sympathy is going to be with her. If I were in your place, I would prefer to be known as her friend rather than as her enemy."

"My dear sir," said the sheriff, "my official position puts me in the attitude of neither friend nor enemy of the unfortunate woman. I have simply a certain duty to do, and that duty I intend to perform."

"Oh, that's all right!" exclaimed the newspaper man, jauntily. "I, for one, am not going to ask you to take a step outside your duties; but an official may do his duty, and yet, at the same time, do a friendly act for a newspaper man, or even for a prisoner. In the language of the old chestnut, 'If you don't help me, don't help the bear.' That's all I ask."

"You maybe sure, Mr. Stratton, that anything I can do to help you I shall be glad to do; and now let me give you a hint. If you want to see Mrs. Brenton, the best thing is to get permission from her lawyers. If I were you I would not see Benham—he's rather a hard nut, Benham is, although you needn't tell him I said so. You get on the right side of Brown. Brown has some political aspirations himself, and he does not want to offend a man on so powerful a paper as the *Argus*, even if it is not a Cincinnati paper. Now, if you make him the same offer you have made to me, I think it will be all right. If he sees your copy before it goes into print, and if you keep your word with him that nothing will appear that he does *not* see, I think you will succeed in getting an interview with Mrs. Brenton. If you bring me a note from Brown, I shall be very glad to allow you to see her."

Stratton thanked the sheriff for his hint. He took down in his note-book the address of the lawyers, and the name especially of Mr. Brown. The two men shook hands, and Stratton felt that they understood each other.

When Mr. Stratton was ushered into the private office of Brown, and handed that gentleman his card, he noticed the lawyer perceptibly freeze over.

"Ahem," said the legal gentleman; "you will excuse me if I say that my time is rather precious. Did you wish to see me professionally?"

"Yes," replied Stratton, "that is, from a newspaper standpoint of the profession."

"Ah," said the other, "in reference to what?"

"To the Brenton case."

"Well, my dear sir, I have had, very reluctantly, to refuse information that I would have been happy to give, if I could, to our own newspaper men; and so I may say to you at once that I scarcely think it will be possible for me to be of any service to an outside paper like the *Argus*."

"Local newspaper men," said Stratton, "represent local fame. That you already possess. I represent national fame, which, if you will excuse my saying so, you do not yet possess. The fact that I am in Cincinnati to-day, instead of in Chicago, shows what we Chicago people think of the Cincinnati case. I believe, and the *Argus* believes, that this case is going to be one of national importance. Now, let me ask you one question. Will you state frankly what your objection is to having a newspaper man, for instance, interview Mrs. Brenton, or get any information relating to this case from her or others whom you have the power of controlling?"

"I shall answer that question," said Brown, "as frankly as you put it. You are a man of the world, and know, of course, that we are all selfish, and in business matters look entirely after our own interests. My interest in this case is to defend my client. Your interest in this case is to make a sensational article. You want to get facts if possible, but, in any event, you want to write up a readable column or two for your paper. Now, if I allowed you to see Mrs. Brenton, she might say something to you, and you might publish it, that would not only endanger her chances, but would seriously embarrass us, as her lawyers, in our defence of the case."

"You have stated the objection very plainly and forcibly," said Stratton, with a look of admiration, as if the powerful arguments of the lawyer had had a great effect on him. "Now, if I understand your argument, it simply amounts to this, that you would have no objection to my interviewing Mrs. Brenton if you have the privilege of editing the copy. In other words, if nothing were printed but what you approve of, you would not have the slightest hesitancy about allowing me that interview."

"No, I don't know that I would," admitted the lawyer.

"Very well, then. Here is my proposition to you: I am here to look after the interests of our paper in this particular case. The *Argus* is probably going to be the first paper outside of Cincinnati that will devote a large amount of space to the Brenton trial, in addition to what is received from the Associated Press dispatches. Now you can give me a great many facilities in this matter if you care to do so, and in return I am perfectly willing to submit to you every line of copy that concerns you or your client before it is sent, and I give you my word of honour that nothing shall appear but what you have seen and approved of. If you want to cut out something that I think is vitally important, then I shall tell you frankly that I intend to print it, but will modify it as much as I possibly can to suit your views."

"I see," said the lawyer. "In other words, as you have just remarked, I am to give you special facilities in this matter, and then, when you find out some fact which I wish kept secret, and which you have obtained because of the facilities I have given to you, you will quite frankly tell me that it must go in, and then, of course, I shall be helpless except to debar you from any further facilities, as you call them. No, sir, I do not care to make any such bargain."

"Well, suppose I strike out that clause of agreement, and say to you that I will send nothing but what you approve of, would you then write me a note to the sheriff and allow me to see the prisoner?"

"I am sorry to say"—the lawyer hesitated for a moment, and glanced at the card, then added—"Mr. Stratton, that I do not see my way clear to granting your request."

"I think," said Stratton, rising, "that you are doing yourself an injustice. You are refusing—I may as well tell you first as last— what is a great privilege. Now, you have had some experience in your business, and I have had some experience in mine, and I beg to inform you that men who are much more prominent in the history of their country than any one I can at present think of in Cincinnati, have tried to balk me in the pursuit of my business, and have failed."

"In that matter, of course," said Brown, "I must take my chances. I don't see the use of prolonging this interview. As you have been so frank as to—I won't say threaten, perhaps warn is the better word—as you have been so good as to warn me, I may, before we part, just give *you* a word of caution. Of course we, in Cincinnati, are perfectly willing to admit that Chicago people are the smartest on earth, but I may say that if you print a word in your paper which is untrue and which is damaging to our side of the case, or if you use any methods that are unlawful in obtaining the information you so much desire, you will certainly get your paper into trouble, and you will run some little personal risk yourself."

"Well, as you remarked a moment ago, Mr. Brown, I shall have to take the chances of that. I am here to get the news, and if I don't succeed it will be the first time in my life."

"Very well, sir," said the lawyer. "I wish you good evening."

"Just one thing more," said the newspaper man, "before I leave you."

"My dear sir," said the lawyer, impatiently, "I am very busy. I've already given you a liberal share of my time. I must request that this interview end at once."

"I thought," said Mr. Stratton, calmly, "that perhaps you might be interested in the first article that I am going to write. I shall devote one column in the *Argus* of the day after to-morrow to your defence of the case, and whether your theory of defence is a tenable one or not."

Mr. Brown pushed back his chair and looked earnestly at the young man. That individual was imperturbably pulling on his gloves, and at the moment was buttoning one of them.

"Our *defence*!" cried the lawyer. "What do you know of our defence?"

"My dear sir," said Stratton, "I know *all* about it."

"Sir, that is impossible. Nobody knows what our defence is to be except Mr. Benham and myself."

"And Mr. Stratton, of the Chicago *Argus*," replied the young man, as he buttoned his coat.

"May I ask, then, what the defence is?"

"Certainly," answered the Chicago man. "Your defence is that Mr. Brenton was insane, and that he committed suicide."

Even Mr. Brown's habitual self-control, acquired by long years of training in keeping his feelings out of sight, for the moment deserted him. He drew his breath sharply, and cast a piercing glance at the young man before him, who was critically watching the lawyer's countenance, although he appeared to be entirely absorbed in buttoning his overcoat. Then Mr. Brown gave a short, dry laugh.

"I have met a bluff before," he said carelessly; "but I should like to know what makes you think that such is our defence?"

"*Think*!" cried the young man. "I don't think at all; I *know* it."

"How do you know it?"

"Well, for one thing, I know it by your own actions a moment ago. What first gave me an inkling of your defence was that book which is on your table. It is Forbes Winslow on the mind and the brain; a very interesting book, Mr. Brown, *very* interesting indeed. It treats of suicide, and the causes and conditions of the brain that will lead up to it. It is a very good book, indeed, to study in such a case. Good evening, Mr. Brown. I am sorry that we cannot co-operate in this matter."

Stratton turned and walked toward the door, while the lawyer gazed after him with a look of helpless astonishment on his face. As Stratton placed his hand on the door knob, the lawyer seemed to wake up as from a dream.

"Stop!" he cried; "I will give you a letter that will admit you to Mrs. Brenton."

7

"There!" said Speed to Brenton, triumphantly, "what do you think of *that*? Didn't I say George Stratton was the brightest newspaper man in Chicago? I tell you, his getting that letter from old Brown was one of the cleverest bits of diplomacy I ever saw. There you had quickness of perception, and nerve. All the time he was talking to old Brown he was just taking that man's measure. See how coolly he acted while he was drawing on his gloves and buttoning his coat as if ready to leave. Flung that at Brown all of a sudden as quiet as if he was saying nothing at all unusual, and all the time watching Brown out of the tail of his eye. Well, sir, I must admit, that although I have known George Stratton for years, I thought he was dished by that Cincinnati lawyer. I thought that George was just gracefully covering up his defeat, and there he upset old Brown's apple-cart in the twinkling of an eye. Now, you see the effect of all this. Brown has practically admitted to him what the line of defence is. Stratton won't publish it, of course; he has promised not to, but you see he can hold that over Brown's head, and get everything he wants unless they change their defence."

"Yes," remarked Brenton, slowly, "he seems to be a very sharp newspaper man indeed; but I don't like the idea of his going to interview my wife."

"Why, what is there wrong about that?"

"Well, there is this wrong about it—that she in her depression may say something that will tell against her."

"Even if she does, what of it? Isn't the lawyer going to see the letter before it is sent to the paper?"

"I am not so sure about that. Do you think Stratton will show the article to Brown if he gets what you call a scoop or a beat?"

"Why, of course he will," answered Speed, indignantly; "hasn't he given him his word that he will?"

"Yes, I know he has," said Brenton, dubiously; "but he is a newspaper man."

"Certainly he is," answered Speed, with strong emphasis; "that is the reason he will keep his word."

"I hope so, I hope so; but I must admit that the more I know you newspaper men, the more I see the great temptation you are under to preserve if possible the sensational features of an article."

"I'll bet you a drink—no, we can't do that," corrected Speed; "but you shall see that, if Brown acts square with Stratton, he will keep his word to the very letter with Brown. There is no use in our talking about the matter here. Let us follow Stratton, and see what comes of the interview."

"I think I prefer to go alone," said Brenton, coldly.

"Oh, as you like, as you like," answered the other, shortly. "I thought you wanted my help in this affair; but if you don't, I am sure I shan't intrude."

"That's all right," said Brenton; "come along. By the way, Speed, what do you think of that line of defence?"

"Well, I don't know enough of the circumstances of the case to know what to think of it. It seems to me rather a good line."

"It can't be a good line when it is not true. It is certain to break down."

"That's so," said Speed; "but I'll bet you four dollars and a half that they'll prove you a raving maniac before they are through with you. They'll show very likely that you tried to poison yourself two or three times; bring on a dozen of your friends to prove that they knew all your life you were insane."

"Do you think they will?" asked Brenton, uneasily.

"Think it? Why, I am sure of it. You'll go down to posterity as one of the most complete lunatics that ever lived in Cincinnati.

Oh, there won't be anything left of you when *they* get through with you."

Meanwhile, Stratton was making his way to the residence of the sheriff.

"Ah," said that official, when they met, "you got your letter, did you? Well, I thought you would."

"If you had heard the conversation between my estimable friend Mr. Brown and myself, up to the very last moment, you wouldn't have thought it."

"Well, Brown is generally very courteous towards newspaper men, and that's one reason you see his name in the papers a great deal."

"If I were a Cincinnati newspaper man, I can assure you that his name wouldn't appear very much in the columns of my paper."

"I am sorry to hear you say that. I thought Brown was very popular with the newspaper men. You got the letter, though, did you?"

"Yes; I got it. Here it is. Read it."

The sheriff scanned the brief note over, and put it in his pocket.

"Just take a chair for a moment, will you, and I will see if Mrs. Brenton is ready to receive you."

Stratton seated himself, and, pulling a paper from his pocket, was busily reading when the sheriff again entered.

"I am sorry to say," he began, "after you have had all this trouble, that Mrs. Brenton positively refuses to see you. You know I cannot *compel* a prisoner to meet any one. You understand that, of course."

"Perfectly," said Stratton, thinking for a moment. "See here, sheriff, I have simply *got* to have a talk with that woman. Now, can't you tell her I knew her husband, or something of that sort? I'll make it all right when I see her."

"The scoundrel!" said Brenton to Speed, as Stratton made this remark.

"My dear sir," said Speed, "don't you see he is just the man we want? This is not the time to be particular."

"Yes, but think of the treachery and meanness of telling a poor unfortunate woman that he was acquainted with her husband, who is only a few days dead."

"Now, see here," said Speed, "if you are going to look on matters in this way you will be a hindrance and not a help in the affair. Don't you appreciate the situation? Why, Mrs. Brenton's own lawyers, as you have said, think her guilty. What, then, can they learn by talking with her, or what good can they do her with their minds already prejudiced against her? Don't you see that?"

Brenton made no answer to this, but it was evident he was very ill at ease.

"Did you know her husband?" asked the sheriff.

"No, to tell you the truth, I never heard of him before. But I must see this lady, both for my good and hers, and I am not going to let a little thing like that stand between us. Won't you tell her that I have come with a letter from her own lawyers? Just show her the letter, and say that I will take up but very little of her time. I am sorry to ask this much of you, but you see how I am placed."

"Oh, that's all right," said the sheriff, good-naturedly; "I shall be very glad to do what you wish," and with that he once more disappeared.

The sheriff stayed away longer this time, and Stratton paced the room impatiently. Finally, the official returned, and said—

"Mrs. Brenton has consented to see you. Come this way, please. You will excuse me, I know," continued the sheriff, as they walked along together, "but it is part of my duty to remain in the room while you are talking with Mrs. Brenton."

"Certainly, certainly," said Stratton; "I understand that."

"Very well; then, if I may make a suggestion, I would say this: you should be prepared to ask just what you want to know, and do it all as speedily as possible, for really Mrs. Brenton is in a condition of nervous exhaustion that renders it almost cruel to put her through any rigid cross-examination."

"I understand that also," said Stratton; "but you must remember that she has a very much harder trial to undergo in the future.

I am exceedingly anxious to get at the truth of this thing, and so, if it seems to you that I am asking a lot of very unnecessary questions, I hope you will not interfere with me as long as Mrs. Brenton consents to answer."

"I shall not interfere at all," said the sheriff; "I only wanted to caution you, for the lady may break down at any moment. If you can marshal your questions so that the most important ones come first, I think it will be wise. I presume you have them pretty well arranged in your own mind?"

"Well, I can't say that I have; you see, I am entirely in the dark. I got no help whatever from the lawyers, and from what I know of their defence I am thoroughly convinced that they are on the wrong track."

"What! Did Brown say anything about the defence? That is not like his usual caution."

"He didn't intend to," answered Stratton; "but I found out all I wanted to know, nevertheless. You see, I shall have to ask what appears to be a lot of rambling, inconsequential questions because you can never tell in a case like this when you may get the key to the whole mystery."

"Well, here we are," said the sheriff, as he knocked at a door, and then pushed it open.

From the moment George Stratton saw Mrs. Brenton his interest in the case ceased to be purely journalistic.

Mrs. Brenton was standing near the window, and she appeared to be very calm and collected, but her fingers twitched nervously, clasping and unclasping each other. Her modest dress of black was certainly a very becoming one.

George thought he had never seen a woman so beautiful.

As she was standing up, she evidently intended the interview to be a short one.

"Madam," said Stratton, "I am very sorry indeed to trouble you; but I have taken a great interest in the solution of this mystery, and I have your lawyers' permission to visit you. I assure you, anything you say will be submitted to them, so that there will be no danger of your case being prejudiced by any statements made."

"I am not afraid," said Mrs. Brenton, "that the truth will injure or prejudice my case."

"I am sure of that," answered the newspaper man; and then, knowing that she would not sit down if he asked her to, he continued diplomatically, "Madam, will you permit me to sit down? I wish to write out my notes as carefully as possible. Accuracy is my strong point."

"Certainly," said Mrs. Brenton; and, seeing that it was not probable the interview would be a short one, she seated herself by the window, while the sheriff took a chair in the corner, and drew a newspaper from his pocket.

"Now, madam," said the special, "a great number of the questions I ask you may seem trivial, but as I said to the sheriff a moment ago, some word of yours that appears to you entirely unconnected with the case may give me a clue which will be exceedingly valuable. You will, therefore, I am sure, pardon me if some of the questions I ask you appear irrelevant."

Mrs. Brenton bowed her head, but said nothing.

"Were your husband's business affairs in good condition at the time of his death?"

"As far as I know they were."

"Did you ever see anything in your husband's actions that would lead you to think him a man who might have contemplated suicide?"

Mrs. Brenton looked up with wide-open eyes.

"Certainly not," she said.

"Had he ever spoken to you on the subject of suicide?"

"I do not remember that he ever did."

"Was he ever queer in his actions? In short, did you ever notice anything about him that would lead you to doubt his sanity? I am sorry if questions I ask you seem painful, but I have reasons for wishing to be certain on this point."

"No," said Mrs. Brenton; "he was perfectly sane. No man could have been more so. I am certain that he never thought of committing suicide."

"Why are you so certain on that point?"

"I do not know why. I only know I am positive of it."

"Do you know if he had any enemy who might wish his death?"

"I doubt if he had an enemy in the world. I do not know of any."

"Have you ever heard him speak of anybody in a spirit of enmity?"

"Never. He was not a man who bore enmity against people. Persons whom he did not like he avoided."

"The poison, it is said, was put into his cup of coffee. Do you happen to know," said Stratton, turning to the sheriff, "how they came to that conclusion?"

"No, I do not," answered the sheriff. "In fact, I don't see any reason why they should think so."

"Was morphia found in the coffee cup afterwards?"

"No; at the time of the inquest all the things had been cleared away. I think it was merely presumed that the morphine was put into his coffee."

"Who poured out the coffee he drank that night?"

"I did," answered his wife.

"You were at one end of the table and he at the other, I suppose?"

"Yes."

"How did the coffee cup reach him?"

"I gave it to the servant, and she placed it before him."

"It passed through no other hands, then?"

"No."

"Who was the servant?"

Mrs. Brenton pondered for a moment.

"I really know very little about her. She had been in our house for a couple of weeks only."

"What was her name?"

"Jane Morton, I think."

"Where is she now, do you know?"

"I do not know."

"She appeared at the inquest, of course?" said Stratton, turning to the sheriff.

"I think she did," was the answer. "I am not sure."

He marked her name down in the note-book.

"How many people were there at the dinner?"

"Including my husband and myself, there were twenty-six."

"Could you give me the name of each of them?"

"Yes, I think so."

She repeated the names, which he took down, with certain notes and comments on each.

"Who sat next your husband at the head of the table?"

"Miss Walker was at his right hand, Mr. Roland at his left."

"Now, forgive me if I ask you if you have ever had any trouble with your husband?"

"Never."

"Never had any quarrel?"

Mrs. Brenton hesitated for a moment.

"No, I don't think we ever had what could be called a quarrel."

"You had no disagreement shortly before the dinner?"

Again Mrs. Brenton hesitated.

"I can hardly call it a disagreement," she said. "We had a little discussion about some of the guests who were to be invited."

"Did he object to any that were there?"

"There was a gentleman there whom he did not particularly like, I think, but he made no objection to his coming; in fact, he seemed to feel that I might imagine he had an objection from a little discussion we had about inviting him; and afterwards, as if to make up for that, he placed this guest at his left hand."

Stratton quickly glanced up the page of his notebook, and marked a little cross before the name of Stephen Roland.

"You had another disagreement with him before, if I might term it so, had you not?"

Mrs. Brenton looked at him surprised.

"What makes you think so?" she said.

"Because you hesitated when I spoke of it."

"Well, we had what you might call a disagreement once at Lucerne, Switzerland."

"Will you tell me what it was about?"

"I would rather not."

"Will you tell me this—was it about a gentleman?"

"Yes," said Mrs. Brenton.

"Was your husband of a jealous disposition?"

"Ordinarily I do not think he was. It seemed to me at the time that he was a little unjust—that's all."

"Was the gentleman in Lucerne?"

"Oh no!"

"In Cincinnati?"

"Yes."

"Was his name Stephen Roland?"

Mrs. Brenton again glanced quickly at the newspaper man, and seemed about to say something, but, checking herself, she simply answered—

"Yes."

Then she leaned back in the armchair and sighed.

"I am very tired," she said. "If it is not absolutely necessary, I prefer not to continue this conversation."

Stratton immediately rose.

"Madam," he said, "I am very much obliged to you for the trouble you have taken to answer my questions, which I am afraid must have seemed impertinent to you, but I assure you that I did not intend them to be so. Now, madam, I would like very much to get a promise from you. I wish that you would promise to see me if I call again, and I, on my part, assure you that unless I have something particularly important to tell you, or to ask, I shall not intrude upon you."

"I shall be pleased to see you at any time, sir."

When the sheriff and the newspaper man reached the other room, the former said—

"Well, what do you think?"

"I think it is an interesting case," was the answer.

"Or, to put it in other words, you think Mrs. Brenton a very interesting lady."

"Officially, sir, you have exactly stated my opinion."

"And I suppose, poor woman, she will furnish an interesting article for the paper?"

"Hang the paper!" said Stratton, with more than his usual vim.

The sheriff laughed. Then he said—

"I confess that to me it seems a very perplexing affair all through. Have you got any light on the subject?"

"My dear sir, I will tell you three important things. First, Mrs. Brenton is innocent. Second, her lawyers are taking the wrong line of defence. Third," tapping his breast-pocket, "I have the name of the murderer in my note-book."

8

"Now," said John Speed to William Brenton, "we have got Stratton fairly started on the track, and I believe that he will ferret out the truth in this matter. But, meanwhile, we must not be idle. You must remember that, with all our facilities for discovery, we really know nothing of the murderer ourselves. I propose we set about this thing just as systematically as Stratton will. The chances are that we shall penetrate the mystery of the whole affair very much quicker than he. As I told you before, I am something of a newspaper man myself; and if, with the facilities of getting into any room in any house, in any city and in any country, and being with a suspected criminal night and day when he never imagines any one is near him—if with all those advantages I cannot discover the real author of that crime before George Stratton does, then I'll never admit that I came from Chicago, or belonged to a newspaper."

"Whom do you think Stratton suspects of the crime? He told the sheriff," said Brenton, "that he had the name in his pocket-book."

"I don't know," said Speed, "but I have my suspicions. You see, he has the names of all the guests at your banquet in that pocket-book of his; but the name of Stephen Roland he has marked with two crosses. The name of the servant he has marked with one cross. Now, I suspect that he believes Stephen Roland committed the crime. You know Roland; what do you think of him?"

"I think he is quite capable of it," answered Brenton, with a frown.

"Still, you are prejudiced against the man," put in Speed, "so your evidence is hardly impartial."

"I am not prejudiced against any one," answered Brenton; "I merely know that man. He is a thoroughly despicable, cowardly character. The only thing that makes me think he would not commit a murder, is that he is too craven to stand the consequences if he were caught. He is a cool villain, but he is a coward. I do not believe he has the courage to commit a crime, even if he thought he would benefit by it."

"Well, there is one thing, Brenton, you can't be accused of flattering a man, and if it is any consolation for you to know, you may be pretty certain that George Stratton is on his track."

"I am sure I wish him success," answered Brenton, gloomily; "if he brings Roland to the gallows I shall not mourn over it."

"That's all right," said Speed; "but now we must be up and doing ourselves. Have you anything to propose?"

"No, I have not, except that we might play the detective on Roland."

"Well, the trouble with that is we would merely be duplicating what Stratton is doing himself. Now, I'll tell you my proposal. Supposing that we consult with Lecocq."

"Who is that? The novelist?"

"Novelist? I don't think he has ever written any novels—not that I remember of."

"Ah, I didn't know. It seemed to me that I remembered his name in connection with some novel."

"Oh, very likely you did. He is the hero of more detective stories than any other man I know of. He was the great French detective."

"What, is he dead, then?"

"Dead? Not a bit of it; he's here with us. Oh, I understand what you mean. Yes, from your point of view, he is dead."

"Where can we find him?"

"Well, I presume, in Paris. He's a first-rate fellow to know, anyhow, and he spends most of his time around his old haunts. In fact, if you want to be certain to find Lecocq, you will generally get him during office hours in the room he used to frequent while in Paris."

"Let us go and see him, then."

"Monsieur Lecocq," said Speed, a moment afterwards, "I wish to introduce to you a new-comer, Mr. Brenton, recently of Cincinnati."

"Ah, my dear Speed," said the Frenchman, "I am very pleased indeed to meet any friend of yours. How is the great Chicago, the second Paris, and how is your circulation?—the greatest in the world, I suppose."

"Well, it is in pretty good order," said Speed; "we circulated from Chicago to Paris here in a very much shorter time than the journey usually occupies down below. Now, can you give us a little of your time? Are you busy just now?"

"My dear Speed, I am always busy. I am like the people of the second Paris. I lose no time, but I have always time to speak with my friends."

"All right," said Speed. "I am like the people of the second Chicago, generally more intent on pleasure than business; but, nevertheless, I have a piece of business for you."

"The second Chicago?" asked Lecocq. "And where is that, pray?"

"Why, Paris, of course," said Speed.

Lecocq laughed.

"You are incorrigible, you Chicagoans. And what is the piece of business?"

"It is the old thing, monsieur. A mystery to be unravelled. Mr. Brenton here wishes to retain you in his case."

"And what is his case?" was the answer.

Lecocq was evidently pleased to have a bit of real work given him.

Speed briefly recited the facts, Brenton correcting him now and then on little points where he was wrong. Speed seemed to think these points immaterial, but Lecocq said that attention to trivialities was the whole secret of the detective business.

"Ah," said Lecocq, sorrowfully, "there is no real trouble in elucidating that mystery. I hoped it would be something difficult; but, you see, with my experience of the old world, and with the privileges one enjoys in this world, things which might be difficult to one below are very easy for us. Now, I shall show you how simple it is."

"Good gracious!" cried Speed, "you don't mean to say you are going to read it right off the reel, like that, when we have been bothering ourselves with it so long, and without success?"

"At the moment," replied the French detective, "I am not prepared to say who committed the deed. That is a matter of detail. Now, let us see what we know, and arrive, from that, at what we do not know. The one fact, of which we are assured on the statement of two physicians from Cincinnati, is that Mr. Brenton was poisoned."

"Well," said Speed, "there are several other facts, too. Another fact is that Mrs. Brenton is accused of the crime."

"Ah! my dear sir," said Lecocq, "that is not pertinent."

"No," said Speed, "I agree with you. I call it very impertinent."

Brenton frowned, at this, and his old dislike to the flippant Chicago man rose to the surface again.

The Frenchman continued marking the points on his long forefinger.

"Now, there are two ways by which that result may have been attained. First, Mr. Brenton may have administered to himself the poison; secondly, the poison may have been administered by some one else."

"Yes," said Speed; "and, thirdly, the poison may have been administered accidentally—you do not seem to take that into account."

"I do not take that into account," calmly replied the Frenchman, "because of its improbability. If there were an accident; if, for instance, the poison was in the sugar, or in some of the viands served, then others than Mr. Brenton would have been poisoned. The fact that one man out of twenty-six was poisoned, and the fact that several people are to benefit by his death, point, it seems to me, to murder; but to be sure of that, I will ask Mr. Brenton one question. My dear sir, did you administer this poison to yourself?"

"Certainly not," answered Brenton.

"Then we have two facts. First, Mr. Brenton was poisoned; secondly, he was poisoned by some person who had an interest in his death. Now we will proceed. When Mr. Brenton sat down to that dinner he was perfectly well. When he arose from that dinner he was feeling ill. He goes to bed. He sees no one but his wife after he has left the dinner-table, and he takes nothing between the time he leaves the dinner-table and the moment he becomes unconscious. Now, that poison must have been administered to Mr. Brenton at the dinner-table. Am I not right?"

"Well, you seem to be," answered Speed.

"Seem? Why, it is as plain as day. There cannot be any mistake."

"All right," said Speed; "go ahead. What next?"

"What next? There were twenty-six people around that table, with two servants to wait on them, making twenty-eight in all. There were twenty-six, I think you said, including Mr. Brenton."

"That is correct."

"Very well. One of those twenty-seven persons has poisoned Mr. Brenton. Do you follow me?"

"We do," answered Speed; "we follow you as closely as you have ever followed a criminal! Go on."

"Very well, so much is clear. These are all facts, not theories. Now, what is the thing that I should do if I were in Cincinnati? I would find out whether one or more of those guests had anything to gain by the death of their host. That done, I would follow the suspected persons. I would have my men find out what each of them had done for a month before the time of the crime. Whoever committed it made some preparation. He did something, too, as you say, in America, to cover up his tracks. Very well. By the keen detective these actions are easily traced. I shall at once place twenty-seven of the best men I know on the track of those twenty-seven persons."

"I call that shadowing with a vengeance," remarked the Chicago man.

"It will be very easy. The one who has committed the crime is certain, when he is alone in his own room, to say something, or to do something, that will show my detective that he is the criminal. So, gentlemen, if you can tell me who those twenty-seven persons are, in three days or a week from this time I will tell you who gave the poison to Mr. Brenton."

"You seem very sure of that," said Speed.

"Sure of it? It is simply child's play. It is mere waiting. If, for instance, at the trial Mrs. Brenton is found guilty, and sentenced, the one who is the guilty party is certain to betray himself or herself as soon as he or she is alone. If it be a man who hopes to marry Mrs. Brenton, he will be overcome with grief at what has happened. He will wring his hands and try to think what can be done to prevent the sentence being carried out. He will argue with himself whether it is better to give himself up and tell the truth, and if he is a coward he will conclude not to do that, but will try to get a pardon, or at least have the capital sentence commuted into life imprisonment. He will possibly be cool and calm in public, but when he enters his own room, when his door is locked, when he believes no one can see him, when he thinks he is alone, then will come his trial. Then his passions and his emotions will betray him. It is mere child's play, as I tell you, and long before there is a verdict I will give you the name of the murderer."

"Very well, then," said Speed, "that is agreed; we will look you up in a week from now."

"I should be pained," said Lecocq, "to put you to that trouble. As soon as I get the report from my men I will communicate with you and let you know the result. In a few days I shall give you the name of the assassin."

"Good-bye, then, until I see you again," answered Speed; and with this he and Brenton took their departure.

"He seems to be very sure of himself," said Brenton.

"He will do what he says, you may depend on that."

The week was not yet up when Monsieur Lecocq met John Speed in Chicago.

"By the look of satisfaction on your face," said Mr. Speed, "I imagine you have succeeded in unravelling the mystery."

"Ah," replied the Frenchman; "if I have the appearance of satisfaction, it is indeed misplaced."

"Then you have not made any discovery?"

"On the contrary, it is all as plain as your big buildings here. It is not for that reason, but because it is so simple that I should be foolish to feel satisfaction regarding it."

"Then who is the person?"

"The assassin," replied the Frenchman, "is one whom no one has seemed to think of, and yet one on whom suspicion should have been the first to fall. The person who did Monsieur Brenton the honour to poison him is none other than the servant girl, Jane Morton."

9

"Jane Morton!" cried Speed; "who is she?"

"She is, as you may remember, the girl who carried the coffee from Mrs. Brenton to monsieur."

"And are you sure she is the criminal?"

The great detective did not answer; he merely gave an expressive little French gesture, as though the question was not worth commenting upon.

"Why, what was her motive?" asked Speed.

For the first time in their acquaintance a shade of perplexity seemed to come over the enthusiastic face of the volatile Frenchman.

"You are what you call smart, you Chicago people," he said, "and you have in a moment struck the only point on which we are at a loss."

"My dear sir," returned Speed, "that is *the* point in the case. Motive is the first thing to look for, it seems to me. You said as much yourself. If you haven't succeeded in finding what motive Jane Morton had for poisoning her employer, it appears to me that very little has been accomplished."

"Ah, you say that before you know the particulars. I am certain we shall find the motive. What I know now is that Jane Morton is the one who put the poison in his cup of coffee."

"It would take a good deal of nerve to do that with twenty-six people around the table. You forget, my dear sir, that she had to pass the whole length of the table, after taking the cup, before giving it to Mr. Brenton."

"Half of the people had their backs to her, and the other half, I can assure you, were not looking at her. If the poison was ready, it was a very easy thing to slip it into a cup of coffee. There was ample time to do it, and that is how it was done."

"May I ask how you arrived at that conclusion?"

"Certainly, certainly, my dear sir. My detectives report that each one of the twenty-seven people they had to follow were shadowed night and day. But only two of them acted suspiciously. These two were Jane Morton and Stephen Roland. Stephen Roland's anxiety is accounted for by the fact that he is evidently in love with Mrs. Brenton. But the change in Jane Morton has been something terrible. She is suffering from the severest pangs of ineffectual remorse. She has not gone out again to service, but occupies a room in one of the poorer quarters of the city—a room that she never leaves except at night. Her whole actions show that she is afraid of the police—afraid of being tracked for her crime. She buys a newspaper every night, locks and bars the door on entering her room, and, with tears streaming from her eyes, reads every word of the criminal news. One night, when she went out to buy her paper, and what food she needed for the next day, she came unexpectedly upon a policeman at the corner. The man was not looking at her at all, nor for her, but she fled, running like a deer, doubling and turning through alleys and back streets until by a very roundabout road she reached her own room. There she locked herself in, and remained without food all next day rather than go out again. She flung herself terror-stricken on the bed, after her room door was bolted, and cried, 'Oh, why did I do it? why did I do it? I shall certainly be found out. If Mrs. Brenton is acquitted, they will be after me next day. I did it to make up to John what he had suffered, and yet if John knew it, he would never speak to me again.'"

"Who is John?" asked Speed.

"Ah, that," said the detective, "I do not know. When we find out who John is, then we shall find the motive for the crime."

"In that case, if I were you, I should try to find John as quickly as possible."

"Yes, my dear sir, that is exactly what should be done, and my detective is now endeavouring to discover the identity of John. He will possibly succeed in a few days. But there is another way of finding out who John is, and perhaps in that you can help me."

"What other way?"

"There is one man who undoubtedly knows who John is, and that is Mr. Brenton. Now, I thought that perhaps you, who know Brenton better than I do, would not mind asking him who John is."

"My dear sir," said Speed, "Brenton is no particular friend of mine, and I only know him well enough to feel that if there is any cross-examination to be done, I should prefer somebody else to do it."

"Why, you are not afraid of him, are you?" asked the detective.

"Afraid of him? Certainly not, but I tell you that Brenton is just a little touchy and apt to take offence. I have found him so on several occasions. Now, as you have practically taken charge of this case, why don't you go and see him?"

"I suppose I shall have to do that," said the Frenchman, "if you will not undertake it."

"No, I will not."

"You have no objection, have you, to going with me?"

"It is better for you to see Brenton alone. I do not think he would care to be cross-examined before witnesses, you know."

"Ah, then, good-bye; I shall find out from Mr. Brenton who John is."

"I am sure I wish you luck," replied Speed, as Lecocq took his departure.

Lecocq found Brenton and Ferris together. The cynical spirit seemed to have been rather sceptical about the accounts given him of the influence that Speed and Brenton, combined, had had upon the Chicago newspaper man. Yet he was interested in the case, and although he still maintained that no practical good would result, even if a channel of communication could be opened between the two states of existence, he had listened with his customary respect to what Brenton had to say.

"Ah," said Brenton, when he saw the Frenchman, "have you any news for me?"

"Yes, I have. I have news that I will exchange, but meanwhile I want some news from you."

"I have none to give you," answered Brenton.

"If you have not, will you undertake to answer any questions I shall ask you, and not take offence if the questions seem to be personal ones?"

"Certainly," said Brenton; "I shall be glad to answer anything as long as it has a bearing on the case."

"Very well, then, it has a very distinct bearing on the case. Do you remember the girl Jane Morton?"

"I remember her, of course, as one of the servants in our employ. I know very little about her, though."

"That is just what I wish to find out. Do you know *anything* about her?"

"No; she had been in our employ but a fortnight, I think, or perhaps it was a month. My wife attended to these details, of course. I knew the girl was there, that is all."

The Frenchman looked very dubious as Brenton said this, while the latter rather bridled up.

"You evidently do not believe me?" he cried.

Once more the detective gave his customary gesture, and said—

"Ah, pardon me, you are entirely mistaken. I have this to acquaint you with. Jane Morton is the one who murdered you. She did it, she says, partly for the sake of John, whoever he is, and partly out of revenge. Now, of course, you are the only man who can give me information as to the motive. That girl certainly had a motive, and I should like to find out what the motive was."

Brenton meditated for a few moments, and then suddenly brightened up.

"I remember, now, an incident which happened a week or two before Christmas, which may have a bearing on the case. One night I heard—or thought I heard—a movement downstairs, when I supposed everybody had retired. I took a revolver in my hand, and went cautiously down the stairs. Of course I had no light, because, if there was a burglar, I did not wish to make myself too conspicuous a mark. As I went along the hall leading to the kitchen, I saw there was a light inside; but as soon as they heard me coming the light was put out. When I reached the kitchen, I noticed a man trying to escape through the door that led to the coal-shed. I fired at him twice, and he sank to the floor with a groan. I thought I had bagged a burglar sure, but it turned out to be nothing of the kind. He was merely a young man who had been rather late visiting one of the girls. I suspect now the girl he came to see was Jane Morton. As it was, the noise brought the two girls there, and I never investigated the matter or tried to find out which one it was that he had been visiting. They were both terror-stricken, and the young man himself was in a state of great fear. He thought for a moment that he had been killed. However, he was only shot in the leg, and I sent him to the house of a physician who keeps such patients as do not wish to go to the hospital. I did not care to have him go to the hospital, because I was afraid the newspapers would get hold of the incident, and make a sensation of it. The whole thing was accidental; the young fellow realized that, and so, I thought, did the girls; at least, I never noticed anything in their behaviour to show the contrary."

"What sort of a looking girl is Jane Morton?" asked Ferris.

"She is a tall brunette, with snapping black eyes."

"Ah, then, I remember her going into the room where you lay," said Ferris, "on Christmas morning. It struck me when she came out that she was very cool and self-possessed, and not at all surprised."

"All I can say," said Brenton, "is that I never noticed anything in her conduct like resentment at what had happened. I intended to give the young fellow a handsome compensation for his injury, but of course what occurred on Christmas Eve prevented that: I had really forgotten all about the circumstance, or I should have told you of it before."

"Then," said Lecocq, "the thing now is perfectly clear. That black-eyed vixen murdered you out of revenge."

10

It was evident to George Stratton that he would have no time before the trial came off in which to prove Stephen Roland the guilty person. Besides this, he was in a strange state of mind which he himself could not understand. The moment he sat down to think out a plan by which he could run down the man he was confident had committed the crime, a strange wavering of mind came over him. Something seemed to say to him that he was on the wrong track. This became so persistent that George was bewildered, and seriously questioned his own sanity. Whenever he sat alone in his own room, the doubts arose and a feeling that he was on the wrong scent took possession of him. This feeling became so strong at times that he looked up other clues, and at one time tried to find out the whereabouts of the servant girls who had been employed by the Brentons. Curiously enough, the moment he began this search, his mind seemed to become clearer and easier; and when that happened, the old belief in the guilt of Stephen Roland resumed its sway again. But the instant he tried to follow up what clues he had in that direction, he found himself baffled and assailed again by doubts, and so every effort he put forth appeared to be nullified. This state of mind was so unusual with him that he had serious thoughts of abandoning the whole case and going back to Chicago. He said to himself, "I am in love with this woman and I shall go crazy if I stay here any longer." Then he remembered the trust she appeared to have in his powers of ferreting out the mystery of the case, and this in turn encouraged him and urged him on.

All trace of the girls appeared to be lost. He hesitated to employ a Cincinnati detective, fearing that what he discovered would be given away to the Cincinnati press. Then he accused himself of disloyalty to Mrs. Brenton, in putting his newspaper duty before his duty to her. He was so torn by his conflicting ideas and emotions that at last he resolved to abandon the case altogether and return to Chicago. He packed up his valise and resolved to leave that night for big city, trial or no trial. He had described his symptoms to a prominent physician, and that physician told him that the case was driving him mad, and the best thing he could do was to leave at once for other scenes. He could do no good, and would perhaps end by going insane himself.

As George Stratton was packing his valise in his room, alone, as he thought, the following conversation was taking place beside him.

"It is no use," said Speed; "we are merely muddling him, and not doing any good. The only thing is to leave him alone. If he investigates the Roland part of the case he will soon find out for himself that he is on the wrong track; then he will take the right one."

"Yes," said Brenton; "but the case comes on in a few days. If anything is to be done, it must be done now."

"In that I do not agree with you," said Speed. "Perhaps everything will go all right at the trial, but even if it does not, there is still a certain amount of time. You see how we have spoiled things by interfering. Our first success with him has misled us. We thought we could do anything; we have really done worse than nothing, because all this valuable time has been lost. If he had been allowed to proceed in his own way he would have ferreted out the matter as far as Stephen Roland is concerned, and would have found that there was no cause for his suspicion. As it is he has done nothing. He still believes, if left alone, that Stephen Roland is the criminal. All our efforts to lead him to the residence of Jane Morton have been unavailing. Now, you see, he is on the eve of going back to Chicago."

"Well, then, let him go," said Brenton, despondently.

"With all my heart, say I," answered Speed; "but in any case let us leave him alone."

Before the train started that night Stratton said to himself that he was a new man. Richard was himself again. He was thoroughly convinced of the guilt of Stephen Roland, and wondered why he had allowed his mind to wander off the topic and waste time with other suspicions, for which he now saw there was no real excuse. He had not the time, he felt, to investigate the subject personally, but he flattered himself he knew exactly the man to put on Roland's track, and, instead of going himself to Chicago, he sent off the following despatch:—

"Meet me to-morrow morning, without fail, at the Gibson House. Answer."

Before midnight he had his answer, and next morning he met a man in whom he had the most implicit confidence, and who had, as he said, the rare and valuable gift of keeping his mouth shut.

"You see this portrait?" Stratton said, handing to the other a photograph of Stephen Roland. "Now, I do not know how many hundred chemist shops there are in Cincinnati, but I want you to get a list of them, and you must not omit the most obscure shop in town. I want you to visit every drug store there is in the city, show this photograph to the proprietor and the clerks, and find out if that man bought any chemicals during the week or two preceding Christmas. Find out what drugs he bought, and where he bought them, then bring the information to me."

"How much time do you give me on this, Mr. Stratton?" was the question.

"Whatever time you want. I wish the thing done thoroughly and completely, and, as you know, silence is golden in a case like this."

"Enough said," replied the other, and, buttoning the photograph in his inside pocket, he left the room.

There is no necessity of giving an elaborate report of the trial. Any one who has curiosity in the matter can find the full particulars from the files of any paper in the country. Mrs. Brenton was very pale as she sat in the prisoner's dock, but George Stratton thought he never saw any one look so beautiful. It seemed to him that any man in that crowded courtroom could tell in a moment that she was not guilty of the crime with which she was charged, and he looked at the jury of twelve supposedly good men, and wondered what they thought of it.

The defence claimed that it was not their place to show who committed the murder. That rested with the prosecution. The prosecution, Mr. Benham maintained, had signally failed to do this. However, in order to aid the prosecution, he was quite willing to show how Mr. Brenton came to his death. Then witnesses were called, who, to the astonishment of Mrs. Brenton, testified that her husband had all along had a tendency to insanity. It was proved conclusively that some of his ancestors had died in a lunatic asylum, and one was stated to have committed suicide. The defence produced certain books from Mr. Brenton's library, among them Forbes Winslow's volume on "The Mind and the Brain," to show that Brenton had studied the subject of suicide.

The judge's charge was very colourless. It amounted simply to this: If the jury thought the prosecution had shown Mrs. Brenton to have committed the crime, they were to bring in a verdict of guilty, and if they thought otherwise they were to acquit her; and so the jury retired.

As they left the court-room a certain gloom fell upon all those who were friendly to the fair prisoner.

Despite the great reputation of Benham and Brown, it was the thought of every one present that they had made a very poor defence. The prosecution, on the other hand, had been most ably conducted. It had been shown that Mrs. Brenton was chiefly to profit by her husband's death. The insurance fund alone would add seventy-five thousand dollars to the money she would control. A number of little points that Stratton had given no heed to had been magnified, and appeared then to have a great bearing on the case. For the first time, Stratton admitted to himself that the prosecution had made out a very strong case of circumstantial evidence. The defence, too, had been so deplorably weak that it added really to the strength of the prosecution. A great speech had been expected of Benham, but he did not rise to the occasion, and, as one who knew him said, Benham evidently believed his client guilty.

As the jury retired, every one in the court-room felt that there was little hope for the prisoner; and this feeling was intensified when, a few moments after, the announcement was made in court, just as the judge was preparing to leave the bench, that the jury had agreed on the verdict.

Stratton, in the stillness of the court-room, heard one lawyer whisper to another, "She's doomed."

There was intense silence as the jury slowly filed into their places, and the foreman stood up.

"Gentlemen of the jury," was the question, "have you agreed upon a verdict?"

"We have," answered the foreman.

"Do you find the prisoner guilty or not guilty?"

"Not guilty," was the clear answer.

At this there was first a moment of silence, and then a ripple of applause, promptly checked.

Mrs. Brenton was free.

11

George Stratton sat in the court-room for a moment dazed, before he thought of the principal figure in the trial; then he rose to go to her side, but he found that Roland was there before him. He heard her say, "Get me a carriage quickly, and take me away from here."

So Stratton went back to his hotel to meet his Chicago detective. The latter had nothing to report. He told him the number of drug stores he had visited, but all without avail. No one had recognized the portrait.

"All right," said Stratton; "then you will just have to go ahead until you find somebody who does. It is, I believe, only a question of time and perseverance."

Next morning he arose late. He looked over the report of the trial in the morning paper, and then, turning to the leader page, read with rising indignation the following editorial:—

"THE BRENTON CASE.

"The decision of yesterday shows the glorious uncertainty that attends the finding of the average American jury. If such verdicts are to be rendered, we may as well blot out from the statute-book all punishment for all crimes in which the evidence is largely circumstantial. If ever a strong case was made out against a human being it was the case of the prosecution in the recent trial. If ever there was a case in which the defence was deplorably weak, although ably conducted, it was the case that was concluded yesterday. Should we, then, be prepared to say that circumstantial evidence will not be taken by an American jury as ground for the conviction of a murderer? The chances are that, if we draw this conclusion, we shall be entirely wrong. If a man stood in the dock, in the place of the handsome young woman who occupied it yesterday, he would to-day have been undoubtedly convicted of murder. The conclusion, then, to be arrived at seems to be that, unless there is the direct proof of murder against a pretty woman, it is absolutely impossible to get the average jury of men to convict her. It would seem that the sooner we get women on juries, especially where a woman is on trial, the better it will be for the cause of justice."

Then in other parts of the paper there were little items similar to this—

"If Mrs. Brenton did not poison her husband, then who did?"

That afternoon George Stratton paid a visit to Mrs. Brenton. He had hoped she had not seen the paper in question, but he hoped in vain. He found Mrs. Brenton far from elated with her acquittal.

"I would give everything I possess," she said, "to bring the culprit to justice."

After a talk on that momentous question, and when George Stratton held her hand and said good-bye, she asked him—

"When do you go to Chicago?"

"Madam," he said, "I leave for Chicago the moment I find out who poisoned William Brenton."

She answered sadly—

"You may remain a long time in Cincinnati."

"In some respects," said Stratton, "I like Cincinnati better than Chicago."

"You are the first Chicago man I ever heard say that," she replied.

"Ah, that was because they did not know Cincinnati as I do."

"I suppose you must have seen a great deal of the town, but I must confess that from now on I should be very glad if I never saw Cincinnati again. I would like to consult with you," she continued, "about the best way of solving this mystery. I have been thinking of engaging some of the best detectives I can get. I suppose New York would be the place."

"No; Chicago," answered the young man.

"Well, then, that is what I wanted to see you about. I would like to get the very best detectives that can be had. Don't you think that, if they were promised ample reward, and paid well during the time they were working on the case, we might discover the key to this mystery?"

"I do not think much of our detective system," answered Stratton, "although I suppose there is something in it, and sometimes they manage in spite of themselves to stumble on the solution of a crime. Still, I shall be very glad indeed to give you what advice I can on the subject. I may say I have constituted myself a special detective in this case, and that I hope to have the honour of solving the problem."

"You are very good, indeed," she answered, "and I must ask you to let me bear the expense."

"Oh, the paper will do that. I won't be out of pocket at all," said Stratton.

"Well, I hardly know how to put it; but, whether you are successful or not, I feel very grateful to you, and I hope you will not be offended at what I am going to say. Now, promise me that you won't!"

"I shall not be offended," he answered. "It is a little difficult to offend a Chicago newspaper man, you know."

"Now, you mustn't say anything against the newspaper men, for, in spite of the hard things that some of them have said about me, I like them."

"Individually or collectively?"

"I am afraid I must say individually. You said you wouldn't be offended, so after your search is over you must let me—. The labourer is worthy of his hire, or I should say, his reward—you know what I mean. I presume that a young man who earns his living on the daily press is not necessarily wealthy."

"Why, Mrs. Brenton, what strange ideas you have of the world! We newspaper men work at the business merely because we like it. It isn't at all for the money that's in it."

"Then you are not offended at what I have said?"

"Oh, not in the least. I may say, however, that I look for a higher reward than money if I am successful in this search."

"Yes, I am sure you do," answered the lady, innocently. "If you succeed in this, you will be very famous."

"Exactly; it's fame I'm after," said Stratton, shaking her hand once more, and taking his leave.

When he reached his hotel, he found the Chicago detective waiting for him.

"Well, old man," he said, "anything new?"

"Yes, sir. Something very new."

"What have you found out?"

"Everything."

"Very well, let me have it."

"I found out that this man bought, on December 10th, thirty grains of morphia. He had this morphia put up in five-grain capsules. He bought this at the drug store on the corner of Blank Street and Nemo Avenue."

"Good gracious!" answered Stratton. "Then to get morphia he must have had a physician's certificate. Did you find who the physician was that signed the certificate?"

"My dear sir," said the Chicago man, "this person is himself a physician, unless I am very much mistaken. I was told that this was the portrait of Stephen Roland. Am I right?"

"That is the name."

"Well, then, he is a doctor himself. Not doing a very large practice, it is true, but he is a physician. Did you not know that?"

"No," said Stratton; "how stupid I am! I never thought of asking the man's occupation."

"Very well, if that is what you wanted to know, here's the detailed report of my investigation."

When the man left, Stratton rubbed his hands.

"Now, Mr. Stephen Roland, I have you," he said.

12

After receiving this information Stratton sat alone in his room and thought deeply over his plans. He did not wish to make a false step, yet there was hardly enough in the evidence he had secured to warrant his giving Stephen Roland up to the police. Besides this, it would put the suspected man at once on his guard, and there was no question but that gentleman had taken every precaution to prevent discovery. After deliberating for a long while, he thought that perhaps the best thing he could do was to endeavour to take Roland by surprise. Meanwhile, before the meditating man stood Brenton and Speed, and between them there was a serious disagreement of opinion.

"I tell you what it is," said Speed, "there is no use in our interfering with Stratton. He is on the wrong track, but, nevertheless, all the influence we can use on him in his present frame of mind will merely do what it did before—it will muddle the man up. Now, I propose that we leave him severely alone. Let him find out his mistake. He will find it out in some way or other, and then he will be in a condition of mind to turn to the case of Jane Morton."

"But don't you see," argued Brenton, "that all the time spent on his present investigation is so much time lost? I will agree to leave him alone, as you say, but let us get somebody else on the Morton case."

"I don't want to do that," said Speed; "because George Stratton has taken a great deal of interest in this search. He has done a great deal now, and I think we should he grateful to him for it."

"Grateful!" growled Brenton; "he has done it from the most purely selfish motives that a man can act upon. He has done it entirely for his paper—for newspaper fame. He has done it for money."

"Now," said Speed, hotly, "you must not talk like that of Stratton to me. I won't say what I think of that kind of language coming from you, but you can see how seriously we interfered with his work before, and how it nearly resulted in his departure for Chicago. I propose now that we leave him alone."

"Leave him alone, then, for any sake," replied Brenton; "I am sure I build nothing on what he can do anyway."

"All right, then," returned Speed, recovering his good nature. "Now, although I am not willing to put any one else on the track of Miss Jane Morton, yet I will tell you what I am willing to do. If you like, we will go to her residence, and influence her to confess her crime. I believe that can be done."

"Very well; I want you to understand that I am perfectly reasonable about the matter. All I want is not to lose any more time."

"Time?" cried Speed; "why, we have got all the time there is. Mrs. Brenton is acquitted. There is no more danger."

"That is perfectly true, I admit; but still you can see the grief under which she labours, because her name is not yet cleared from the odium of the crime. You will excuse me, Speed, if I say that you seem to be working more in the interests of Stratton's journalistic success than in the interests of Mrs. Brenton's good name."

"Well, we won't talk about that," said Speed; "Stratton is amply able to take care of himself, as you will doubtless see. Now, what do you say to our trying whether or not we can influence Jane Morton to do what she ought to do, and confess her crime?"

"It is not a very promising task," replied Brenton; "it is hard to get a person to say words that may lead to the gallows."

"I'm not so sure about that," said Speed; "you know the trouble of mind she is in. I think it more than probable that, after the terror of the last few weeks, it will be a relief for her to give herself up."

"Very well; let us go."

The two men shortly afterwards found themselves in the scantily furnished room occupied by Jane Morton. That poor woman was rocking herself to and fro and moaning over her trouble. Then she suddenly stopped rocking, and looked around the room with vague apprehension in her eyes. She rose and examined the bolts of the door, and, seeing everything was secure, sat down again.

"I shall never have any peace in this world again," she cried to herself.

She rocked back and forth silently for a few moments.

"I wish," she said, "the police would find out all about it, and then this agony of mind would end."

Again she rocked back and forth, with her hands helplessly in her lap.

"Oh, I cannot do it, *I cannot do it!*" she sobbed, still rocking to and fro. Finally she started to her feet.

"I *will* do it," she cried; "I will confess to Mrs. Brenton herself. I will tell her everything. She has gone through trouble herself, and may have mercy on me."

"There, you see," said Speed to Brenton, "we have overcome the difficulty, after all."

"It certainly looks like it," replied Brenton. "Don't you think, however, that we had better stay with her until she *does* confess? May she not change her mind?"

"Don't let us overdo the thing," suggested Speed; "if she doesn't, come to time, we can easily have another interview with her. The woman's mind is made up. She is in torment, and will be until she confesses her crime. Let us go and leave her alone."

George Stratton was not slow to act when he had once made up his mind. He pinned to the breast of his vest a little shield, on which was the word "detective." This he had often found useful, in a way that is not at all sanctioned by the law, in ferreting out crime in Chicago. As soon as it was evening he paced up and down in front of Roland's house, and on the opposite side of the road. There was a light in the doctor's study, and he thought that perhaps the best way to proceed was to go boldly into the house and put his scheme into operation. However, as he meditated on this, the light was turned low, and in a few moments the door opened. The doctor came down the steps, and out on the pavement, walking briskly along the street. The reporter followed him on the other side of the thoroughfare. Whether to do it in the dark or in the light, was the question that troubled Stratton. If he did it in the dark, he would miss the expression on the face of the surprised man. If he did it in the light, the doctor might recognize him as the Chicago reporter, and would know at once that he was no detective. Still, he felt that if there was anything in his scheme at all, it was surprise; and he remembered the quick gasp of the lawyer Brown when he told him he knew what his defence was. He must be able to note the expression of the man who was guilty of the terrible crime.

Having made up his mind to this, he stepped smartly after the doctor, and, when the latter came under a lamp-post, placed his hand suddenly on his shoulder, and exclaimed—

"Doctor Stephen Roland, I arrest you for the murder of William Brenton!"

13

Stephen Roland turned quietly around and shook the hand from his shoulder. It was evident that he recognized Stratton instantly.

"Is this a Chicago joke?" asked the doctor.

"If it is, Mr. Roland, I think you will find it a very serious one."

"Aren't you afraid that *you* may find it a serious one?"

"I don't see why I should have any fears in the premises," answered the newspaper man.

"My dear sir, do you not realize that I could knock you down or shoot you dead for what you have done, and be perfectly justified in doing so?"

"If you either knock or shoot," replied the other, "you will have to do it very quickly, for, in the language of the wild and woolly West, I've got the drop on you. In my coat pocket is a cocked revolver with my forefinger on the trigger. If you make a hostile move I can let daylight through you so quickly that you won't know what has struck you."

"Electric light, I think you mean," answered the doctor, quietly. "Even a Chicago man might find it difficult to let daylight through a person at this time in the evening. Now, this sort of thing may be Chicago manners, but I assure you it will not go down here in Cincinnati. You have rendered yourself liable to the law if I cared to make a point of it, but I do not. Come back with me to my study. I would like to talk with you."

Stratton began to feel vaguely that he had made a fool of himself. His scheme had utterly failed. The doctor was a great deal

cooler and more collected than he was. Nevertheless, he had a deep
distrust of the gentleman, and he kept his revolver handy for fear
the other would make a dash to escape him. They walked back without saying a word to each other until they came to the doctor's
office. Into the house they entered, and the doctor bolted the door
behind them. Stratton suspected that very likely he was walking
into a trap, but he thought he would be equal to any emergency
that might arise. The doctor walked into the study, and again locked
the door of that. Pulling down the blinds, he turned up the gas to
its full force and sat down by a table, motioning the newspaper
man to a seat on the other side.

"Now," he said calmly to Stratton, "the reason I did not resent
your unwarrantable insult is this: You are conscientiously trying
to get at the root of this mystery. So am I. Your reason is that you
wish to score a victory for your paper. My motive is entirely different, but our object is exactly the same. Now, by some strange
combination of circumstances you have come to the conclusion that
I committed the crime. Am I right?"

"You are perfectly correct, doctor," replied Stratton.

"Very well, then. Now, I assure you that I am entirely innocent. Of course, I appreciate the fact that this assurance will not in
the slightest degree affect your opinion, but I am interested in
knowing why you came to your conclusion, and perhaps by putting our heads together, even if I dislike you and you hate me, we
may see some light on this matter that has hitherto been hidden. I
presume you have no objection at all to co-operate with me?"

"None in the least," was the reply.

"Very well, then. Now, don't mind my feelings at all, but tell
me exactly why you have suspected me of being a murderer."

"Well," answered Stratton, "in the first place we must look for
a motive. It seems to me that you have a motive for the crime."

"And might I ask what that motive is, or was?"

"You will admit that you disliked Brenton?"

"I will admit that, yes."

"Very well. You will admit also that you were—well, how shall I
put it?—let us say, interested in his wife before her marriage?"

"I will admit that; yes."

"You, perhaps, will admit that you are interested in her now?"

"I do not see any necessity for admitting that; but still, for the purpose of getting along with the case, I will admit it. Go on."

"Very good. Here is a motive for the crime, and a very strong one. First, we will presume that you are in love with the wife of the man who is murdered. Secondly, supposing that you are mercenary, quite a considerable amount of money will come to you in case you marry Brenton's widow. Next, some one at that table poisoned him. It was not Mrs. Brenton, who poured out the cup of coffee. The cup of coffee was placed before Brenton, and my opinion is that, until it was placed there, there was no poison in that cup. The doomed man was entirely unsuspicious, and therefore it was very easy for a person to slip enough poison in that cup unseen by anybody at that table, so that when he drank his coffee nothing could have saved him. He rose from the table feeling badly, and he went to his room and died. Now, who could have placed that poison in his cup of coffee? It must have been one of the two that sat at his right and left hand. A young lady sat at his right hand. She certainly did not commit the crime. You, Stephen Roland, sat at his left hand. Do you deny any of the facts I have recited?"

"That is a very ingenious chain of circumstantial evidence. Of course, you do not think it strong enough to convict a man of such a serious crime as murder?"

"No; I quite realize the weakness of the case up to this point. But there is more to follow. Fourteen days before that dinner you purchased at the drug store on the corner of Blank Street and Nemo Avenue thirty grains of morphia. You had the poison put up in capsules of five grains each. What do you say to that bit of evidence added to the circumstantial chain which you say is ingenious?"

The doctor knit his brows and leaned back in his chair.

"By the gods!" he said, "you are right. I did buy that morphia. I remember it now. I don't mind telling you that I had a number of experiments on hand, as every doctor has, and I had those capsules put up at the drug store, but this tragedy coming on made me forget all about the matter."

"Did you take the morphia with you, doctor?"

"No, I did not. And the box of capsules, I do not think, has been opened. But that is easily ascertained."

The doctor rose, went to his cabinet, and unlocked it. From a number of packages he selected a small one, and brought it to the desk, placing it before the reporter.

"There is the package. That contains, as you say, thirty grains of morphia in half a dozen five-grain capsules. You see that it is sealed just as it left the drug store. Now, open it and look for yourself. Here are scales; if you want to see whether a single grain is missing or not, find out for yourself.

"Perhaps," said the newspaper man, "we had better leave this investigation for the proper authorities."

"Then you still believe that I am the murderer of William Brenton?"

"Yes, I still believe that."

"Very well; you may do as you please. I think, however, in justice to myself, you should stay right here, and see that this box is not tampered with until the proper authorities, as you say, come."

Then, placing his hand on the bell, he continued—"Whom shall I send for? An ordinary policeman, or some one from the central office? But, now that I think of it, here is a telephone. We can have any one brought here that you wish. I prefer that neither you nor I leave this room until that functionary has appeared. Name the authority you want brought here," said the doctor, going to the telephone, "and I will have him here if he is in town."

The newspaper man was nonplussed. The Doctor's actions did not seem like those of a guilty man. If he were guilty he certainly had more nerve than any person Stratton had ever met. So he hesitated. Then he said—

"Sit down a moment, doctor, and let us talk this thing over."

"Just as you say," remarked Roland, drawing up his chair again.

Stratton took the package, and looked it over carefully. It was certainly just in the condition in which it had left the drug store; but still, that could have been easily done by the doctor himself.

"Suppose we open this package?" he said to Roland.

"With all my heart," said the doctor, "go ahead;" and he shoved over to him a little penknife that was on the table.

The reporter took the package, ran the knife around the edge, and opened it. There lay six capsules, filled, as the doctor had said. Roland picked up one of them, and looked at it critically.

"I assure you," he said, "although I am quite aware you do not believe a word I say, that I have not seen those capsules before."

He drew towards him a piece of paper, opened the capsule, and, let the white powder fall on the paper. He looked critically at the powder, and a shade of astonishment came over his face. He picked up the penknife, took a particle on the tip of it, and touched it with his tongue.

"Don't fool with that thing!" said Stratton.

"Oh, my dear fellow," he said, "morphia is not a poison in small quantities."

The moment he had tasted it, however, he suddenly picked up the paper, put the five grains on his tongue, and swallowed them.

Instantly the reporter sprang to his feet. He saw at once the reason for all the assumed coolness. The doctor was merely gaining time in order to commit suicide.

"What have you done?" cried the reporter.

"Done, my dear fellow? nothing very much. This is not morphia; it is sulphate of quinine."

14

In the morning Jane Morton prepared to meet Mrs. Brenton, and make her confession. She called at the Brenton residence, but found it closed, as it had been ever since the tragedy of Christmas morning. It took her some time to discover the whereabouts of Mrs. Brenton, who, since the murder, had resided with a friend except while under arrest.

For a moment Mrs. Brenton did not recognize the thin and pale woman who stood before her in a state of such extreme nervous agitation, that it seemed as if at any moment she might break down and cry.

"I don't suppose you'll remember me, ma'am," began the girl, "but I worked for you two weeks before—before—"

"Oh yes," said Mrs. Brenton, "I remember you now. Have you been ill? You look quite worn and pale, and very different from what you did the last time I saw you."

"Yes," said the girl, "I believe I have been ill."

"You *believe*; aren't you sure?"

"I have been very ill in mind, and troubled, and that is the reason I look so badly,—Oh, Mrs. Brenton, I wanted to tell you of something that has been weighing on my mind ever since that awful day! I know you can never forgive me, but I must tell it to you, or I shall go crazy."

"Sit down, sit down," said the lady, kindly; "you know what trouble I have been in myself. I am sure that I am more able to sympathize now with one who is in trouble than ever I was before."

"Yes, ma'am; but you were innocent, and I am guilty. That makes all the difference in the world."

"Guilty!" cried Mrs. Brenton, a strange fear coming over her as she stared at the girl; "guilty of *what*?"

"Oh, madam, let me tell you all about it. There is, of course, no excuse; but I'll begin at the beginning. You remember a while before Christmas that John came to see me one night, and we sat up very late in the kitchen, and your husband came down quietly, and when we heard him coming we put out the light and just as John was trying to get away, your husband shot twice at him, and hit him the second time?"

"Oh yes," said Mrs. Brenton, "I remember that very well. I had forgotten about it in my own trouble; but I know that my husband intended to do something for the young man. I hope he was not seriously hurt?"

"No, ma'am; he is able to be about again now as well as ever, and is not even lame, which we expected he would be. But at the time I thought he was going to be lame all the rest of his life, and perhaps that is the reason I did what I did. When everything was in confusion in the house, and it was certain that we would all have to leave, I did a very wicked thing. I went to your room, and I stole some of your rings, and some money that was there, as well as a lot of other things that were in the room. It seemed to me then, although, of course, I know now how wicked it was, that you owed John something for what he had gone through, and I thought that he was to be lame, and that you would never miss the things; but, oh! madam, I have not slept a night since I took them. I have been afraid of the police and afraid of being found out. I have pawned nothing, and they are all just as I took them, and I have brought them back here to you, with every penny of the money. I know you can never forgive me, but I am willing now to be given up to the police, and I feel better in my mind than I have done ever since I took the things."

"My poor child!" said Mrs. Brenton, sympathetically, "was that *all*?"

"All?" cried the girl. "Yes, I have brought everything back."

"Oh, I don't mean that, but I am sorry you have been worried over anything so trivial. I can see how at such a time, and feeling that you had been wronged, a temptation to take the things came to you. But I hope you will not trouble any more about the matter. I will see that John is compensated for all the injury he received, as far as it is possible for money to compensate him. I hope you will keep the money. The other things, of course, I shall take back, and I am glad you came to tell me of it before telling any one else. I think, perhaps, it is better never to say anything to anybody about this. People might not understand just what temptation you were put to, and they would not know the circumstances of the case, because nobody knows, I think, that John was hurt. Now, my dear girl, do not cry. It is all right. Of course you never will touch anything again that does not belong to you, and the suffering you have gone through has more than made up for all the wrong you have done. I am sure that I forgive you quite freely for it, and I think it was very noble of you to come and tell me about it."

Mrs. Brenton took the package from the hands of the weeping girl, and opened it. She found everything there, as the girl had said. She took the money and offered it to Jane Morton. The girl shook her head.

"No," she cried, "I cannot touch it. I cannot, indeed. It has been enough misery to me already."

"Very well," said Mrs. Brenton. "I would like very much to see John. Will you bring him to me?"

The girl looked at her with startled eyes.

"You will not tell him?" she said.

"No indeed, I shall tell him nothing. But I want to do what I can for him as I said. I suppose you are engaged to be married?"

"Yes," answered the girl; "but if he knew of this he never, never would marry me."

"If he did not," said Mrs. Brenton, "he would not be worthy of you. But he shall know nothing about it. You will promise to come here and see me with him, will you not?"

"Yes, madam," said the girl.

"Then good-bye, until I see you again."

Mrs. Brenton sat for a long time thinking over this confession. It took her some time to recover her usual self-possession, because for a moment she had thought the girl was going to confess that she committed murder. In comparison with that awful crime, the theft seemed so trivial that Mrs. Brenton almost smiled when she thought of the girl's distress.

"Well," said John Speed to Mr. Brenton, "if that doesn't beat the Old Harry. Now I, for one, am very glad of it, if we come to the real truth of the matter."

"I am glad also," said Brenton, "that the girl is not guilty, although I must say things looked decidedly against her."

"I will tell you why I am glad," said Speed. "I am glad because it will take some of the superfluous conceit out of that French detective Lecocq. He was so awfully sure of himself. He couldn't possibly be mistaken. Now, think of the mistakes that man must have made while he was on earth, and had the power which was given into his hands in Paris. After all, Stratton is on the right track, and he will yet land your friend Roland in prison. Let us go and find Lecocq. This is too good to keep."

"My dear sir," said Brenton, "you seem to be more elated because of your friend Stratton than for any other reason. Don't you want the matter ferreted out at all?"

"Why, certainly I do; but I don't want it ferreted out by bringing an innocent person into trouble."

"And may not Stephen Roland be an innocent person?"

"Oh, I suppose so; but I do not think he is."

"Why do you not think so?"

"Well, if you want the real reason, simply because George Stratton thinks he isn't. I pin my faith to Stratton."

"I think you overrate your friend Stratton."

"Overrate him, sir? That is impossible. I love him so well that I hope he will solve this mystery himself, unaided and alone, and that in going back to Chicago he will be smashed to pieces in a railway accident, so that we can have him here to congratulate him."

15

"I suppose," said Roland, "you thought for a moment I was trying to commit suicide. I think, Mr. Stratton, you will have a better opinion of me by-and-by. I shouldn't be at all surprised if you imagined I induced you to come in here to get you into a trap."

"You are perfectly correct," said Stratton; "and I may say, although that was my belief, I was not in the least afraid of you, for I had you covered all the time."

"Well," remarked Roland, carelessly, "I don't want to interfere with your business at all, but I wish you wouldn't cover me quite so much; that revolver of yours might go off."

"Do you mean to say," said Stratton, "that there is nothing but quinine in those capsules?"

"I'll tell you in a moment," as he opened them one by one. "No, there is nothing but quinine here. Thirty grains put up in five-grain capsules."

George Stratton's eyes began to open. Then he slowly rose, and looked with horrified face at the doctor.

"My God!" he cried; "who got the thirty grains of morphia?"

"What do you mean?" asked the doctor.

"Mean? Why, don't you see it? It is a chemist's mistake. Thirty grains of quinine have been sent you. Thirty grains of morphia have been sent to somebody else. Was it to William Brenton?"

"By Jove!" said the doctor, "there's something in that. Say, let us go to the drug store."

The two went out together, and walked to the drug store on the corner of Blank Street and Nemo Avenue.

"Do you know this writing?" said Doctor Roland to the druggist, pointing to the label on the box.

"Yes," answered the druggist; "that was written by one of my assistants."

"Can we see him for a few moments?"

"I don't know where he is to be found. He is a worthless fellow, and has gone to the devil this last few weeks with a rapidity that is something startling."

"When did he leave?"

"Well, he got drunk and stayed drunk during the holidays, and I had to discharge him. He was a very valuable man when he was sober; but he began to be so erratic in his habits that I was afraid he would make a ghastly mistake some time, so I discharged him before it was too late."

"Are you sure you discharged him before it was too late?"

The druggist looked at the doctor, whom he knew well, and said, "I never heard of any mistake, if he did make it."

"You keep a book, of course, of all the prescriptions sent out?"

"Certainly."

"May we look at that book?"

"I shall be very glad to show it to you. What month or week?"

"I want to see what time you sent this box of morphia to me."

"You don't know about what time it was, do you?

"Yes; it must have been about two weeks before Christmas."

The chemist looked over the pages of the book, and finally said, "Here it is."

"Will you let me look at that page?"

"Certainly."

The doctor ran his finger down the column, and came to an entry written in the same hand.

"Look here," he said to Stratton, "thirty grains of quinine sent to William Brenton, and next to it thirty grains of morphia sent to Stephen Roland. I see how it was. Those prescriptions were mixed up. My package went to poor Brenton."

The druggist turned pale.

"I hope," he said, "nothing public will come of this."

"My dear sir," said Roland, "something public will *have* to come of it. You will oblige me by ringing up the central police station, as this book must be given in charge of the authorities."

"Look here," put in Stratton, his newspaper instinct coming uppermost, "I want to get this thing exclusively for the *Argus*."

"Oh, I guess there will be no trouble about that. Nothing will be made public until to-morrow, and you can telegraph to-night if we find the box of capsules in Brenton's residence. We must take an officer with us for that purpose, but you can caution or bribe him to keep quiet until to-morrow."

When the three went to William Brenton's residence they began a search of the room in which Brenton had died, but nothing was found. In the closet of the room hung the clothes of Brenton, and going through them Stratton found in the vest pocket of one of the suits a small box containing what was described as five-grain capsules of sulphate of quinine. The doctor tore one of these capsules apart, so as to see what was in it. Without a moment's hesitation he said—

"There you are! That is the morphia. There were six capsules in this box, and one of them is missing. William Brenton poisoned himself! Feeling ill, he doubtless took what he thought was a dose of quinine. Many men indulge in what we call the quinine habit. It is getting to be a mild form of tippling. Brenton committed unconscious suicide!"

16

A group of men, who were really alive, but invisible to the searchers, stood in the room where the discovery was made. Two of the number were evidently angry, one in one way and one in another. The rest of the group appeared to be very merry. One angry man was Brenton himself, who was sullenly enraged. The other was the Frenchman, Lecocq, who was as deeply angered as Brenton, but, instead of being sullen, was exceedingly voluble.

"I tell you," he cried, "it is not a mistake of mine. I went on correct principles from the first. I was misled by one who should have known better. You will remember, gentlemen," he continued, turning first to one and then the other, "that what I said was that we had certain facts to go on. One of those facts I got from Mr. Brenton. I said to him in your presence, 'Did you poison yourself?' He answered me, as I can prove by all of you, 'No, I did not.' I took that for a fact. I thought I was speaking to a reasonable man who knew what he was talking about."

"Haven't I told you time and again," answered Brenton, indignantly, "that it was a mistake? You asked me if I poisoned myself. I answered you that I did not. Your question related to suicide. I did *not* commit suicide. I was the victim of a druggist's mistake. If you had asked me if I had taken medicine before I went to bed, I should have told you frankly, 'Yes. I took one capsule of quinine.' It has been my habit for years, when I feel badly. I thought nothing of that."

"My dear sir," said Lecocq, "I warned you, and I warned these gentlemen, that the very things that seem trivial to a thoughtless person are the things that sometimes count. You should have told me *everything*. If you took anything at all, you should have said so. If you had said to me, 'Monsieur Lecocq, before I retired I took five grains of quinine,' I should have at once said; 'Find where that quinine is, and see if it *is* quinine, and see if there has not been a mistake.' I was entirely misled; I was stupidly misled."

"Well, if there was stupidity," returned Brenton, "it was your own."

"Come, come, gentlemen," laughed Speed, "all's well that ends well. Everybody has been mistaken, that's all about it. The best detective minds of Europe and America, of the world, and of the spirit-land, have been misled. You are *all* wrong. Admit it, and let it end."

"My dear sir," said Lecocq, "I shall not admit anything. I was not wrong; I was misled. It was this way—"

"Oh, now, for goodness' sake don't go over it all again. We understand the circumstances well enough."

"I tell you," cried Brenton, in an angry tone, "that—"

"Come, come," said Speed, "we have had enough of this discussion. I tell you that you are all wrong, every one of you. Come with me, Brenton, and we will leave this amusing crowd."

"I shall do nothing of the kind," answered Brenton, shortly.

"Oh, very well then, do as you please. I am glad the thing is ended, and I am glad it is ended by my Chicago friend."

"Your Chicago friend!" sneered Brenton, slightingly; "It was discovered by Doctor Stephen Roland."

"My dear fellow," said Speed, "Stephen Roland had all his time to discover the thing, and didn't do it, and never would have done it, if George Stratton hadn't encountered him. Well, good-bye, gentlemen; I am sorry to say that I have had quite enough of this discussion. But one thing looms up above it all, and that is that Chicago is ahead of the world in everything—in detection as well as in fires."

"My dear sir," cried Lecocq, "it is not true. I will show you in a moment—"

"You won't show *me*," said Speed, and he straightway disappeared.

"Come, Ferris," said Brenton, "after all, you are the only friend I seem to have; come with me."

"Where are you going?" asked Ferris, as they left.

"I want to see how my wife takes the news."

"Don't," said Mr. Ferris—"don't do anything of the kind. Leave matters just where they are. Everything has turned out what you would call all right. You see that your interference, as far as it went, was perfectly futile and useless. I want now to draw your attention to other things."

"Very well, I will listen to you," said Brenton, "if you come with me and see how my wife takes the news. I want to enjoy for even a moment or two her relief and pleasure at finding that her good name is clear."

"Very well," assented Ferris, "I will go with you."

When they arrived they found the Chicago reporter ahead of them. He had evidently told Mrs. Brenton all the news, and her face flushed with eager pleasure as she listened to the recital.

"Now," said the Chicago man, "I am going to leave Cincinnati. Are you sorry I am going?"

"No," said Mrs. Brenton, looking him in the face, "I am not sorry."

Stratton flushed at this, and then said, taking his hat in his hand, "Very well, madam, I shall bid you good day."

"I am not sorry," said Mrs. Brenton, holding out her hand, "because I am going to leave Cincinnati myself, and I hope never to see the city again. So if you stayed here, you see, I should never meet you again, Mr. Stratton."

"Alice," cried Stratton, impulsively grasping her hand in both of his, "don't you think you would like Chicago as a place of residence?"

"George," she answered, "I do not know. I am going to Europe, and shall be there for a year or two."

Then he said eagerly—

"When you return, or if I go over there to see you after a year or two, may I ask you that question again?"

"Yes," was the whispered answer.

"Come," said Brenton to Ferris, "let us go."

COACHWHIP PUBLICATIONS

COACHWHIPBOOKS.COM

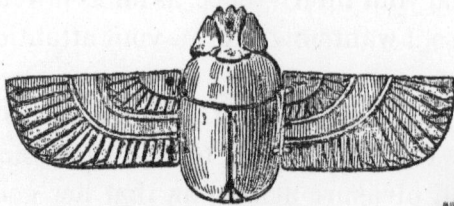

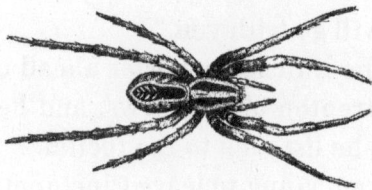

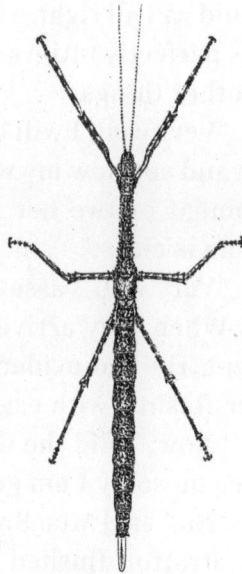

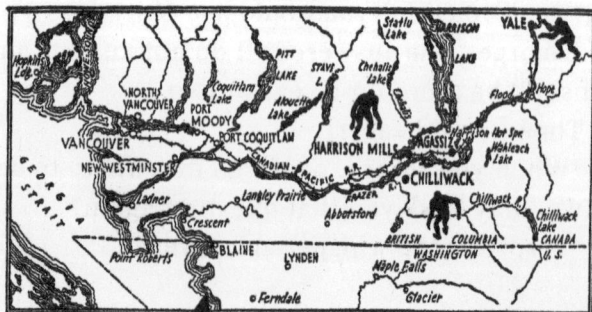

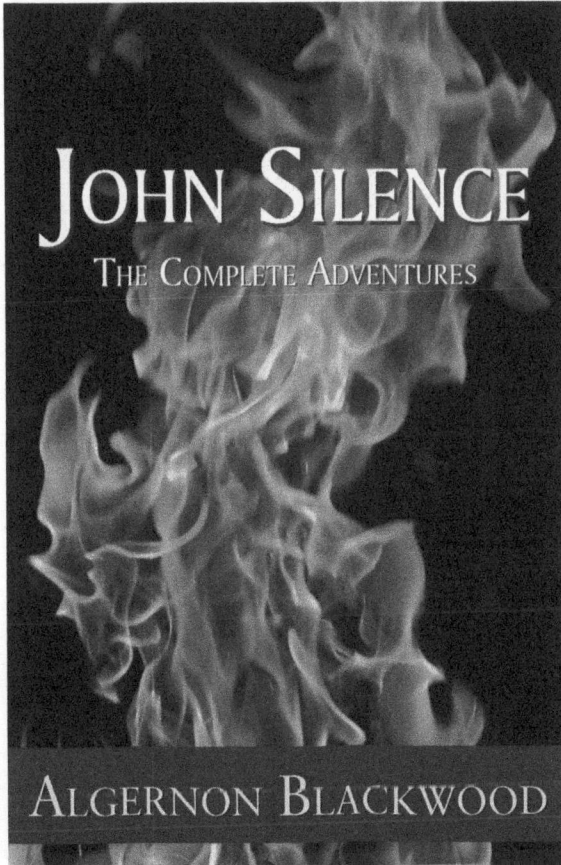

John Silence: The Complete Adventures
ISBN 1-930585-90-X

Coachwhip Publications

Also Available

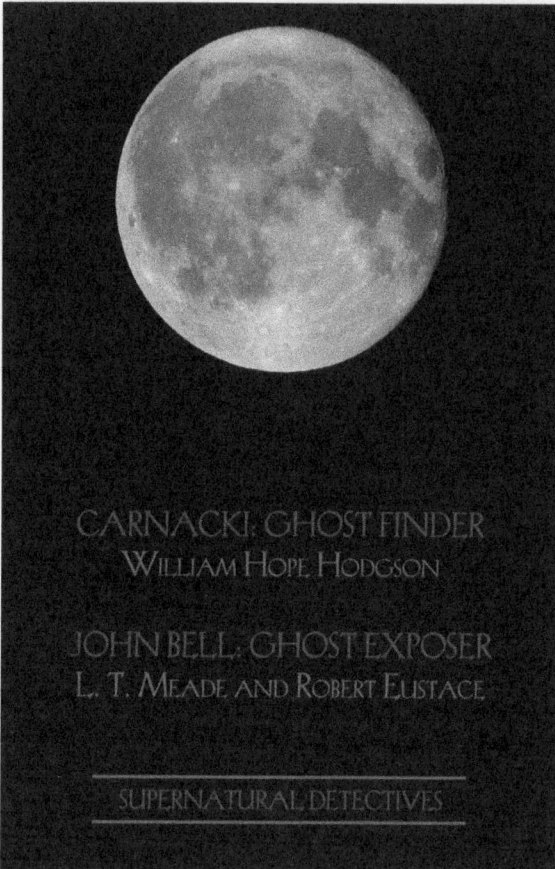

Supernatural Detectives 1:
Carnacki / John Bell
ISBN 1-61646-086-5

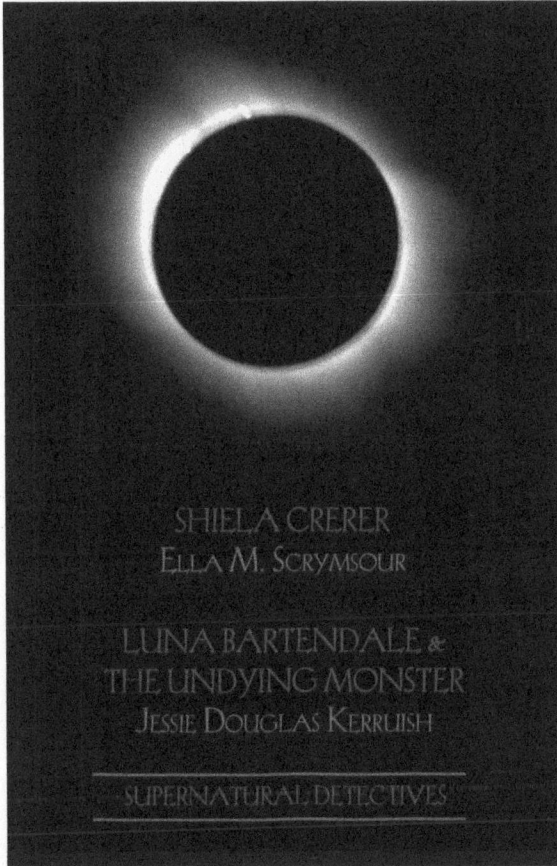

Coachwhip Publications

Also Available

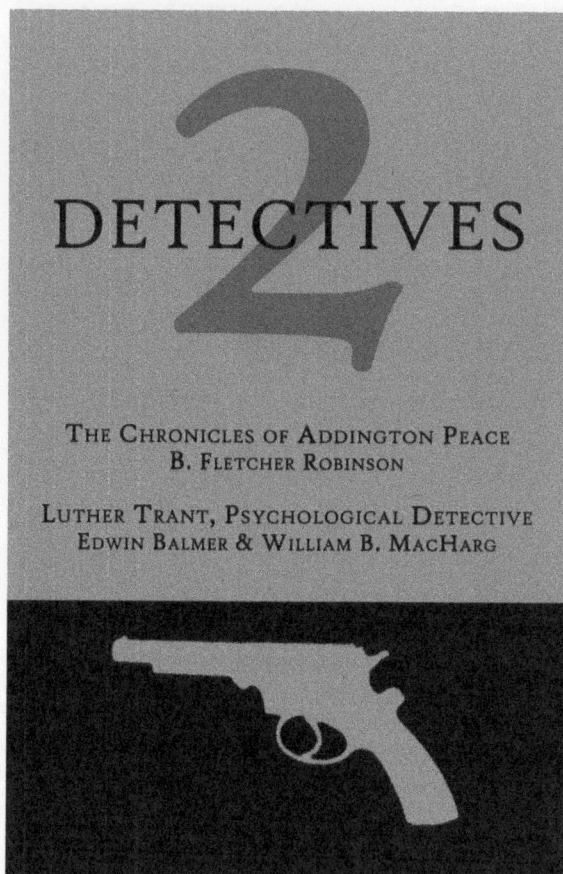

2
DETECTIVES

The Chronicles of Addington Peace
B. Fletcher Robinson

Luther Trant, Psychological Detective
Edwin Balmer & William B. MacHarg

2 Detectives:
Addington Peace / Luther Trant
ISBN 1-61646-097-0

COACHWHIP PUBLICATIONS

ALSO AVAILABLE

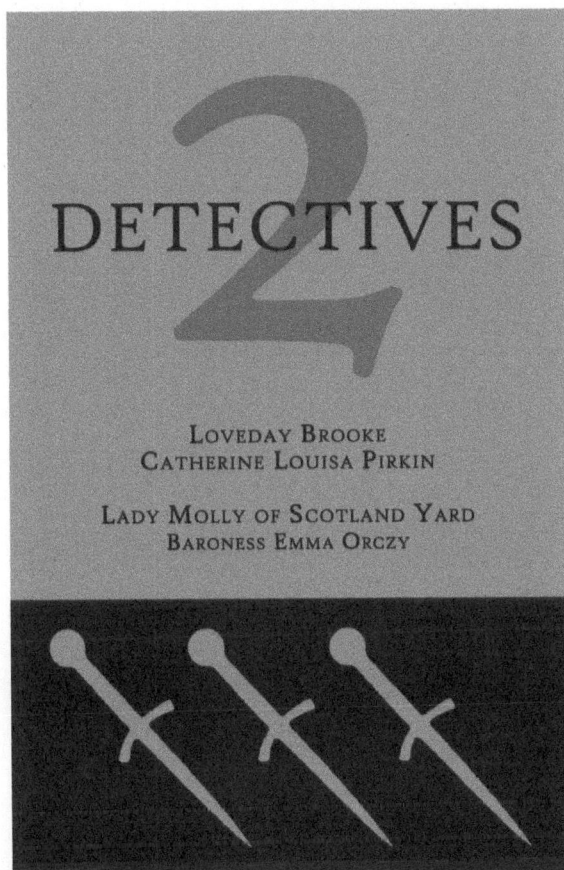

2 Detectives:
Loveday Brooke / Lady Molly
ISBN 1-61646-112-8

Printed in July 2021
by Rotomail Italia S.p.A., Vignate (MI) - Italy